TRAPPED

Also by Rhonda Pollero

TRAPPED

RHONDA POLLERO

FOREVER
YOURS

New York   Boston

Forever Yours
Hachette Book Group
1290 Avenue of the Americas
New York, NY 10104
forever-romance.com
twitter.com/foreverromance

First published as an ebook and print on demand edition: November 2017

Forever Yours is an imprint of Grand Central Publishing. The Forever Yours name and logo are trademarks of Hachette Book Group, Inc.

The publisher is not responsible for websites (or their content) that are not owned by the publisher.

The Hachette Speakers Bureau provides a wide range of authors for speaking events. To find out more, go to www.hachettespeakersbureau.com or call (866) 376-6591.

ISBN 978-1-4555-5542-0 (ebook edition)
ISBN 978-1-4555-9763-5 (print on demand edition)

For Bob and Amy Fetzer, thank you from the bottom of my heart.

TRAPPED

TRAPPED

PROLOGUE

Chasyn Summers parked her Prius on the street adjacent to the courthouse on East Ocean Boulevard. Her best friend and fellow witness, Kasey, was belted into the passenger side.

"Are you nervous?" Kasey asked.

Chasyn thought for a minute while she checked her makeup in the rearview mirror. The state's attorney had warned them to wear subdued clothing and modest makeup. He'd said something about making them seem more sympathetic to the grand jury. So, she had chosen a navy skirt and a cream-colored blouse and she had fore-gone eye makeup save for a touch of mascara, and applied just a hint of blush-nude lipstick to complete the look. Her blond hair was pulled tight into a neat ponytail. She couldn't look more matronly if she tried. "I feel like a school marm."

"Tell me about it. I spent over a hundred dollars on this dress and it really needs to be hemmed. After we testify, I'll take it to the seamstress and have her turn it into a proper little black dress."

"Well, for now we are not two twenty-somethings out at a bar at two a.m.; we're upstanding citizens who witnessed a murder."

Kasey shivered. "I still have nightmares about that."

"Me too," Chasyn said. "But at least this will help them arrest Dr. Lansing. Thanks to us, or more specifically you."

"Should be a cake walk," Kasey said. "Except remember, the state's attorney said the defense attorney would probably attack both of us because we'd been drinking that night."

"Hours earlier and only two drinks. I mean how many times does a girl turn twenty-nine?" Chasyn asked. "We were both stone cold sober when we walked out of that restaurant and found that poor girl on the pavement." She smoothed a wayward hair. "Ready?"

"Sure." They exited the car and walked the short distance to the courthouse. It was made up of two buildings separated by a breezeway. Chasyn knew from earlier meetings with the state's attorney that they needed to enter on the left side of the Martin County, Florida courthouse.

As they approached the buildings, she heard a loud pop, and suddenly found herself falling forward. Chasyn felt pressure but no real pain to go with her total sense of shock. A split second later she heard a second pop and Kasey fell next to her. Kasey's eyes were open but blood was trickling out of her mouth.

Chasyn was vaguely aware of people screaming and running. A pool of blood was starting to form around her face. She smelled burned flesh and her ears were ringing.

After what seemed like a long time, someone came over to her and whispered, "You've been shot in the head. Try not to move."

CHAPTER ONE

Chasyn opened her eyes slowly, wincing against the harsh light overhead. At first, her vision was blurred, but it slowly cleared. She heard the beeps of machines and then a nurse said, "Doctor, the patient is awake."

An attractive woman in scrubs appeared at her bedside wearing a stethoscope and a smile. "You're at St. Mary's Medical Center," she explained.

Chasyn's brain throbbed as she started putting pieces together. "I got shot," she said incredulously.

"You got lucky," the doctor corrected. "The bullet entered the back-right side of your head. A fraction of an inch either way and you probably would have died immediately."

"Kasey?!" she asked, reaching out to clutch the doctor's arm. The action caused the IV in her hand to pull painfully.

"Your family is outside," the doctor replied evasively.

Chasyn felt a knot of fear in her stomach as her mind replayed the events on the courthouse steps. The knot grew

larger when her parents were ushered into the room, their
faces etched with concern. She could tell her mother had been
crying and her father, normally jovial, looked positively stoic.

"Baby," her mother cooed as she carefully avoided the IV
lines and brushed Chasyn's cheek with the back of her hand.
Her father moved to the other side of the bed and rubbed
her arm. "We've been frantic."

"Don't be," Chasyn insisted. "The doctor said I was very
lucky. What about Kasey?"

Her mother's mouth pulled into a taut line and her father's hand went still on her arm. Chasyn felt a sharp pain
in her chest. She and Kasey had been inseparable for the last
sixteen years. They'd met on their first day of kindergarten
and now worked at the law firm of Keller and Mason together. Both litigation paralegal specialists, they'd shared an
office and often worked the same cases.

"Did she die?" Chasyn asked with a hitch in her voice.
"Did she?"

"I'm sorry, baby," her mother said. "They couldn't save her."

"Did they catch the shooter?" she asked as tears began to
fall from the corners of her eyes.

Her father shook his head. "All the police are saying is
that according to witnesses, it was some sort of drive-by."

"Her poor father," Chasyn said. "After losing his wife to
cancer last year, losing Kasey must be a terrible blow to him.
They were so close."

"Her funeral is this afternoon."

Chasyn blinked up at her mother. "Today?"

"Jewish tradition," she explained. "They rushed the autopsy so Mr. Becker could lay his daughter to rest in accordance with his religious beliefs."

"In one day?"

"You've been here for almost eighteen hours," her mother explained.

"But I have to go," Chasyn said as she started to scoot herself up into a seated position. The exertion produced an immediate, pounding headache.

Her mother placed her hands firmly on her shoulders and placed her down flat. "You aren't going anywhere. You're scheduled for surgery this afternoon to remove the bullet from your head."

Chasyn fought back burning tears. She couldn't imagine life without Kasey. Nor could she make sense of being shot. Or of the confusion spinning in her head. She'd obviously lost nearly a day. Her head hurt but the pounding acted like a metronome for her racing thoughts. First and foremost, her heartbreak over Kasey. How could they be chatting casually one second and the next second be gunned down? And, she felt with a measure of guilt, why had she been lucky? Why hadn't she died and Kasey lived? Tears fell from her eyes. For the first time, Chasyn reached up and felt her head. There was a large bandage at the back of her head; when she felt her forehead she found a distinct bulge just at her hairline. With very little effort, she could make out the outline of a bullet. "Can't they remove it tomorrow?" she asked. "I'll go to Kasey's service and then come right back."

Her father looked even more concerned. Deep lines furrowed his brow. "Chase, the police don't think it's a very good idea for you to be out and about."

She let that sink in. "I'm still in danger?" About a thousand scary scenarios flashed in her mind. Had it been just wrong place, wrong time, or was there some crazed killer after her specifically? Her whole body began to tremble as fear lodged in her throat and the tears kept coming. She wanted to hide under something or get as far away from West Palm as possible. She felt like a sitting duck in the hospital. *If they think I'm still in danger, are they implying that the shooter is still after me? What if he comes back?* That thought very nearly paralyzed her.

"Possibly," he said. "There's a police officer outside your room and your mom and I have agreed that we'll take the extra step and hire private security for you as well."

"You're scaring me, Daddy."

"Well, until they find the person who shot you, we don't want to take any chances with your safety. I'm a pharmaceutical salesman, Chase. I don't know anything about keeping you safe but I've hired the best in the business to keep you alive."

"But Kasey's service…"

"We'll go," he said. "We'll pass on your condolences to Mr. Becker."

"And I just lie here doing nothing?"

"The police and the state's attorney want to talk to you and then you'll have your surgery. They should release you from the hospital tomorrow."

Chasyn felt an immediate sense of dread. Now that Kasey was dead, she'd have to come clean with the police and the state's attorney. She'd have to admit that she'd been shot for no reason.

* * *

Declan Kavanaugh exited the elevator and walked briskly toward room 207. He saw an officer perched on a chair outside one of the rooms and figured that was his destination. He greeted the deputy and showed him his credentials. "I'm Miss Summers' bodyguard."

"Heard you were coming," the younger, smaller man said. "She just got back from surgery. Go on in."

He opened the door. The room was dimly lit; only the small light behind the bed was on. The woman in the bed looked small and vulnerable. Her blonde hair was fanned out on the pillow, giving her an ethereal look. Her eyes were closed but her long lashes rested against her cheeks. She had flawless skin. In fact, it if weren't for the bandage at her temple, she would have been perfect. Only not for him. Petite blondes just weren't his type.

Soundlessly, he sat in the padded chair at the end of the bed and watched her breathing. For a long time it was a rhythmic sound, then suddenly a small moan escaped her parted lips and she began to thrash.

Declan got to his feet, went over to her, and gently grabbed her shoulders to shake her awake from whatever nightmare was haunting her. She was thinner than he had originally thought; his beefy hands practically encircled her shoulders.

* * *

Chasyn opened her eyes with a start to find a huge man standing over her, trying to shake the life out of her. She let out a loud scream that reverberated in her head as she took her fist and punched him in the vicinity of his groin.

He let out a *whoosh* of air and his hands dropped away. At the same moment the officer who'd been guarding her from outside the door entered the room, flipping the switch to flood the room with painful light. The huge man was doubled over near her bed. Her pulse raced and she felt trapped in her hospital bed, with serious danger lurking nearby. Even the presence of the officer was of little comfort. At this point she was in a perpetual state of fear.

"He was trying to kill me!" she told the officer on a rush of breath.

The officer reholstered his weapon and smiled. "This is your bodyguard, Miss Summers."

She was instantly awed by the man's sheer size. He had to be at least six-four and his forearms were the size of her thighs. Then she looked up and noted he had the most beautiful blue eyes she had ever seen. Especially since they were rimmed in inky lashes that mirrored the color of his close-cropped black hair. The only flaw she could detect was a slight flush on his cheeks, no doubt a result of her punch to the groin.

She suddenly felt terribly guilty for noticing something like the shade of the man's eyes when she'd just lost Kasey. Maybe the bullet did more damage than they were letting on.

"Oh, God," she muttered, feeling her own cheeks warm. "I'm so sorry. But you had your hands on me and—"

"You were having a nightmare," he explained in a deep, incredibly sexy voice that she felt deep in the pit of her stomach.

Chasyn thought for a few seconds and let the memory come flooding back. "It wasn't a nightmare; I was reliving the shooting."

"Miss Summers?" the officer asked.

"Yes?"

"The detectives and the state's attorney asked me to call them when you woke up. They should be here in a few minutes." With that he left the room.

"I'm Declan Kavanaugh," her bodyguard introduced himself.

"Chasyn," she replied in as normal a tone as she could muster. "I really am sorry for punching you in the..."

He waved his hand. "No big deal. So why did you look so horrified when the deputy told you the police and the prosecutor were coming?"

This guy didn't miss a trick. "I'm just tired of dealing with them. I mean, look what happened. My best friend is dead. I got shot. And now I'm afraid of my own shadow because Dr. Lansing is still roaming free."

"Lansing?"

"He's a forensic psychiatrist. He killed the girl in the parking lot. Kasey and I were supposed to testify before the grand jury so they could finally arrest him."

Declan stroked his chin. "And you think Lansing was the one who shot at you at the courthouse?"

She shrugged. "It isn't like I have any other enemies. Neither did Kasey."

"No jilted boyfriends? Stalkers?"

"Kasey's been dating a guy on and off for about six months. Nothing serious. I haven't had a boyfriend in two years and that relationship ended by mutual agreement."

"Anything strange happen recently? Get the feeling someone was following you?"

She shook her head. "No one following me, but seeing that poor dead girl in the parking lot qualifies as strange. I had never seen a dead body before. It was horrible." Chasyn turned to look at the closed blinds covering the window. "And now Kasey. It seems surreal. Do you have any idea what it's like to see your best friend gunned down?"

"Yes," he said softly.

She was in her own world because Chasyn's heart actually hurt. She was just devastated over Kasey. In her mind she saw a slideshow of their time together that felt as if it lasted an hour. Lots of laughter and deep conversation. Chasyn couldn't imagine her life with Kasey gone. "It was different from the girl in the alley. A tragedy, but not as personal."

"So you didn't know the girl in the alley?"

"Casually," Chasyn replied. "Kasey and I went to that restaurant often. She waited on us a few times. She was working her way through law school. She seemed really nice and—"

The door opened and in stepped two men. With a grimace she recognized the older of the two: state's attorney Nelson Hammond. He was flanked by Detective Burrows. "I remember," Chasyn said.

Hammond was a stocky, round man with a shock of white hair and a distracting moustache. Burrows wasn't in much better shape; his belly protruded over his belt and his tie was a few inches too short. Burrows had a small notepad in one hand and a stubby pencil in the other.

"Good evening Chasyn," the state's attorney greeted. "I'm sorry about Kasey."

Chasyn felt the comment stab her in the gut. "Was it Dr. Lansing?" she asked.

Burrows and Hammond looked from her to Declan. Burrows said, "Declan."

"How are you, Hank?" he responded.

"I'm fine, but we need some privacy to interview Miss Summers."

"Sorry. I stay. Client's orders."

All three men looked at her. "He can stay," she said after a brief pause.

Neither Hammond nor Burrows seemed pleased but Chasyn wasn't concerned about their territorial pissing contest. She was fixated on what she had to do. What she didn't want to do.

Burrows, pencil poised, asked, "Can you tell us what happened yesterday morning?"

Chasyn pressed the button on the handrail and raised the back of the bed so she was nearly sitting upright. The change in position brought on a sudden pounding in her head. She waited for it to subside slightly, then explained. "Kasey and I got ready for court. We drove to the courthouse, parked, then when we were walking up the steps, someone shot at us."

"Did you happen to notice if a car was following you on your way to the courthouse?"

"No."

"No, you didn't notice, or no, there wasn't anyone? Did you hear anything when you were walking? A car stopping? Anything?"

She gingerly shook her head. "We were talking and joking and then suddenly I hit the pavement and a second later I saw Kasey fall, too."

Hammond shifted his weight from foot to foot. "How long do the doctors expect your recovery to take?"

"They'll release me in the morning."

"Then I'll reschedule the grand jury for day after tomorrow if you think you'll be up to it."

Chasyn met the expectant eyes of the prosecutor. "That's not a good idea."

"You need more time?"

"I need to correct my statement," she said quickly.

"Correct your statement?" Burrows asked, his voice slightly raised. "Since Dr. Lansing has refused to provide a DNA sample, your testimony is the only thing tying him to the murder."

"I wasn't completely truthful the night of the murder," Chasyn admitted.

Burrow frowned. "If the shooting's scared you off—"

"No," she interrupted. "See, Kasey and I were on the way out and I remembered I'd left my credit card in the little booklet for our check. When I came back outside the girl was already dead and all I saw were taillights racing away from the scene."

Burrows and Hammond exchanged furious looks. "So, you *lied* about recognizing the killer?" Burrows seethed.

"*Kasey* recognized Dr. Lansing from a case we worked a few months back but she was afraid to say anything unless I agreed to back her up. Kasey wouldn't lie about that, so when you interviewed me, I simply answered your questions honestly without expounding on anything."

Burrows was redfaced. "I asked you if Dr. Lansing killed Miss Jolsten!"

"And he did. Kasey saw the whole thing and I believed her, so I technically wasn't lying to you."

"You're splitting hairs," Hammond remarked. "I should charge you with giving a false police report. Do you know what this means? Dr. Lansing is probably going to get away with murder."

"What about Kasey's murder?" Chasyn said. "Can't you investigate him for that?"

"Did you see Lansing?" Burrows demanded.

"No."

"So far we haven't found anyone who saw him either. All we have is a white SUV with or without a Hispanic male in the passenger seat. Know who that could be?"

Chasyn shook her pounding head. "No."

Hammond sighed heavily. Burrows put away his notepad. "Good luck to you, Miss Summers. Something tells me you're going to need it."

As soon as they left the room, Chasyn looked at Declan. He gave her a half-smile. It was very sexy in an unintentional way. She wondered how she could feel so bereft and yet so aware of this man at the same time.

"Looks like the state's attorney and the detective are a little bit pissed at you."

"I did a stupid thing. But I thought it was important for Kasey to come forward and the only way she'd do that was if I backed her up. Maybe all that did was get her killed."

"You can't blame yourself for that. Tell me more about this Lansing case."

"Lansing is a big deal in the criminal defense world. He's a renowned expert witness but a total asshole. He testified for one of our clients and charged a fortune, but the jury didn't believe him even though our client had been on schizophrenic meds for years before he snapped. Lansing made it sound like a manageable disease.

"Anyway, we were leaving the restaurant when I realized I'd forgotten to grab my card so Kasey went on ahead to the parking lot. I was *maybe* thirty seconds behind her. From what Kasey told me, she walked out and saw Lansing and the waitress at the back of the waitress's car. He stabbed her. One quick one to the back. I learned from the detective that it was a 'kidney kill,' a military-style move that causes such pain you can't even scream." She shivered. "So, when I came out a few seconds later, I saw the taillights racing out of the parking lot. I went over to where Kasey was trying to help the girl but she was bleeding so badly."

Chasyn closed her eyes for a minute. "At her autopsy, they discovered she was six weeks pregnant. The police think Lansing was having some sort of fling with the waitress when she got pregnant. They got DNA from the fetus but without Lansing's to match it against, they can't arrest him. No probable cause, then, but the theory is that Lansing couldn't risk his marriage, so he killed the girl thinking it would solve all his problems. Since Lansing has refused to cooperate in any way, the state's attorney decided to present the case to a grand jury using our testimony to get an indictment so they could compel Lansing to fork over his DNA."

Declan was quiet for a moment, then said, "Sounds as if Lansing is the logical suspect in your shooting."

"How do I prove that?" she asked. Especially since she was completely frustrated by her own lack of observation. She hadn't heard a car or noticed anything sinister on the walk to the courthouse. Chasyn just knew she couldn't let Lansing get away with another murder. She owed Kasey that much and more.

"You don't; I do."

"You do what, exactly?" Chasyn asked, her question tinged with the frustration gripping her body. Her head wasn't pounding as badly but her heart was broken and at that moment, knowing she no longer had the support of the police or the prosecutor, she felt very vulnerable and alone.

Declan shifted his weight from one foot to the other. "My job is to keep you safe and to investigate the shooting at the courthouse."

"Forgive my skepticism, but how do you plan on doing that when the cops have been trying for months?"

"I have a few tricks the cops don't have and I've never lost a client. And I don't intend to start now."

CHAPTER TWO

Chasyn glanced in the mirror as she carefully attempted to brush her hair. She had to avoid the stitches at the base of her skull as well as those at her right temple. A dull headache, which the medical staff assured her was normal, throbbed slightly in the background.

The headache wasn't the only thing in the background. Her small hospital room was filled with the presence of Declan Kavanaugh. For such a large man, he moved with great stealth. She could see him in the mirror of the tiny hospital bathroom, lingering in the room behind her. He seemed perfectly relaxed. Chasyn, on the other hand, was a ball of nerves and emotions. Part of that was due to the fact that Detective Burrows had pulled the officer outside off guard duty, promising only that he'd step up patrols around her apartment. Chasyn felt this was no doubt supposed to be her penance for the way she had evaded telling the full truth about the waitress's murder. The other part was the constant fear that now seemed to be as much a part of her as her right arm.

She'd had a fitful night. Her nightmares, full of the trauma of the shooting and losing Kasey, mixed with the disturbing images of watching the waitress die, were more than her overloaded senses could handle. And now there was another strong and palpable layer of fear: She was nearly paralyzed at the thought of leaving the relative safety of the hospital. If and until they had evidence to arrest Lansing, there was every reason to think he might try to kill her again. She was sure she hadn't been shot by mistake. Someone had killed Kasey and then deliberately attempted to kill her, too. That hadn't been a stray bullet; there was no way she could make herself believe that she'd merely gotten in the way. The shooter had wanted *both* of them dead. They'd succeeded with her friend. They'd try again, Chasyn knew.

Thanks to her mother, she had a fresh pair of jeans and a T-shirt, as well as sandals and her makeup bag. The police had confiscated her clothing, which was fine with her. It wasn't as if she wanted to wear that school marm getup any time again soon.

"You about ready?" Declan called from the other room.

"Almost," she said as she slipped her cosmetics back into the pouch and zipped it closed. Chasyn took one last look in the mirror and decided she'd done the best she could under the circumstances. She still had to wait an additional twenty-four hours to shower, so she wasn't having the best hair day ever.

"Ready," she said as she came out of the bathroom. "What exactly *is* the plan?"

"We'll stop by your place so you can pack."

"Pack for what?"

He cocked his head and his eyes bored into her. "You can't stay at your apartment. It's a safe bet that the shooter knows where you live."

No shit. "So *where* are you taking me?"

"For starters, my place."

She wasn't so sure that would be a safe place either. Her attraction to him couldn't have come at a worse time. "But what about my job?" Her head spun. "And my car. My car is still parked at the courthouse." Trivial crap, true, but thinking about that was easier than dealing with the reality of what her life had recently become.

"I'll have one of my men pick it up and park it at your place. As for your job, too risky for you to stick to your normal schedule."

Chasyn's shoulders slumped. "They'll fire me."

His response was an *oh well* shrug. "My priority is your safety."

"Well," she sighed. "My *safety* only has about three thousand dollars in the bank and rent and a car payment. That'll go quickly."

"You can get another job but you can't come back from the dead."

Chasyn rubbed her arms at the chilling thought.

"Let's go," Declan placed his hand at the small of her back.

Her body reacted to his innocent touch. It jolted her nerve endings and it was everything she could do not to jump from the contact. Of course she was being stupid. It was probably just a screwy reaction because she was so tightly coiled given recent events. Still, she quickened her step so his hand fell away.

Chasyn assumed he'd worked something out with the hospital because contrary to procedure, they took a back staircase out instead of a wheelchair out the front door. Declan blocked the exit, peered out, then gave her the go ahead to follow him to a black SUV with heavily tinted windows. The heavy tint wasn't uncommon in south Florida, but it made the car seem as if it was some part of a presidential motorcade.

Chasyn had to hoist herself up into the passenger seat, grasping the handle above the door while holding her plastic bag of belongings in the other. Very quickly, Declan slipped into the driver's side and gunned the engine.

Compared to her Prius, she felt like she was in a tank. Only this particular tank smelled of woodsy cologne.

* * *

While Chasyn had slept, he'd done a little background so he knew the way to her apartment in West Palm Beach. It was just off Blue Heron and I-95. In less than twenty minutes, he was pulling into a neatly manicured apartment complex. She had been quiet during the brief trip. Made sense. She'd been through hell and back and was probably scared shitless. And for good reason. He had a bad feeling about this case.

"That's my assigned spot," she told him, pointing to one of the spaces under an awning about ten yards from the front of the building.

He didn't like the setup. Too open. "Can you give me a list of what you need from your apartment?" he asked.

"Not really, why?"

"That's a long way to the front door. A long time to be out in the open."

Chasyn nervously looked around. "Then park in the first spot. Jeremy is at work this time of day."

He looked at her. "Jeremy?"

"My neighbor."

"Any problems with him?"

She shook her head and offered a half-smile. "He's a nice guy who loves to cook and brings…*brought* food to Kasey and me all the time. I can't believe I'm talking about her in the past tense." Her smile faded as again a wave of anguish washed over her. She went still but felt Declan's eyes on her. "I still can't believe she's gone. I feel like someone cut a piece of my heart out of my chest."

"It's tough to lose someone close to you," Declan replied in a subdued tone that hinted he might know something about personal loss.

"Kasey and I did everything together."

"So we work hard and find the guy who did this."

"You mean Lansing," she said with a flash of genuine anger. "It had to be him; Kasey didn't have enemies. Everyone loved her. So how do you propose we prove Lansing was behind the shooting?"

"We park, then we run. Is the vestibule door opened or locked?"

"Locked. And how does running help convict Lansing?"

"Once you're safe, we can turn our attention to Lansing. Give me the key."

Chasyn dug into the plastic hospital bag and produced her keys. She placed them in his outstretched palm and in the process, her knuckles brushed his fingers. Declan felt a jar of desire pulse through his system. *Weird.* And not very smart, he told himself as he took the keys. The last thing this woman needed was him lusting after her.

"I'll get out first, then you slide across, okay?"

She did as she was told and Declan used his body to shield her during the quick dash to the door. He slipped the key in the lock and they were inside in a matter of seconds. He followed her up the stairs to the second floor and then gave her back the keys when they reached apartment 212.

When they entered, he could tell something was wrong when she stopped short.

"We've been robbed," she said.

They walked down the short hallway, past the galley-style kitchen into a living room/dining room combination. There was a blank space on the wall where a flat screen had been mounted and various DVDs strewn about. If there'd been a dining room table, it wasn't there now.

He followed her into a tidy bedroom. It was untouched, including a flat screen and a decent stereo. Then they went into the bedroom on the opposite side of the apartment, and it was empty save for a few wire hangers in the closet.

She turned and looked up at him. "I don't understand. All of Kasey's stuff is gone."

"Just her things?"

She nodded. "It must have been her dad. Mr. Becker," she said on a sad sigh.

He followed her back into the living room where she retrieved her purse from the hospital bag. Chasyn scrolled through her contacts, then pressed the speaker button. He heard the phone ring three times until a weak male voice said, "Hello?"

"Mr. Becker, this is Chasyn."

"Oh."

"I'm so sorry about Kasey and I'm so sorry I couldn't attend the service."

"Yes, well…How are you doing?"

"I'm fine, except there's something wrong here at the apartment. All of Kasey's things are gone. Even her toiletries."

"I hired a company to remove her things. I wanted everything of hers with me. Does that make any sense?"

Her heart tugged at the thought of a father having to arrange for someone to pack up his daughter's belongings. Mr. Becker—the whole Becker family—had been so good to her over the years. They'd taken her on vacations and included her in family events. She thought of Mr. Becker as a second father, so just hearing the strain in his voice was enough to make her cry. Losing Kasey so close to when he'd lost his wife must be unbearable. Chasyn cleared her throat of the lump of emotion before saying, "Of course. I would have taken care of that for you."

"You've done enough, Chasyn," he assured her. "Now you just have to focus on feeling better."

"I'll be fine," she told him.

"Then take care," Mr. Becker said, then the line went dead.

"Is he always that glum?" Declan asked.

She gaped up at him. "He just lost his only child. Eight months after his wife succumbed to cancer. How is he supposed to sound?" she asked defensively. When he did not reply, she challenged him further. "Well?"

He just muttered, "Never mind. Pack what you need for at least a week."

"A week? That long?"

"Probably longer, but I have a washer and dryer, so it shouldn't be a problem."

* * *

Shouldn't be a problem? Who was he kidding? Chasyn thought as she went into her bedroom and tried to make a mental list of what she might need. It was March, so that meant cool mornings and evenings, but daytime highs in the mid-seventies. Taking a large suitcase out of her closet, she began to fill it with an assortment of clothes, shoes, bathroom stuff, accessories and everything else she could possibly think of. By the time she was finished, the suitcase weighed a ton and nearly refused to zip. She grabbed a matching tote for her computer and her cell phone accessories. Chasyn made a trip through the apartment and checked to see if there was anything else she might need while she was away.

"I'm impressed," Declan said when he saw her. "I was expecting a suitcase, not a tote."

She gave him a sidelong glance. "The suitcase is in the bedroom. The tote is just for last-minute things." Like the cosmetics pouch she retrieved from her hospital bag. Oh, and the extra bandages and tape they'd given her to redress her wounds until they removed the stitches in five days.

"Jesus H. Christ," she heard him say from the bedroom. "Did you pack all your worldly possessions?"

"A girl likes to have choices," she insisted.

Declan rolled the bag into the now empty dining room just as she was placing her phone charger into her purse. "Stay off the phone unless you check with me first, okay?"

"I have to stay in touch with my parents," she said.

"I'll be in touch with them. After all, they're paying my bill."

"Do I want to know what that is?"

"Probably not. But your safety is their only concern right now. And I told them you'd be difficult to reach until we get this sorted out."

She tilted her head back to look into his eyes. The motion made the stitches at the back of her skull pinch. "If you're babysitting me, how do you propose to sort this out?"

"I have five operatives and I can multitask."

She let out a slow breath. "If only the police had been able to get a DNA sample. None of this would have happened."

"My guys will sit on Lansing twenty-four-seven."

"How does that help?" she asked.

"If Lansing takes a drink or puts his trash out, they'll find something to run DNA on."

"The police tried that for a week and nothing," she told him. "They said he was very cagy when it came to his DNA."

"Which means he knows it will incriminate him. If they

can prove he's the father of the waitress's baby, that gives him motive to kill her."

"Motive times ten if you add in his wife's money."

Declan gave her a quizzical look.

She hoisted the tote up onto her shoulder. "Dr. Lansing's wife comes from old money. If anyone were to prove he was having an affair, she'd probably divorce him and take her money with her."

"What kind of money are we talking about?"

"She has an estate on Jupiter Island. In the area of tens of millions."

Declan whistled. "No wonder he didn't want you and Kasey to testify against him."

"What if I go public with the fact that I can't actually identify him? Wouldn't that stop him from trying to kill me?"

"You won't have to go public. The state's attorney isn't going to go forward with the grand jury without a witness or some other evidence. Lansing will figure that out in no time. His other problem now being linked to Kasey's murder and your attempted murder."

"Well, I can't do that," she said, feeling defeated. "I was so distracted talking to Kasey that I didn't notice anything."

"What about the white SUV?" he pressed. "Maybe you saw one that morning or a day or two before you were supposed to testify?"

Chasyn pressed her lips together and tried to think. "No, nothing."

"We'd better go. I don't want to stay here long enough for whoever to find you again."

She shivered. "When you talk like that I get really scared."

His expression softened. "Let me worry about the tough stuff. All you have to do is follow my instructions."

"Like I have a choice."

His thumb and forefinger looped her chin, gently forcing her head back so he could look into her eyes. "You're right. For now, you don't have a choice and I'm sorry about that. But I'm the one with the experience here, so you'll just have to trust me."

"I'm trying."

"Okay. We're going downstairs. I'll load the car and then come back for you. Stay away from the glass doors until I come for you. Understood?"

She nodded and they left the apartment.

Chasyn stood in the shadows of the vestibule with her heart pounding in her ears. Her headache was a dull throb yet adrenaline had her practically jumping out of her skin. She held her breath as Declan went out and put her suitcase and tote in the back of his SUV. Then he jogged back and she stepped forward to open the door.

As soon as she yanked the handle open, she heard a *whoosh* and a *ping*. Then glass from the door splintered all around them. Declan threw himself on her and they tumbled back on the ground as a second *whoosh* and *ping* split the air.

He'd knocked the air out of her so all she could say was, "What…is…happening?"

"Rifle fire! Keep your head down!"

Chasyn wasted a few seconds trying to get her breath.

Not an easy task when she was scared out of her wits as bullets kept flying. Instantly her mind went back to the horrible scene on the courthouse steps, and she wasn't sure she could get lucky a second time. She buried her face in his chest and waited to die.

CHAPTER THREE

It took several seconds for her brain to register that the shooting had stopped. The eerie silence that followed was almost as frightening as the hail of bullets. Where was the shooter? Was he walking closer, intent on finishing the job?

Chasyn's body began to shake, and abject fear—as well as the weight of Declan's large body on hers—made it difficult to breathe. When he didn't move immediately, she thought the worst. With some effort and a growing sense of panic, she gave his shoulder a shove. "Declan?"

Once the shooting stopped Declan rolled off her, reached into an ankle holster, and produced a gun.

"Why didn't you take that out sooner?" she asked in a huff.

"I was a little preoccupied covering your body with mine. You're welcome, by the way."

Leaving her lying on the glass-strewn floor, he moved along the wall, toward the now shattered vestibule doors. Several long seconds passed before he said, "All clear."

He shot her a glance. "Are you hurt?" he demanded.

Relieved that neither of them was dead or riddled with bullets, she shook her head. "Just...had...the...wind...knocked...out of me." With difficulty, she sipped air until her constricted lungs no longer felt constricted.

At about that same moment, she could hear a cacophony of sirens growing closer. Careful to avoid the glass shards, she stood on shaky legs.

"You're bleeding," Declan tucked his gun into the back of his waistband.

Chasyn looked down and saw a steady stream of blood dripping off her middle finger. She turned her palm up and noted a small piece of glass protruding from her hand.

Declan took her hand in his and examined the wound. "This may hurt a little," he said before he grabbed the edge of the glass and pulled it free. "Sorry," he mumbled.

"It doesn't hurt," she insisted. She lifted the edge of her T-shirt and applied pressure to the wound. While she waited for the bleeding to stop, she watched Declan move toward the back of the vestibule. He got down on his haunches and examined something shiny on the ground. "What is it?" she asked.

"Projectiles from a thirty-ought-six, is my guess."

"In English?"

He stood, his handsome features suddenly strobed in red and blue lights as an ambulance and several police cars came to a screeching halt in the parking lot. Before he could answer, Chasyn heard someone on a megaphone say, "West Palm Beach Police!"

Declan gripped her elbow and led her out of the building. The officers had taken up defensive positions behind their open car doors. Perhaps a half-dozen guns were trained in their direction.

Because she'd seen it on TV and in the movies, Chasyn reflexively raised her hands. A small stream of blood trickled from her palm. Her surrender seemed to relax the atmosphere just as an unmarked car came rushing onto the scene.

A familiar face emerged from the car. Detective Burrows stepped from the dark blue, American-made sedan with his ever-present notepad in one hand. He did not look happy.

Chasyn lowered her arms and absently wiped her injured palm on her T-shirt again. With each step she took she could hear a slight jingling noise. It took her a few seconds to realize it was the sound of glass shards falling from her hair onto the pavement. Between her bloody shirt, bloody hand, and incessant shaking, she was definitely a hot mess.

Burrows pulled Declan aside for a statement while Chasyn was sent to the paramedics to have her hand bandaged. "Sorry, I'm trying to keep my hand still, but I've got the shakes," she said as the EMT placed a couple of butterfly bandages over the cut.

"It's adrenaline," he explained. "It will dissipate soon."

Burrows came over to her, pencil poised above his pad. "So, tell me what happened."

"We were in the vestibule when someone shot at us. *Shot at me.*"

"Did you see the shooter?"

She shook her head. As she did so, Declan came up quietly behind Burrows. "I didn't see or hear anything until the bullets when whizzing past my head."

"Nothing? Not even the sound of a car?"

"No."

Declan stepped forward. "The guy didn't necessarily fire from the parking lot. If I'm right, the ammunition used can be fired from as far as a thousand yards away. This was no amateur."

Chasyn felt a chill creep down her spine. "Are you saying a *professional* hit man has tried to kill me twice?"

Burrows thumbed through his notebook. "The bullets recovered from the other shooting were nine millimeters."

Confused Chasyn looked at Declan "He changed guns?"

"Yes," Burrows said.

"Or two different shooters," Declan corrected. "Which begs the question. How did this guy know where to find you? The only person who knew when I'd be bringing her by the apartment is me and I didn't tell anyone."

Burrows looked in her direction. "Did you tell anyone your plans, Miss Summers?"

"No. Well…" She hesitated for a minute. "I think I said something to the nurse who helped me this morning."

"Which nurse?"

Chasyn let her head fall to one side. "Seriously? Why would some nurse I met exactly three times get involved with a murder attempt?"

"We have to follow every lead."

Declan's expression changed to a hard, intimidating scowl. "You wouldn't be chasing ghosts if you hadn't pulled your man off Chasyn. You should have left a man at the hospital."

Burrows' face flushed. "If it happened the way you say it did, then having an officer on site wouldn't have made a difference."

Declan reached around Burrows and said, "C'mon, Chasyn. Let's get out of here."

"I'm not finished with my questioning," Burrows objected.

While she began to walk past the detective, Declan took out his wallet and produced a business card. He presented it to Burrows. "If you have any more questions for either of us, you can call this attorney."

As soon as they were out of earshot, Chasyn asked, "I have an attorney?"

"My brother," Declan explained. "Jack has an office in Stuart."

"But how can he represent me if he hasn't met me?"

Declan shrugged and opened the car door for her. "He trusts me *and* he owes me one."

As Declan slalomed through the emergency vehicles, he reached into the back of his waistband and pulled out the gun, leaving it to rest on the console between them. It made Chasyn nervous. "What if that thing goes off?" she asked.

"The safety is on. I take it you don't have any experience with guns."

"No. Unless you count the two times I've been shot at and the fact that they removed a bullet from my head."

He let out a little half-laugh. "I see your point."

Chasyn shifted in her seat and looked at him in profile. As predicted, the adrenaline rush had subsided and now she just felt an overwhelming exhaustion. Her limbs felt heavy and her mind wandered aimlessly as she regarded him. He was handsome in a classical statue kind of way. Chiseled angles. His shoulders were broad and the fabric of his shirt was pulled taut across his expansive chest and his well-defined upper arms. She could see the outline of his six-pack as his torso narrowed at his waist. The same was true of his thighs—muscle pressed an outline against fabric. Her attention lifted to his mouth and her frazzled brain produced a vivid image of what it might be like to be kissed by him.

It wouldn't be soft or tentative. No, she pegged him for the deep, thrusting kind of kiss that would have the ability to curl her toes in nothing flat. Chasyn cheeks grew warm and she twisted back in her seat and kept her eyes front. Lusting after this man was a really bad idea. It wasn't part of her plan. And she never deviated from her life plan. Yet she lifted her hand to her mouth and could almost feel the lingering effect of the non-existent kiss.

Declan made two calls from the car. One to his office and another to his brother Jack. Both calls were short and to the point. He made arrangements for his team to follow Dr. Lansing and the call to his brother was just a heads-up should Burrows contact him. The easy banter between the brothers left her with a pang of envy. She was an only child and Kasey had been the closest thing she'd ever had to a sister. And now she was gone.

* * *

He had to admit—at least to himself—that there was something not quite right about the situation. The change in MO troubled Declan. If he was right and the first attempt on Chasyn's life had been a professional job, then the second attempt should have followed a similar pattern. It was a whole different skill set going from a nine-millimeter used in a drive-by to a thirty-ought-six fired from a long distance, high-powered rifle. It wasn't unheard of for a killer to switch from a firearm to a knife or vice versa, but it was odd to change weapons in midstream. Why go from an easily concealed handgun to a high-powered rifle when Chasyn was the target? That fact gnawed at his thoughts. Not to mention his personal take on the change in weapons. A nine millimeter can do some damage but a two-two-three shell is designed for the infliction of maximum damage. Whoever had shot at her today wanted her dead. *Real* dead. It would be easy enough to check if Lansing had any firearms training but he assumed that would be a dead end. No, the way to catch Lansing would come from DNA and/or a financial trail leading to the hit man. Or more optimally, Declan could chase him down and beat the crap out of him before turning him over to the police.

He glanced over at Chasyn. She sat in silence, eyes front. Too bad. She had beautiful eyes. They reminded him of the ocean. Hell, if he was being totally honest, she was beautiful, period. He normally went for the dark, exotic type but there was something about the mix of strength and vulnerability that piqued his interest. And it didn't hurt that she was positively stunning. Declan gave himself a mental bitch slap as he reached up to the visor and pressed the button to open the gate in the stucco fence that surrounded his home.

* * *

Chasyn wasn't sure what she'd been expecting, but it wasn't the home set back from the road. As they pulled in the drive and waited for the garage door to open, she spotted at least a half-dozen security cameras mounted on the beige stucco house with the barrel tile roof. Very Florida.

"Where are we?" she asked.

"Unincorporated Palm Beach County," he replied.

"I meant, is this your house?"

"Yes," he said as he pulled into the garage.

The walls were lined with pegboard and an assortment of tools hung in precise order. There was a surfboard leaning against the back wall and scuba gear to the right of that.

She started to open the door when Declan reached out and closed his hand over her wrist. "Wait until the garage door closes."

"You think the killer will look for me here?"

"Doubtful," he said. "The property is in the name of my company and I made sure we weren't followed on the way over here."

She let out a sigh of relief just as the garage door rumbled to a stop. Grabbing her tote, she slipped out of the SUV. Not an easy chore; it was more like a dismount than a graceful exit. Declan retrieved her suitcase, then led her through the door.

They passed through a laundry room that then opened to a spacious kitchen, complete with light marble counter tops. Obviously private detecting paid well. But it didn't decorate well. It was immediately apparent that a man had selected the furnishings and other décor. Everything was big and masculine with lots of leather and there was an adjacent family room with the biggest TV she'd ever seen.

Declan rolled her suitcase down the hallway off the family room, flipped on lights, and showed her the guest room and the guest bath. "There's towels and stuff in the hall closet."

"Thank you," she said as she eyed the sleigh bed dominating the room. There was a large window over the bed, obscured by plantation shutters.

"I'll let you get settled, then join me in the family room, okay?"

She nodded, then watched his back as he left the room.

Chasyn spent about twenty minutes changing out of her bloody shirt and unpacking and setting up her things in the bathroom. While there she took a look at herself in the mirror and groaned. Her hair was mussed and her lip gloss was long gone. And the bandage at her temple didn't exactly heighten her appearance. It shouldn't have mattered. Declan was her bodyguard, not her date. Still, she took the time to brush her hair and reapply nude gloss before re-emerging to the family room.

The gigantic television was on, but instead of a normal screen, this screen was split into nine images, stacked in three rows of three. Declan was in the kitchen with a dish towel over his shoulder and a whisk in his hand.

He smiled at her and she just about melted. Recovering quickly, she asked, "What smells so good?"

"An omelet. I'm afraid it's the only thing I know how to cook well. And I figured you'd be hungry."

"I am," she admitted, rubbing her belly for emphasis. "May I help?"

He shook his head and whisked the eggs. He poured them into a pan, then allowed them to cook for a minute or so before adding cheese. It smelled wonderful and also worked as an effective distraction from her silly fixation on his physique.

As he was plating the food, he asked, "Coffee, water?"

"Water's fine."

Declan grabbed one plate and stopped at the fridge on the way to the kitchen table and grabbed a bottle of water for her. He made a second trip and retrieved his plate and a mug of steaming coffee.

"What's with the television?" she asked.

"My security system," he explained. "Before I forget," he paused to reach into his pocket, then passed her a fob with a red button on it. "This is the panic button. Keep it with you at all times when we're in the house. One press and this place lights up like the fourth of July."

Chasyn curled her fingers around the fob, then dove into the omelet. It was a wonderful change after two days of hospital food. When she looked up, she found Declan staring at her mouth. It was a tad distracting. Then again, her nerves were shot and she wasn't exactly in the best frame of mind to try to decipher what that look was all about. When her belly did a flip-flop, she chalked it up to her stomach thanking her for the good food. The alternative was to acknowledge that in the midst of her grief and fear she was actually attracted to him, and that wasn't an option. Still, all of her nerve endings sizzled at once.

CHAPTER FOUR

Chasyn abandoned her half-eaten omelet, rinsed the plate in the sink, then claimed a sudden, urgent need to lie down. All this was done under the laserlike eyes of Declan, who probably wasn't buying her excuse for a quick getaway. At least that was the impression she got from the sexy half-smile he offered at her feeble excuse.

Once she was safely hidden behind the bedroom door, she sat on the edge of the bed, mentally berating herself for her behavior. "Maybe being shot *has* scrambled my brain." A man like Declan was way out of her league. Not to mention the fact that he wasn't part of her master plan. No, Chasyn pretty much had her life worked out in stages and none of those stages included a distraction like Declan.

She scooted back on the bed, gently rested her head on the pillow and covered her eyes with one bent arm. In no time, she fell into an exhausted sleep.

When she next opened her eyes, she was momentarily

disoriented. Then the reality came streaming back like the streaks of moonlight filtering in from the slats in the shutters. Glancing at the bedside table, she read the blue digits illuminated on the clock. Nine-fifty-seven. She'd been asleep for more than six hours. "How did that happen?" she wondered as she stood.

She slipped into the bathroom, brushed her teeth, and fixed her smudged makeup. The tape around her Band-Aid-sized dressing was beginning to peel. Slipping her hand beneath her hair, she felt for the edges of the other dressing. It too was peeling. They needed to be changed but she didn't think she could manage the one on the back of her head on her own. Ironically, the stitches were no longer tender, just tight. Amazing how fast the body could heal.

Given the way she had all but run from the room, Chasyn took care to practice an easy smile before she exited the bathroom. As soon as she entered the family room she stopped in her tracks. There was a stunning blonde sitting at the kitchen table flipping through a magazine. Unlike Chasyn, this woman was tall and almost regal looking—more like Grace Kelly in her heyday. She felt like a bandaged freak.

The woman looked up and smiled easily. "Hello."

"Hi," she managed, wondering if this woman knew Declan was such a smarmy flirt when she wasn't around. Her opinion of her bodyguard went right down the toilet.

"I'm Darby. You must be Chasyn." She stood and extended her hand.

Chasyn stepped forward and greeted the woman with a

mild smile. "Nice to meet you. What happened to Declan?" she asked.

Darby crooked her head in the direction of the opposite hallway. "He's in the office with Jack. Probably discussing strategy. Coffee?"

Jack. She remembered the name from earlier in the day. Jack Kavanaugh was the name on the business card Declan had handed to Burrows. "Coffee would be great."

When Darby stood and pivoted toward the counter top, Chasyn noted the gun sticking out of her waistband. "You have a gun,'" she blurted out.

"Given the situation," Darby said. "It only seemed prudent. Don't worry; I'm an excellent shot. Just ask my fiancé."

Fiancé?! "Declan is your fiancé?"

She laughed. "He's my soon-to-be brother-in-law. Jack is my fiancé. Declan marry someone? That would take a very large miracle. Declan has taken an oath never to marry. He's one of those guys who is content to live a life of debauchery," she said with a laugh. "He's all about his work but that doesn't stop him from attracting some of the most beautiful women in Palm Beach County. I'm guessing you noticed he's pretty easy on the eyes and he's a nice guy to boot. He just doesn't subscribe to marriage or anything that remotely resembles commitment. What about you?" she asked as she flipped on a Keurig and took two mugs out of a cabinet.

"Not married. I wouldn't even consider it until after I reach my professional goal."

"Which is?"

"I want to head the litigation department at my firm."

"You're a lawyer?"

Chasyn shook her head. "Paralegal."

"That must be interesting." The coffee maker spit out two steaming mugs of coffee in rapid succession. "Cream? Sugar?"

"Black is good." Darby delivered the mug and Chasyn wrapped her hands around it, enjoying the warmth. "Thank you."

"No problem. Are you hungry?"

Chasyn shook her head gently. "Ouch."

"Stitches pulling?" Darby asked.

"Yep. Annoying little suckers."

Darby sat at the table and motioned for Chasyn to join her. "That's actually a good sign. It means the wounds are healing."

"Are you a doctor?"

"Kind of. I'm a vet, so I know a little bit about sutures."

"Don't let her kid you," came an unfamiliar male voice. "She knows a lot about a lot."

Chasyn looked up and immediately knew she was seeing Declan's brother Jack. The family resemblance was strong, though in her opinion Declan was the more handsome of the two. Jack wasn't as tall nor was his body as impressively defined. Jack came over and placed an unselfconscious kiss on his fiancée's slightly parted lips. It was quick but easily conveyed an enviable amount of intimacy.

Declan appeared with a pile of papers in his hands. His brow was furrowed and he seemed a little preoccupied. "Did you get some rest?"

Chasyn nodded.

"This your attorney, Jack. He'll be providing interference with the police and the state's attorney's office."

"Okay, but shouldn't I trust the police?" she asked. "Why am I going it alone?" Fear surged through her.

"First off," Jack began, "the state's attorney and the cops are super pissed at you right now for giving a false statement. Second, Declan has better resources and a better chance at getting the dirt on your shooter than the cops and the state's attorney's investigators combined. Your parents didn't pick his name out of a phone book. They obviously did their homework and hired the best."

Declan shrugged. The motion pulled the fabric of his shirt tight against his broad chest. "Don't worry about the cops. They'll do their thing and we'll do ours."

Darby patted Jack's hand on her shoulder. "We have to get home to relieve the babysitter."

"Family life calls," he agreed. "Need anything else?" he asked his brother.

"Not right now, but thanks for calling in those favors."

* * *

"What favors?" Chasyn asked him as he watched Jack and Darby exit the driveway and the gate close behind their car.

He turned and looked at her. Strain was evident around her eyes and it had the uncharacteristic result of tugging on his gut. He didn't like the reaction. It was as if his body and his brain had suffered a serious disconnect. One glance at her and he was practically aching with need. He wondered if her hair would feel as silky as it looked. If her mouth would be as soft and pliant. The memory of brushing her lips with his thumb was seared on his sex-addled brain. It wasn't just the physical contact; it was her reaction. Watching the way her eyes had shimmered with pent-up desire as the pad of his thumb moved over her skin had almost got him hard.

But that reaction was quickly doused when he reminded himself why she was here. It was his job to keep her safe, not try to get her into bed. A fact he needed to keep at the forefront.

"Let me show you," he said as he joined her at the table and began spreading out a variety of documents. "I've got copies of the police reports from the waitress's murder as well as the shooting at your apartment complex this afternoon."

"Aren't those private?"

He smiled. "Between Jack and me, we called in some favors so we can be on the same page as the cops."

"Did you learn anything?" Chasyn asked.

"According to the autopsy report, Mary Jolsten, the waitress, was stabbed once in the kidney. A very specific method was used in the stabbing."

"Are you saying it wasn't Dr. Lansing?"

Declan shook his head. "No, I'm saying whoever did it most likely had some sort of military training. And," he paused and shuffled some of his papers. "Dr. Lansing did four years in the Marine Corps before going to college and then med school."

"And he would have learned this kidney kill thing there?"

"Standard training for Marines."

"But not enough for a warrant for his DNA," Chasyn acknowledged. "What else?"

"I watched all the news footage and read all the print coverage at the time of the murder. Clearly Lansing was the prime suspect but without DNA tying him to the Jolsten woman's unborn fetus, the cops hit a wall. And Lansing hired Don Younger as his attorney and cut off all cooperation with the investigation."

She looked up at him and again he was struck by her unusually pale blue eyes. "Don Younger is an excellent defense attorney," she said. "He's legendary for getting one of his clients acquitted even after the police caught the defendant driving around with the corpse in his trunk."

"I've done a little work for Younger. I know how talented he is."

"You work for guilty people?" she said with censure.

"Your firm represents criminal defendants and you're a litigation specialist, so don't you do the same thing?" he challenged gently.

She pursed her lips for a second. "Kasey did criminal work. I do personal injury litigation."

"Never criminal?"

She shrugged. "A few cases, but it isn't my normal specialty."

"But I heard you tell Darby that you want to be the head litigation paralegal. So, wouldn't that mean that you'd be overseeing all kinds of litigation, criminal defense included?"

She sighed. "Okay. I take back my snarky remark about you working for guilty people."

"You're forgiven," he said with a half-laugh. "Anyway, I

got Lansing's phone records and his financials. If he was having an affair with the Jolsten woman, he covered his tracks. No calls to or from her phone or the phone at the restaurant. No unusual charges on his credit card statements. If he was wining and dining her, it wasn't coming out of his joint checking account with his wife or his business account."

"So he was careful."

"Or," Declan reached in and took out a sheet of paper with the name William Jolsten printed across the top. "Mary Jolsten had another man in her life, maybe an ex-husband."

"How ex?" Chasyn asked.

"Divorce was final seven months ago. I'm waiting for a copy of the divorce decree; it should come tomorrow."

Chasyn tilted her head and her hair fell over her shoulder, catching the light. "I don't care," she said fiercely. "Kasey knew Dr. Lansing and she was positive he was the one she saw stab that poor woman. I don't care if she had an unhappy ex-husband."

"Her ex-husband is stationed at MacDill."

"He's military?"

Declan nodded. "Which I'm sure Younger would use to create reasonable doubt. Lansing's military career was twenty-plus years ago, while Mary Jolsten's ex is active duty with the same training."

"Have the police talked to William Jolsten?"

Declan let out a breath. "NCIS interviewed him and forwarded a single paragraph report asserting Captain Jolsten was on duty the night of the murder."

"You don't seem convinced."

"I'd like it a lot better if they had included a duty roster or a witness placing Jolsten at a specific location at the time of the killing. That kind of detail verification would eliminate Jolsten as an alternative suspect."

"Kasey wouldn't have lied," Chasyn insisted. "She had no reason to falsely identify Lansing."

"There was a mention in one of the articles that the witness had a prior relationship with Dr. Lansing."

"Relationship?" Chasyn scoffed. "Kasey didn't care for him because she thought his lackadaisical testimony and arrogant attitude caused our client to get a twenty-seven to life sentence instead of a not guilty by reason of insanity."

"So, she had a grudge?"

"Not a grudge," she said, voice slightly raised. "She just thought the guy was a jerk because he refused to do a prep session with her and didn't get his written report to her until two days before his testimony."

"But they had words at the courthouse?"

"*Word*," she corrected. "When she ran into him in the hallway she called him an asshole. He got all affronted and caused a scene, demanding the firm fire her for insubordination. He even threatened to bring a defamation suit."

"Anything come of that?"

"HR put a memo in her personnel file."

"How did Kasey take that?"

"Not well," she admitted. "You have to understand; Kasey was very dedicated to her job. We shared that value. Having a note in her permanent record pissed her off royally."

"Any chance she could have been mistaken the night of the murder?"

Chasyn shook her head vehemently. "No way. She was honest to a fault. When she told me it was Lansing, I believed her. Period. Now how do we prove it when the cops have hit a brick wall?"

"We?" he asked, trying not to laugh when her spine stiffened.

"I want him held accountable for killing Kasey and I don't want to see her name and reputation smeared by Younger or anyone else. I owe that to her father. And to myself. If only I hadn't gone back for my credit card…"

"Well, you'll have to leave things to me. You're staying here under guard until I can nail Lansing for the attempts on your life."

"I'm under house arrest?"

"Think of it more like protective custody."

"I'm not a sidelines kind of girl," she argued.

"Would you rather be a moving target? Out in the open?"

She mulled over his logical argument for a few seconds. "I'd rather be proactive. No offense, but you're being paid to guard me, not keep me prisoner. Besides, I'd be an excellent asset to the investigation."

"No."

"It wasn't a request."

"It isn't an option."

"Well, it is now." She stood. "You're the professional. You figure out the logistics, but with or without you, I'm going to prove that Lansing killed Kasey."

"And get yourself killed in the process."

"Not if you're as good as you think you are."

CHAPTER FIVE

Do you have a legal pad?" she asked. He gave her a confused look. "I think better with a pad and pen."

Declan went back to his office and returned with a pad and pen. "Now what?"

"We need a plan."

"A plan for what?" He sat next to her as she drew column lines on the page. She gave each column a header—Mary's Murder, Kasey's Murder, Dr. Lansing. "All we have to do is find the link between these three things and we'll be able to turn Lansing over to the authorities tied in a neat bow."

"Do you always make lists?" The tinge of amusement in his voice annoyed her.

"Lists, plans, graphs, charts. Whatever it takes to stay focused on my goals."

His smile reached his eyes. "Sounds a tad anal."

"No, it's rational. I have my entire life planned out. Until a few days ago, I was solidly on track."

"For what?"

She let out an exasperated sigh. "Reaching my goals."

"Which are?" he asked as he leaned back in the chair and crossed his massive arms over his chest.

She shrugged. "The usual stuff. Establishing a career. Marriage at thirty-five. Children by forty. Planning for retirement."

"Sounds boring," he observed. "And isn't forty cutting it a bit close?"

"No." She regarded him for a few seconds. "Oh, so you're one of those 'take life as it comes' types?"

"My way isn't so bad. I've got a successful business. I own this place outright. I'm a pretty content guy."

"So, what happens when you're too old to chase bad guys? Do you have savings? A 401K?"

"You're pretty hung up on planning for the future, aren't you?"

She nodded. "I have every intention of following the example set by my parents."

"Ah, that explains a lot."

Her temper flared. "What's that supposed to mean?"

Lifting his arms, Declan laced his fingers together and rested them behind his head. "Father, Thomas John Summers. Mother, Debra (nee Chasyn) Summers. Married thirty-three years. Thomas is a salesman for Gruber Pharmaceuticals, mother is a retired teacher. One daughter—you. Impressive investment portfolio. Some real estate ventures and—"

"You did a background check on my family?"

"Standard practice for me. I don't like surprises."

"Did you check me out, too?" she challenged.

"Born and bred in Florida. Attended Florida Atlantic University. Graduated with honors. Hired directly out of college by Keller and Mason. Steady climb up the corporate ladder."

"I could have told you all that."

He cocked his head to one side. "Like you told me you only had three thousand in the bank?"

Chasyn sighed but didn't back down. "That's what's in my checking account."

"But you have another eleven grand in savings and a modest 401K. Saving for a rainy day?"

"A condo," she admitted. "Why did you run my financials?"

"To make sure you were on the up and up. I also ran Kasey's finances."

"And?"

He shook his head. "Nothing of note other than a serious problem with buying expensive shoes."

Chasyn smiled. "Kasey never met a designer pump she didn't like."

"Tough on the budget."

"Kasey didn't stick to a budget. It made her father crazy."

"He subsidized her expenses?"

She nodded. "Mr. Becker adored Kasey. He couldn't stand to see her go without something she wanted. But she wasn't spoiled or anything. Kasey just liked nice things and her parents had the money. Mr. Becker owns a chain of car washes."

"Thirty-nine of them in four states," Declan supplied.

She met and held his gaze. "Is there anything you don't already know?"

"Not much," he admitted easily.

"That remains to be seen," she grumbled as she lowered her eyes back to her paper and began making bullet points in the columns. "So we know where and how Mary was killed. We know she was six weeks pregnant at the time she was killed and we know Dr. Lansing was the baby's father."

"*Think* Lansing is the father; can't prove it," he corrected.

"What other motive would he have for killing her?" Chasyn asked. Under the 'Dr. Lansing' column, she wrote: *Uber-rich wife.* "Mary having Lansing's baby would cost him dearly. His wife is Martha Hamilton Lansing, sole heir to the Hamilton Foods empire, and she might have taken issue with her husband fathering a child as a result of an adulterous affair." There was censure in her tone that inspired a small smile from Declan.

"But Lansing is a doctor," he said. "I've never met a poor doctor in West Palm."

She shook her head emphatically. "He doesn't practice. He writes articles about criminal insanity and earns hefty fees for expert testimony but that's a drop in the bucket compared to the billions his wife controls."

"Judging by their joint checking account, his wife keeps him on a pretty short leash. If he doesn't practice, why does he keep an office in West Palm Beach?" Declan asked after consulting a report in his hands. He seemed perplexed by what he read.

"For show?" Chasyn speculated. "I guess there is no real reason for it. Just for show, and Lansing is all about show."

"Put that in the Lansing column."

She smiled. "Are you admitting my system is effective?" She felt a surge of pride.

He gave her a sidelong look and a sexy half-smile. "I'm considering the fact that your anal-retentive bent might be helpful."

The 'Kasey' column was pretty light. She wrote down the date and time and the fact that she was killed by a nine-millimeter projectile. "Do I include the white SUV with the possibly Hispanic passenger as the gunman?" she asked. A chill danced along her spine at the memory. "Even though I didn't see it?"

"Sure, just put a question mark next to it." Declan got up and refilled his coffee. "Want some?" he asked.

"No, but I'd love some water."

He retrieved a bottle from the refrigerator and placed it on the table next to her pad. "Add Captain William Jolsten under Mary's column," he suggested. "Our first stop should be MacDill to get some background on Mary."

"Our?"

"Can I stop you from getting involved?" he asked with one dark brow arched.

"No," she answered with conviction. "My best friend is dead. I want Lansing to pay."

"Fine. But we're doing it my way."

"Which is?"

He paused to take a sip from his mug. "You do whatever I tell you to do, whenever I tell you to do it."

"But—"

He raised a finger to his lips. "No buts. No negotiation. You're in my world now. My world, my rules."

She sat up straighter. "Anyone ever tell you you're a tad dictatorial?"

"Maybe. But at least I haven't turned my life into a rigid timeline."

"You're probably just jealous because I've got a plan and you're cruising through life," she scoffed.

"What do you know about my life?" He challenged her with obvious amusement.

"I'm guessing you're in your mid-thirties. You live in a tech-overload house that's decorated like a big man-cave and your chosen career leaves you open to the potential for sporadic employment."

"Ouch."

"Well, you asked."

"Enough about me," he said dismissively. "Time for a little prep work. Come with me."

He led her into his office. It was a sparse room with a desk and a credenza, two filing cabinets and a couple of mismatched leather chairs. There was a phone, a fax machine, and a laser printer.

Declan crouched by the credenza, slid open one door and revealed a small safe. After punching in a code, a short beep sounded and he pulled open the door. Inside she saw an array of firearms and clips. He selected a black one and removed the clip, then slid the barrel to clear the chamber before standing.

"Ever fire a gun?"

She shook her head. "I've never even held one."

"You only point it where you're planning to shoot," he said as he came around to where she stood. He handed her the gun by the grip, then moved behind her.

"It's not as heavy as I thought it would be," she said with mild surprise.

"It isn't loaded. Now, stand with your feet shoulders' width apart."

She followed his instruction and was focused on the task at hand until he pressed up behind her and reached his arms around so that his hands covered hers. Chasyn was afraid to breathe when she felt his solid body against hers. She could feel coiled muscle and heat and her body instantly reacted by sending a surge of heightened awareness through her system. Her nerve endings were firing strobelike messages to her brain. Chasyn was aware of everything: the slight callouses on his fingertips where they brushed the back of her hands, the corded muscles of his forearms, the very male scent of him. It was almost overwhelming to her senses.

"Farther apart," he said, his voice slightly deeper and close enough to her ear that she could feel the heat of his breath.

Chasyn moved lead legs into position. "What next?" she asked.

"Palms against the grip."

Chasyn was so distracted by Declan that she barely noticed the pinch from the small glass cut on her hand as she gripped the gun as instructed.

Slowly, he moved his hands up her arms, searing a trail of tingling sensations along the way. He cupped her elbows and raised her arms higher. In the process, his forearms brushed the sides of her breasts, making her breath catch in her throat. She stood perfectly still, praying he didn't notice her reaction.

"Look down the barrel and you'll see the sight."

She tried to focus, but it was a challenge. She was practically being strangled by the lump of desire in her throat. God, she was reacting like some awkward teenager fumbling through her first time. She started a mental list. Of course she was overreacting. Nearly two years of celibacy would do that to a girl. Declan was an attractive man, so of course she wouldn't be immune to him. All she needed to do was get a freaking grip on herself.

"I see it."

"Good. Tomorrow morning I'll take you out and let you shoot a few rounds."

"You mean actually fire the gun?"

He stepped back and she felt abandoned.

"Unless you plan on *throwing* it at the bad guys."

* * *

Declan slept fitfully, mainly because he was mentally bashing himself over his behavior the previous evening. He stepped into his jeans, yanked them up, and heard the guest shower running. He knew where Chasyn was and his mind conjured vivid images of her naked body under the steamy spray.

Thinking about her naked was unprofessional and unproductive. His job was to keep her safe, not bed her. "So, what was that gun thing about?" he muttered to himself. The answer came to him instantly. He simply wanted to be close to her. To feel her against him. "You, my friend, are a glutton for punishment."

Declan pulled on a black T-shirt and jeans and went into

the kitchen. After making a pot of coffee, he poured a mug and sat down at the table and began to look over the notes Chasyn had made the previous night. Though he'd teased her about it, he had to admit that her organizational skills were impressive and had the potential to be of use. Especially when the case involved three separate and distinct crime scenes as well as three different weapons.

He re-read the coroner's report. Mary's wounds had been consistent with the use of a K-Bar-type knife. According to the autopsy report on Kasey, the weapon had been a nine-millimeter handgun. He and Chasyn had been shot at with a sniper rifle. He rubbed his freshly shaved chin. "Why the change-up?" he wondered aloud. At the top of Chasyn's page he wrote: *Three Killers???*

Chasyn emerged wearing white jeans and a blush-colored top that left her shoulders bare. Her hair was up in a towel and she had bandages in her hand. "Mind helping me?" she asked.

Declan stood and took the supplies while she unwound the towel. She held her damp hair up, revealing the small row of stitches where the bullet had entered the back of her skull.

"It looks good," he told her.

"I'm sure it's stunning," she quipped.

"You were one lucky person," he said on an expelled breath. "Or you have a very hard head."

"Neither," she said. "It was a fluke."

"A lucky fluke." Or a warning?

"Definitely," she said with more confidence than she felt. A few millimeters either way and she wouldn't be alive. The thought made her shiver. Or was it the feel of Declan's hand brushing her neck? God, she was confused. Unrelated thoughts seemed to buzz around her head. Maybe this was a result of being shot. Made sense. The alternative was admitting she was attracted to a man with whom she had absolutely nothing in common. And who didn't fit into her life plan. Declan was a lot of things, first and foremost—dangerous.

* * *

Chasyn struggled to stay still while he applied the new bandage. As if his hands weren't distracting enough, she could feel his warm breath wash over her exposed neck and shoulders. She longed to tilt her head to the side to invite a kiss. Perhaps a gentle nibble or nuzzle. Any kind of contact would work. She just wanted to feel his mouth on her body.

"Am I hurting you?"

In ways that have nothing to do with my injuries. "No."

When he finished, she couldn't step away fast enough. She had hoped her long shower would wash away the remnants of her lingering lust. Apparently not. That feeling chased her back to the bedroom. Chasyn took her time drying her hair and applying her makeup. She knew she was dawdling but she really needed the time to regroup. After nearly an hour and a long mental chat with herself, she reemerged and found Declan on the phone.

He turned and looked at her with concern etched in his eyes.

"What?" she mouthed.

He cupped the receiver and said, "Someone broke into your apartment last night."

CHAPTER SIX

Lansing was in my house?" Chasyn asked incredulously.

Declan shook his head as he replaced the phone on its cradle. "No, I have him under surveillance. He never left his home last night."

"Then he's paying someone."

"Most likely," he agreed.

Chasyn took a few steps closer. "How bad is it? Can I go check out the damage?"

"Too dangerous," Declan explained. "It could be a trap."

"Trap?" she repeated.

He took a brief sip from his mug, then said, "It could be a ploy to get you back to the apartment. Right into the crosshairs of the sniper."

Chasyn rubbed her bare upper arms. "You're scaring me."

He did a half-turn and leaned against the countertop. "Don't worry; you're insulated and we're going to take every precaution."

"'We're'?"

"My team and me," he clarified, setting down his empty mug on the counter. "Are you ready to go?"

"Go where?"

"We have to swing by my office and then up to MacDill to see Mary's ex."

"Let me just throw a few things in a bag." She pivoted back toward the bedroom. Her hands shook as she pulled her tote from the closet and filled it with her wallet and keys, though she doubted either of them were necessary. She added a small cosmetics bag and rejoined Declan, who was standing by the door.

"My car is still in the parking lot of the courthouse," she said suddenly.

"I'll send one of the guys for it."

"I have to stop by an ATM to get cash out for the parking fee," she said. "Or I may have to finance it. Depending on how many days they charge me for." Why, she wondered, was she obsessing over her car when she had a sniper after her?

"No ATM withdrawals," Declan told her. "You need to calm down."

"Easy for you to say. No one is trying to kill you." She rubbed her arms and hated that her voice cracked just a little. She struggled to keep the warm tears behind her eyes from spilling out over her cheeks. Abject fear was not good company.

"And my job is to make sure no one kills *you*."

She tilted her head back and met his gaze. "Aren't you

afraid of being shot in the crossfire?" The idea of him being hurt or worse because of her caused a tightness in her belly. She already felt guilty about Kasey's death; she didn't want to entertain the idea of someone else getting hurt because Lansing wanted her dead.

"I'm a big boy," he replied with a grin. "And this isn't my first rodeo."

Chasyn placed one hand on her hip. "Mine either. *I* was the one who convinced Kasey she had to testify. If it wasn't for me, she wouldn't have been at the courthouse the other day. She wouldn't be dead."

"That's crazy," Declan argued. "How could you possibly have known the lengths Lansing would go to cover his ass? No one but Lansing is responsible for Kasey's death."

"But as you so eloquently pointed out last night, we can't *prove* that."

"Yet."

Chasyn dropped her hand. "So, what's the plan?"

Declan took out his cell phone and made a quick call to arrange for her car to be retrieved from the downtown garage. Tamping down her fears, Chasyn gathered the legal pad with her notes and shoved it into her tote. She didn't like feeling so vulnerable. Her well-ordered life was spinning out of her control and she wasn't exactly equipped for that. She couldn't remember a time when her life wasn't planned to a 'T.' She always knew the next step, the next goal. She ticked them off like pickets on a passing fence. It was completely disconcerting to have that stability and structure ripped out from beneath her feet.

"Let's go."

She followed him out to the car and half-expected to be shot on sight. When she climbed up into the passenger seat, her heart was pounding in her ears. "How long does this abject terror last?" she asked as he started the engine.

He put the car in gear, then his hand fell to her thigh and he gave a gentle squeeze. "Believe it or not, you'll probably get used to it."

She felt the warmth of his touch and it spread through her, chasing away the fear and replacing it with something different. And not in a good way. No, her mind wandered to what it would feel like to have his hands all over her. It was a powerful and vivid image and totally inappropriate. Luckily, his hand dropped away, quelling her impure thoughts.

Chasyn fiddled with the handle of her tote as they waited for the iron gate to open so they could leave his well-protected home. In no time, they were heading toward a second location in the western part of Palm Beach County.

Communities gave way to small farms, then the population became more sporadic as they continued to drive. "Where are we going?"

"A little place I have out in the sticks," he said.

"With plenty of places a sniper could hide?"

"If you think my house is secure, you'll be awed by the warehouse."

"Warehouse?"

He turned left down an unmarked road. After about half a mile, they came upon a high fence topped with razor wire. As far as the eye could see, chain-link fencing drew a straight line through the fields. Warning signs and a clearly marked representation cautioned that the fence was electrified. Declan reached into the glove box and took out a remote, depressing the button. A gate swung open with a rattle and a hum.

They drove about another quarter mile before Chasyn caught sight of a massive warehouse with a giant satellite dish mounted on the roof. The building was about half the size of an airplane hangar, with triple garage doors to the left, embedded in concrete walls. It did look like a warehouse.

"Hang on a second," Declan said as he placed the SUV in park and went over to a keypad mounted by one of the garage walls.

He punched in a series of numbers, then one of the triple doors slowly opened. Back into the car, he drove it inside the building, then parked next to a half-dozen other cars.

Chasyn emerged from the vehicle and caught a whiff of engine exhaust before the garage door closed. She cautiously glanced around the unfamiliar surroundings as she followed Declan across the concrete floor. The din of muffled voices came from the far end of the space, and she saw a frosted glass wall up ahead. Harsh fluorescent bulbs lined the ceiling leading to the glassed-in area.

Declan opened the door and then stepped aside for her to enter first. What she found looked very much like an ordinary office. The walls were lined with file cabinets and there were desks set up at equal intervals. At the far end of the room she noted a portion of the wall was covered by three large computer monitors. Then she became aware of the three men and one woman with their eyes trained on her.

"Everyone, this is Chasyn."

The first person to step forward with his hand extended was like Declan, tall and well-muscled. "Gavin," he greeted her, extending his hand. His smile reached his dark brown eyes.

"Hello."

Declan absently placed one hand at the small of her back. To Chasyn, it felt like branding, but she managed to keep her expression bland.

"Don't let his boyish good looks fool you. Gavin is ex-Special Forces. He can kill you with an eyelash."

Chasyn dropped her hand and when she did, Gavin offered up a playful wink.

A smaller man with shoulder-length blond hair pulled into a man-bun came over and offered his hand. "This is Chuck. He's my resident expert on finding people and things."

"Ma'am."

Chasyn smiled.

"This," Declan said as a third man stepped forward, "is Adam. He's my right-hand guy and basically keeps this place running smoothly."

Adam was deeply tanned and looked more like a surfer than a business associate. "Nice to meet you, Chasyn."

"And last but not least," Declan said. "This is Ziggy. She's the resident geek and the best hacker in the business."

The thin brunette grinned but didn't offer her hand. She seemed socially awkward so Chasyn didn't press it. Instead she just said, "Nice to meet all of you."

Declan moved past her and leaned on the edge of one of the desks. "So, where are we?"

"Tom took pictures at the apartment, then picked up Chasyn's car. He should be here in about forty minutes," Adam said. "Any idea what Lansing would want from your apartment?" he asked, his eyes focused on her.

She shook her head, much like she shook off the memory of Decan's hand on her back. "I don't have anything of any real value."

"Maybe the photos will tell us what he was looking for," Declan suggested. "What about Mary's ex? I really want to talk to him."

Ziggy spoke up. "He's on duty until six and I found the address to the house he rents off-base."

Declan stroked his chin. "Anything hinky with his financials?"

"Actually, yes," Ziggy said, jogging back to the computer area and returning with a small stack of pages. "Two days after Mary's death, he invested five grand in cash in his mutual fund."

"Can you trace the cash?"

Ziggy shook her head, causing a few strands of her dark hair to come free from a hastily created updo. "No. And nothing strange since then. Just direct deposits from the Marine Corps into his checking account."

"Go back to before Mary's death," Declan said. "See if Mr. Jolsten has supplemented his income in the past."

Declan glanced over at Gavin. "Anything on the weapons used?"

"Other than the fact that most killers don't change MOs with every attempt?"

Declan nodded. "That bothers me, too."

"But," Chasyn interjected, "couldn't it just be that he didn't kill me in the drive-by so he switched to a different tactic?"

Declan shrugged his broad shoulders. "Possible. But I'm thinking Lansing killed Mary himself and now he's hired someone to clean up his mess."

Adam agreed. "That would explain the different weapons."

"However," Ziggy countered, "I've crawled all up into his finances and I can't find any method of payment."

"Maybe payment on completion?" Adam suggested.

Chasyn shivered. "That's a cheery thought."

"Or," Declan said. "He's got some source of cash flow we haven't found yet. Ziggy, keep digging. I'm going to take Chasyn to the range. Let me know when Tom gets back with her car." He stood to his full, impressive height. "Leave your bag here," he told her.

Chasyn followed him back through the garage. He went to a black Hummer and opened the back. Inside there was a long metal box with a combination lock. Declan dialed in the code, then lifted the top.

"Jesus," Chasyn said on an expelled breath when she saw the mini-arsenal stored in the case. "You could start a war with all that stuff."

"Just a few handguns and a couple of rifles." He selected a gun that looked very much like the one he'd given her last night. Only this time he didn't remove the clip or clear the chamber. "Let's go see what you've got."

"Go where?" she asked.

"There's a range out back."

"Your neighbors must love you."

"We're sitting on five acres. No neighbors to complain."

They took a side door outside and Chasyn blinked against the mid-morning sunlight. There was a decent breeze and just a hint of pine in the air. She followed him into an area petitioned by a fence with a thatched overhang. Wooden pedestals were lined up in a row of four. Beyond the pedestals, there was a rope and pulley system strung between the overhang and some targets that seemed very far in the distance. Beyond the targets was a huge mound of dirt.

"Ready?" he asked.

She almost put her hands behind her back. "No."

"Buck up. There's nothing to it."

"Says the man who *wasn't* shot in the head." With a sigh, Chasyn stepped up, spread her feet shoulder-width apart and gingerly took the gun from Declan, being careful to keep it pointed away from him and her own feet. "It's heavier with bullets."

"First," he said as he came up behind her. "Take it off safety."

Chasyn was struggling to stay focused. Not only could she feel him pressed against her, his breath was warm against her bared shoulders and threatening to send a shiver the full length of her spine. She clicked the lever to its new position. "Okay, safety off."

"Site the target."

She closed one eye and brought the outline into focus. "Got it."

"Pull the trigger."

She did and instantly slammed back against his solid form. If he hadn't been standing there, she would have fallen on her ass. "You didn't warn me about that."

"Sorry. On the next one, adjust to for the recoil."

Again she sighted the target, then adjusted her stance before pulling the trigger. This time she was ready and managed to hold her ground. "I hit it!" she practically squealed.

"You hit the white part," Declan remarked with amusement. "Let's see if you can hit the actual outline."

It took her a dozen more tries before she winged the outline in the shoulder. She was no Annie Oakley but she was getting the hang of it. "This is a lot harder than I thought it would be."

"It's a skill," he said. "Keep practicing and you'll get better." He reached around and cautiously took the gun from her. Once he put it back on safety, he shoved it into the back of his waistband. "Tom should be back by now," he said, leading her back to the gate.

Declan was correct. Tom was back and so was her pale, metallic blue Prius. It looked small and out of place parked among the SUVs, sedans, and the rolling arsenal Hummer. Tom turned out to be a young man she thought was about her age, with a full beard and dark, curly hair. They shared introductions.

"What do you want first?" Tom asked. "The apartment or the car?"

"Something happened to my car?" Chasyn demanded as she took a quick look at the vehicle.

Tom pulled his phone out of his front pocket and pulled up a photograph. It appeared to be the front wheel well of her car but there was a small black box with a tiny antenna and a red light on the box.

"High end," Declan remarked.

"High end what?" Chasyn asked.

"GPS tracker," Declan explained.

"I got the serial number off it in case Ziggy can do anything with it," Tom said.

"Where is it now?" Chasyn asked.

Tom grinned. "Attached to a seat on one of the trolleys that goes back and forth through West Palm."

"How long will that deter him?" Chasyn asked.

"Not long," Declan said. "But it's a good sign."

"Of what?"

"That he doesn't know where you are."

Chasyn let out a breath. "Yet."

CHAPTER SEVEN

And my apartment?" Chasyn asked.

Declan was impressed by how well she was keeping it together. He could just imagine how difficult this must be on someone used to a boring, orderly life. But, he thought as he looked her up and down, there was nothing bland about the woman herself. No, she was nothing if not intriguing and he couldn't quite understand why he was so curious about a woman who was the exact opposite of what normally piqued his interest. For one, she was a petite woman. He'd always gone for women closer to five-eight or taller. With her spine straight, Chasyn barely hit the five-four mark, nearly a foot shorter in stature than himself. That alone should have turned him off, but it didn't. On the contrary, he was nearly consumed by a visceral need to protect her. And not for the money. Just because he couldn't stand the look of fear clouding those incredible blue-green eyes. The fact that she had a killer body didn't hurt either.

Tom swiped through a series of photographs. Basically, they showed her ransacked apartment. Drawers were dumped, cushions tossed. A general mess. Declan asked, "How did he get in?"

"There were tool marks on the doorknob and the deadbolt." Tom turned his attention on Chasyn. "One of your neighbors noticed the door ajar this morning and called the cops."

"Who probably want to talk to me. *Again*."

She was rubbing her arms again, a 'tell' he now recognized when she was attempting to tamp down her anxiety. "They'll have to get through Jack," Declan reminded her. "And he'll keep them off our asses, no problem. Any idea what he was looking for in your apartment?"

She scanned the photos a second time. "Most of the chaos is in the kitchen. I don't know; maybe he wanted my grandmother's meatloaf recipe."

Declan smiled as he flipped back to the picture of the kitchen floor. Items strewn about included batteries, rubber bands, a small flashlight, chip clips, note pads and one of those rubber things used to coax open a jar lid. "Junk drawer?" he asked.

She nodded. "Odds and ends."

A cold chill ran through him. "No address book?"

She shook her head. "I keep mine on my phone and sync it to my laptop."

"There's no laptop in any of these photos."

Chasyn pointed to her car. "It's locked in my trunk."

Declan relaxed. "That's good. No way you want this guy getting a hold of your personal information."

Her face registered concern. "What about my parents?" she asked on a quick breath.

"That was probably the first place he looked."

Again, she was rubbing her arms. "Are they in danger?"

"A pro isn't going to risk that kind of collateral damage. It's not good for business." Declan reached out and placed his hand over one of hers. The rubbing immediately stopped when he made contact with her warm, smooth skin. Normally he wasn't a touchy-feely guy but he already knew that his touch distracted her, and right now he wanted to divert her attention away from her fears.

As expected, Chasyn seemed to switch her focus from victim to activist. "So how do I stay one step ahead of this lunatic?"

"That's my job," Declan assured her as he reluctantly let his hand fall away. He had an almost overwhelming desire to pull her into his arms and kiss away her unease. *Who was he kidding? He wanted her in his arms, period.*

* * *

Her car and her apartment had been violated by some unknown dirtbag with orders to kill her and all Chasyn could think was how much she missed the feel of Declan's touch. Clearly she was going crazy. But acknowledging that didn't stop her from ogling him when he wasn't looking. He was so unlike the young professionals she normally dated. The kinds of men with 9-to-5 corporate jobs and upward mobility. Men like her. Boring men. *Where did that come from?*

She wondered as she silently admired Declan's dark good looks, which were accentuated by his black T-shirt and black jeans. That outfit, stretched across corded muscle, made him seem large and invincible. And sexy as hell. *And I am going to burn in hell for my impure thoughts.*

Quelling the urge to reach up and brush a lock of his ebony hair from his forehead, Chasyn clasped her hands together and stood as casually as possible among Declan and his team. Well, his team minus one, but that was quickly rectified. Ziggy came rushing out from the office area waving a sheet of paper in the air.

"Who is the Queen of All Knowledge?" she asked with a wide grin on her otherwise unremarkable face. Her hair was pulled back into a hasty ponytail now and a pencil protruded from where the elastic secured her hair.

"Share with the group," Declan said.

Excitedly, she said, "I traced the serial number on the GPS tracker."

"Is that a new record for you?" Declan asked with a smile that Chasyn felt in the pit of her stomach.

"Maybe," Ziggy sighed dramatically. "Purchased at Spy Zone in Palm Beach Gardens five days ago. And, I've already spoken to the store manager and even though it was a cash transaction, they have video of the sale. I told him you'd be there in twenty minutes."

Declan took the sheet of paper from Ziggy with the address, then placed his hand at the center of Chasyn's back and guided her to the Hummer. Her mind was spinning. A real lead was an exciting development but it seemed to pale badly in comparison to the sensation of Declan's hand splayed at her back. She could feel the heat from his touch through the thin fabric of her top. She quickened her step to try to put some distance between them. She needed to regain her footing; stop fixating on the impressive physicality of the man just behind her. This was an extreme and temporary situation. She didn't do extreme and she certainly didn't do temporary. Too many complications.

As she climbed into the Hummer, Declan replaced the gun in the locker in the back of the car. Ziggy appeared at her door, holding out her tote. "You forgot this," she said. Then she handed Chasyn a nondescript black cellphone "This is a burner phone. I pre-programmed it with all our numbers."

"I have a cellphone," she said. "Or rather Declan confiscated it."

Ziggy shrugged her boney shoulders. "This one is untraceable. No way for our guy to track you via your phone."

"But I have password protection on my phone."

"With your parents, your job and several friends on speed dial."

"How do you know that?"

"I hacked your phone. Anything that connects you to the Internet connects you to hackers and my guess is the guy who's after you has some skills." Ziggy told her as casually as if she was explaining the best way to grow basil on a windowsill.

"This just keeps getting better and better," she grumbled as Declan slipped behind the wheel.

"Ready?" he asked.

"Why are we switching cars?" she asked as she tucked the phone into her tote.

"It's safer for you."

"Wait," Chasyn said. "Can I get my sunglasses and my laptop out of my car?"

"I'll get them," Declan got out and went over to her lonely little Prius. He was back in seconds with her things and in no time, they were heading out of the compound.

The air was thick with the subtle scent of his cologne. Chasyn kept sneaking glances at his profile. It was impressive. Though his face was sharp and angled, he had a rugged quality about him that seemed to soften the edges. Sunlight glistened off his thick, ebony hair. Chasyn was tempted to reach out and run her fingers through it but thought better of it. *Focus!* She chided herself. "I know this spy shop," she said. "When I was doing matrimonial work, we often referred clients there. They have lots of easily hidden cameras for sale."

"To catch cheating husbands in the act?"

"Or cheating wives. Compromising photographs make for quick settlements."

"Did you like doing divorces?" he asked as he steered the car back onto the main road.

"Nope. Too many people who hate each other more than they love their children."

"Marriage can do that to you," he opined.

"Not marriage material?" She immediately wanted to take back the question.

"Probably not," he answered. His voice held a tinge of derision.

She wondered if that was from a bad experience or just a general feeling. But she didn't want to pry any further. No good reason to confuse the professional with the personal. Though she was at a clear disadvantage. He knew everything about her, and that didn't seem fair.

As promised, they reached Palm Beach Gardens and the Spy Shop in just under twenty-five minutes. It was a small shop in the center of a strip mall on Alternate A-1-A. Chasyn stepped down from the Hummer and immediately felt a surge of fear since she was out in the open. She practically ran to the door of the store, yanking it open and nearly tripping inside.

It was a rectangular space with a variety of glass cabinets lining each wall. Down the center were sales racks with a variety of items on hooks and pegs. It smelled faintly of coffee and cherry air freshener. She pushed her glasses high on her head and waited for her pulse to return to normal.

Declan stepped in front of her, introduced himself to the clerk, and then asked, "May we see the manager? He's expecting us."

The male clerk, who was tall, young, thin and a redhead crooked his head in the direction of a door at the back of the store marked PRIVATE. Passing a collection of binoculars and night vision goggles, they reached the door and Declan knocked.

A man she guessed was about sixty opened the door and smiled at Declan. The action caused the nub of a cigar clamped in the corner of his mouth to shift position. What hair he had left was graying and the top of his head mirrored the bright light overhead.

He ushered them inside a storeroom, through to a small office. The scent of cherry deodorizer was stronger in the back. So was the smell of stale coffee. "How long has it been, Declan?"

"A while," he answered. "Mickey, this is Chasyn."

Mickey turned and looked at her, then nodded. "Right, the chick on the news who walked away from a bullet to the brain."

"I'll have to remember to add that to my résumé," she returned with a forced smile.

"Yeah, well, sorry about the other chick."

"Do you have the tape queued up?" Declan asked.

Mickey moved to his computer keyboard, punched in a few commands and then a video opened on his monitor. "This is him entering the store just past noon," he narrated.

The image was clear but the man's face was completely obscured by a baseball cap. He moved with purpose directly to the cabinet with GPS trackers. He seemed to know where the cameras were, because none of the three angles of the transaction revealed his face.

"Does the strip mall have external security cameras?" Declan asked. "Maybe I can get a picture of him going to his car."

"They don't," Mickey explained. "There's cameras mounted on the buildings but they aren't connected. Stupid, cheap bastard. I even offered to get him the recording equipment at cost. Back to your guy: I was working the register and I vaguely remember him."

"Why?" Declan asked.

"When I started to explain to him that he needed software to track the GPS he said he already had it. Seemed to be in a real hurry to get in and get out."

"What did he look like?"

"Early thirties, maybe. Medium build. Dark hair. No beard but that five o'clock shadow from not standing close enough to his razor. Oh, and his hat was an Atlanta Braves cap."

Chasyn felt her shoulders slump. This wasn't much of a lead.

"If he comes in again, give me a call," Declan said.

"Will do," Mickey said. "Sorry I wasn't more help."

Chasyn offered a tepid smile. "Thank you anyway."

"Take care, young lady. You're in good hands with this one."

As soon as they left the store, Declan asked, "Anything about that guy seem familiar to you?"

"Nothing."

"What about the possible Atlanta connection?"

Chasyn shook her head as she moved quickly to get back inside the relative safety of the car. "I've only been to Atlanta once and that was almost seven years ago."

"Vacation?"

"Paralegal Association conference. Kasey and I went together, thanks to her dad." She clicked her seatbelt into place. "We couldn't swing the conference fee and the hotel so her mom and dad rented a suite and went to Atlanta with us."

"They attended a paralegal conference?"

"No," she sighed. "The Beckers have four car washes in the metro Atlanta area. They did their thing and we did ours."

Declan was quiet for a minute. "Was that normal?"

She regarded him for a minute. "Going someplace with the Beckers?"

"Yeah."

"Uh-huh. They've been taking me on vacations and trips with them since I was a teenager. And vice-versa. Kasey travelled with my family as well." Chasyn felt the sting of tears and discreetly dabbed at them, then shoved her sunglasses on her face. "I still can't believe she's gone."

Declan's knuckles turned whitish as he gripped the steering wheel more tightly. Chasyn could sense he was upset and guessed it was because she was crying. Again. Apparently Declan didn't like crying women and sadness seemed to be her go-to emotion right now. "Let's head up to MacDill and see what Captain Jolsten has to say about his ex-wife."

"What if he's in his mid-thirties and wearing an Atlanta Braves cap?" Chasyn asked as she began to rub her arms against the chill of fear that suddenly surged through her.

"Then my job here will be done."

CHAPTER EIGHT

The March sun heated the mid-morning air to near ninety degrees inside the car, and Declan adjusted the A/C. Chasyn, her phone out and her legal pad balanced on her lap, smiled. "Oh God, that cold air feels good, thanks. The base is approximately four miles south-southwest of Tampa. The most direct route to MacDill is the Turnpike to I-4, then—"

"Thanks Magellan, but I know how to get to MacDill," Declan assured her. "Plus I have this," he added, tapping on the GPS display encased in the car's dashboard. "And we won't be going on the base. At least not unless we have to talk directly to the NCIS folks who did the actual interview with Mary's ex William."

"You mean they didn't speak directly to the Martin County Sheriffs?" Chasyn found that odd.

"Military protocol," Declan explained. "Captain Jolsten is active duty Marines. NCIS has jurisdiction over all criminal matters concerning personnel."

Chasyn gently smoothed her hair off her forehead, refusing the temptation to rip off the small bandage and scratch the three stitches beneath. "I thought NCIS was Navy. Isn't MacDill an Air Force base?"

"Yes, but it is also home to the Hurricane Hunters, U.S. Central Command, U.S. Special Ops Command, and a whole host of other collocated services."

Chasyn angled in her seat. Unfortunately his mirrored aviators prevented her from seeing his eyes, so she felt at a distinct disadvantage. Not to mention that she missed the enjoyable side benefit of staring into their ice-blue depths. She settled for an unrestricted view of his handsome profile. "Are you some sort of military junkie?"

"I did a stint in the service."

There was something in his tone that warned her off further inquiry. Chasyn reached over and pressed the A/C button, allowing a sliver of fresh air to enter the car. It was a nice diversion from the numbing din of the Hummer cruising up the turnpike. Declan was pushing beyond the speed limit as the air filled with the scent of freshly mowed grass punctuated occasionally by the sweet smell of orange blossoms in bloom. The ride was flat and monotonous, broken only by the *thud-thud* of the tires passing over roadway joints.

"We should have taken my car," she mused as she glanced out the window at a small herd of cows standing around in a fenced field abutting the roadway. "It's more fuel efficient. What does this thing get, like twelve miles to a gallon?"

"Pretty much," he answered with amusement. "But your potential assassin isn't looking for a black Hummer."

"One with an arsenal in the back."

"Perfectly legal," he assured her. "Everything is permitted and I have a conceal-and-carry permit."

Just then his phone rang and she silently listened as he uttered a series of *Uh-huh*s and *okay*s.

When he ended the call, he asked, "Have you turned on your laptop?"

She shook her head. "Not yet, why?"

"The killer may have your IP address. You don't want to risk a trace."

Chasyn rubbed her arms for a minute, then asked, "Are all determined killers this tech savvy?"

"No," he assured her. "You seem to have lucked into a true pro."

"But that doesn't make any sense," she argued. "I didn't actually see Lansing kill Mary and I sure as shit didn't see the guy who shot me."

"He can't take that chance," Declan reasoned. "What exactly did you see the night of the waitress's murder?"

"I saw the girl lying in the parking lot, bleeding out, and I got a split-second look at the taillights as the car sped away from the parking lot."

"Think you could identify the taillights?" he asked.

Chasyn sucked in a breath and let it out slowly. Just reliving the events of that night tensed every muscle in her body. "I'm not really good with cars. I think it was a dark car, maybe blue, maybe black. The taillights were kinda rectangular, a red frame around the white part. Oh, and there was some sort of lettering below the light."

"Make or model?"

"It was a 2012, metallic blue Mustang GT with white wall mag wheels. Custom sunroof, a scratch on the right rear fender, and the license plate was 12A79." She ticked off the details efficiently.

His head swiveled and he saw her deadpan expression. "Holy shit. You saw all that?" he asked, clearly excited.

She let out a breath and rolled her eyes. "Hell no! The best I can do is it was some kind of sedan. Four door, I'm pretty sure."

He gave her a scowl, then made a call to his office and asked them to get a list of any cars Dr. Lansing owned or had access to.

When he was finished, Chasyn said, "The police already did that. None of the pictures they showed me matched the taillights I saw that night."

Declan rubbed the stubble on his chin. "Guess it could have been a rental."

"Again," she said with frustration, "The police checked that angle too and didn't come up with anything."

Declan reached out and closed his hand over her knee and gave a gentle squeeze. Chasyn knew it was supposed to be reassuring but her body didn't get the memo. Her skin warmed where he touched and carried that warmth throughout her entire body. This was crazy. There was no way she should be so fixated on a man who a) she'd just met, and b) was very temporary. The pull she felt might be strong but she knew better than to involve herself in something that didn't further her goals.

"Hungry?"

You have no idea. "I could eat," she said with an admirably calm voice.

Declan waited until they had cleared Orlando traffic, then pulled off I-4 and into the parking lot of a Cracker Barrel. It was mid-afternoon, so there was no wait. Per Declan's request, they were seated at a window table and he positioned himself so that he could surveille the parking lot.

Chasyn pushed aside the golf tee brainteaser and accepted a tri-fold menu from a seasoned waitress. The smell of coffee hung in the air. She ordered a veggie plate while Declan opted for a high-protein, high-carb selection. They both ordered iced tea, which was delivered quickly along with a small plate of freshly cut lemon wedges.

"You have a huge advantage in this relationship," she said as she draped her napkin in her lap.

"Really?" he asked as he hooked his sunglasses on the neck of his shirt.

"You know everything about me but I don't know much about you, other than that you drive a gas-guzzling car, shoot guns, and did some time in the service."

"You forgot the vestibule of your apartment building," he said with a wry smile. "I also have catlike reflexes."

"And a modest ego," she teased. "I'm serious. Tell me something about you so this doesn't feel so one-sided to me."

"I spent eight years in the Army," he said reluctantly.

"I'm guessing you weren't a cook." *Not with biceps the size of tree trunks.*

He shook his head and said, "Special Forces."

Chasyn regarded him for a few seconds, trying to decipher the flash of something she read in his eyes. "I've heard of them but I don't really know what they do."

Declan shrugged uncomfortably. "The kind of stuff that doesn't make the news," was his cryptic response.

This appeared to be an area he didn't like to discuss, but Chasyn was undeterred. After all, he knew what kind of toilet tissue she ordered online. It was only fair for her to know some of his past. "How old were you when you joined the military?"

"Eighteen." His mouth grew into a taut line.

"Were you planning on making it a career?" she pressed.

"Initially."

Chasyn sighed. "Are you going to give me one word answers to every question?"

"Probably."

"Then I'll just sit here and hope our food arrives soon."

As if on cue, the friendly waitress delivered three plates. One for Chasyn and the other two were placed side by side in front of Declan. She guessed there were about five thousand calories in his meal. But judging by his impressive body, he burned it; he didn't store it. Chasyn, on the other hand, had to run an extra mile if she so much as thought about a Reese's cup.

Aside from, "Pass the pepper," the meal progressed in relative silence, though Chasyn was keenly aware of two things: Declan in general, and his ability to eat and keep vigil at the same time. His fork stopped in mid-air only once, when a thirtyish man with dark hair parked in the lot and started for the building. She noticed Declan tense for a second until a young child emerged from the car's backseat and joined his father.

Chasyn ventured into the ladies' room while Declan paid the bill. It had taken just under an hour before they were back headed northwest toward MacDill.

"Do you like being an only child?" Declan asked after they'd driven for about fifteen minutes in relative silence.

"Not when my parents are worried sick and I probably don't want to know what they're paying you." She turned and took in his angled profile. "What about you? Is Jack your only sibling?"

He shook his head. "I have one older brother, Michael, and then Jack and Conner are younger."

"Jack is a lawyer; what about the other two?"

Immediately his brow furrowed. "Conner is a sheriff in north Florida and Michael is a convicted murderer."

A killer? Well, Chasyn was at a loss for words. *What was the right response to that bit of information? And who did he kill and why? Was there a dark side to the Kavanaugh family? Declan did have a thing for danger. And guns.* Good lord, her mind was spinning.

Her silence must have prompted him to add, "Convicted, but it wasn't murder."

"What was it?"

"Our father was a mean drunk who liked to beat on our mother. One night he pulled out a shotgun and was going to make good on his years of threats to kill her. Michael intervened, grabbed the weapon, and during the struggle, my father managed to pull the trigger. My mother was killed. They continued struggling, the gun went off a second time, and my father was killed in the altercation."

"That's horrible," Chasyn said with a shiver. "If it was an accident, how did he get convicted?"

"The jury system at its worst. His parole hearing is next week."

"How long has he been in prison?"

"Fifteen years."

That sounded like a lifetime, especially given the circumstances. What a horrible fate for Michael and clearly it weighed heavily on Declan. And that tugged at her. It was Chasyn's turn to reach out. She patted his thigh since she couldn't think of anything profound to say.

* * *

Declan figured his reaction to the feel of her touch was stronger than normal because talking about Michael was always difficult. Still, even through the denim, he could feel the warmth of her delicate hand on his leg and it brought more than just comfort. Which was nuts since Chasyn was a client, nothing more. He didn't like complications in his life or in relationships. There was a reason why he preferred exotic women and temporary arrangements. They suited his lifestyle and his needs. Chasyn seemed more the home-and-hearth type. Hell, she even had a timetable that included a marriage target date and children planned down to the minute. Definitely out of his comfort zone. Why, then, did he spend the rest of the drive to Tampa wondering what it would be like to strip the clothes from her enticing body?

It was rush hour by the time they reached Tampa, so traffic was thick and slow. Ziggy called with a good lead.

It turned out William Jolsten used his credit card at a bar called the Zone almost every evening after work. Armed with that info, Declan keyed the address into the GPS and followed the voice commands.

They pulled into a gravel parking lot adjacent to a single-story building. The minute they stepped from the car, the stench of stale beer and cigarette smoke greeted them. There was a mixture of cars, trucks, and motorcycles parked outside, and the place looked in need of some fresh paint and window cleaning.

He held the door for Chasyn and stepped out of bright sunlight into a dimly lit room with a horseshoe-shaped bar. Beyond this space was a back area with three pool tables and a dart board along the far wall. Neon signs touting various brands hung above the worn wooden bar, and the stools were nearly filled with customers. Many of the patrons were in some variation of military uniform. Obviously, this was a popular place with the MacDill gang.

Declan scanned the room and spotted his target sitting on a stool by the waitress stand. He was nursing a half-full bottle of beer and flipping a book of matches in his hand. Declan purposefully placed a possessive hand on Chasyn's shoulder as he guided her toward Mary's ex-husband. She'd drawn attention the minute she stepped inside the male-dominated bar and the last thing he needed was some fool hitting on her.

"Captain Jolsten?"

The man turned. Declan put his age at about thirty. He was tall, maybe six foot, with dark hair and dark eyes, so he couldn't rule him out as the guy from the spy shop. Well, not until he watched as the other man took a look at Chasyn.

There was nothing subtle about the way he was checking her out, but there was nothing familiar about it either. Declan was fairly certain this wasn't the professional killer after Chasyn.

"What do you need?" he asked as he took a swig of his beer.

Declan took out his credentials and showed them to the Marine. "I'm looking into the murder of your wife."

"Ex-wife," Jolsten corrected without emotion.

"Mind if I ask you a few questions about her?" Declan asked as he pulled out a nearby stool for Chasyn.

Jolsten shrugged and said, "I already went through all this with NCIS." He swiveled on his stool and extended his hand to Chasyn. "My friends call me Bill."

Declan inserted himself between them. "She isn't your friend," he said in a low tone. "What can you tell me about Mary?"

Jolsten went back to his beer. "She's dead."

"You don't seem very torn up about it," Declan said.

"Because I'm not. That woman was nothing but trouble. Whoever killed her did me a favor."

"How so?"

"Mary always had an angle," Jolsten explained. "She played me but good. Only stayed married to me long enough to bleed out my savings."

"Then what?" Declan pressed.

"Then nothing. By the time I figured out that she was syphoning off money, she was long gone. The bank just fore-closed on my house. I'm back living on base," he said, hostil-ity in his brown eyes.

"Why didn't you have her prosecuted?"

"Can't get blood out of a turnip," he mused.

"Mary never gave you any money?"

He grunted a laugh. "Hardly. Last I heard she was waiting tables. What was I supposed to do? Garnish her tips and wait twenty years to get my forty grand back?"

Declan glanced down at the badges pinned to his uniform shirt. "You're a marksman," he observed.

"Yes. But since NCIS said my ex was stabbed, I don't see how that's relevant."

In the distance, he heard the opening break of a game of pool. "But you would have gotten K-BAR training as part of your basic combat training."

"Like I told NCIS, I was on duty from twenty-four-hundred hours until I was relieved at O-seven-hundred hours. More than a dozen people verified that." Jolsten took another pull on his beer. "Are we done here?" he asked, clearly getting irritated.

"Almost. What did you mean when you said Mary was always working an angle?"

"I mean just that. Look," he said as he spun his stool. "Mary grew up dirt poor and she was pretty determined to change her lot in life. I was just a stepping stone to something better. And, from what I read about her murder, she had herself mixed up with some rich doctor. Shouldn't you be grilling him?"

"He's on my list," Declan said noncommittally.

"Then we're done here," Jolsten said.

Declan placed one hand on the back of Jolsten's stool. "One last thing. You deposited five grand into your account, in cash, two days before your ex was killed. Care to explain that?"

CHAPTER NINE

Jolsten stopped flipping the matchbook in his hand and balled his fist. A sure physical tell as far as Declan was concerned. "What aren't you sharing with the class?" he pressed.

"Nothing," Jolsten insisted.

But in Declan's assessment, he was a pretty lame liar. "Five thousand dollars' worth of nothing."

Jolsten was silent for a few seconds, then he unballed his fist and turned to meet Declan's gaze. "The money wasn't mine," he admitted. "Well, half of it wasn't." He shifted his weight.

Declan gave him a hard look. "What was it for?"

Jolsten took a pull on his beer, swallowed, and answered. "My share of a scam Mary cooked up."

"Let's go over to a booth," Declan grabbed the man's beer with one hand and placed his other on Chasyn's back. Once the trio was settled in, Declan said, "Explain. And start from the beginning."

Jolsten rubbed the short-cropped hair on his head. "It started when Mary found out she was pregnant."

"With your baby?" Chasyn asked.

Jolsten grunted and shook his head. "No way. She never came out and told me who the father was, just that he was loaded *and* married."

"And you're sure she never told you it was Dr. Lansing's baby?"

"Positive," Jolsten answered. "But she figured he'd pay big time to keep the pregnancy and the baby a secret. She told me his wife was the one with the real bucks and she'd toss him out on his ear if she found out he'd been screwing around again."

"That has to be Lansing," Chasyn said with a small measure of excitement.

"So, Lansing gave Mary five grand?"

Jolsten hung his head and shook it at the same time. "That money came from a couple in Boca Raton. The Wellingtons."

"I don't follow," Declan said.

Jolsten lifted his brown eyes and met Declan's stare. "Mary's plan B."

"Which was?" Declan countered.

"Maybe five seconds after she passed her pee-on-a-stick test, Mary already had an angle. She didn't tell me everything, but she needed my help with part of her scheme. All I know was she planned to string the baby daddy along but she had no intention of keeping the kid. Mary didn't have a maternal bone in her body. So." Jolsten paused and took a sip of his beer. "She responded to an ad in the paper. A childless couple willing to pay for a baby to adopt."

"That's illegal," Chasyn inserted.

Jolsten shook his head. "Mary researched it. So long as the money was to be used for the care, living, and medical expenses of the mother during the pregnancy, it's all nice and legal. The couple supports her for nine months and then they get to adopt the baby."

"So, Mary had no intention of keeping her baby?" Declan asked.

Jolsten sighed. "No, Mary had every intention of keeping that kid. Said it was her ticket to an easy life. She was going to screw the adoptive family. She planned on collecting from them during her pregnancy, then telling them she'd changed her mind when the kid was born."

"So, the five thousand was a down payment?" Chasyn asked.

Jolsten nodded. "Mary said she couldn't risk the baby's father finding out about the phony adoption scam. So, in return for me hiding the money, Mary was going to pay back some of what she owed me."

"Did you tell all this to NCIS?" Declan asked.

"I couldn't," Jolsten insisted.

"Why? Especially in light of the fact that she was murdered." Chasyn pressed.

Jolsten's shoulders slumped. "Mary had me bent over a rock."

"How so?" Declan leaned in closer to the man. "What did she have on you?"

"Are you going to repeat this to NCIS?" he asked. "Because if you do, I'm totally screwed."

Declan shook his head. "I'm not after you."

On a breath, Jolsten explained, "Mary and I were married for about a year when I found out she was cheating on me. I was so pissed I went out and cheated on her. Stupid, I know, but at the time it seemed like a good idea. Only the woman I cheated with was one of my superiors *and* she was married."

"And Mary found out?" Declan supplied.

"Oh, she did more than that," Jolsten said, resigned. "She managed to get pictures of me and the woman. Compromising pictures."

Chasyn clasped her hands and rested them on the worn wooden tabletop. "I don't understand," she said. "If you were both unfaithful, how was that a problem?"

"Military code," Jolsten answered. "Adultery is a crime. At the very least it would have ended both of our careers. That's why I didn't put up a fight when Mary started robbing me blind."

Declan stroked his chin. "So where are the photos now?"

Jolsten shrugged. "They must not have been in her apartment or the cops would have found them. Ever since she died I've been waiting for them to surface."

"Did Mary have anyone close to her that she would have entrusted them to?" Chasyn asked.

"Not that I know of. But that's not unusual. Mary never was very good at making or keeping friends."

Declan began to slide out of the booth. "Thank you for your time, Captain Jolsten."

The other man grabbed his wrist. "If you happen to find those photographs…"

Declan felt for the guy. "I don't see any reason to make them public."

Relief washed over Jolsten's face. "Good luck finding evidence against Dr. Lansing."

* * *

"Maybe Mary has a safe deposit box," Chasyn suggested shortly after they were back on the road. "If she does, there might be some sort of proof that it was Lansing's baby."

"We ran down her financials," Declan said. "No safe deposit box rentals in her name."

Chasyn felt frustrated. "Please tell me your team will be able to get his DNA."

"They're on him twenty-four-seven, but Lansing isn't stupid. Last night he went to dinner with his wife and actually took his own silverware into the restaurant. Drank water with a straw and took the silverware and the straw with him when he left."

"Well, that pretty much screams guilty to me. We have to prove Lansing killed Mary and Kasey, and is pretty determined to kill me, too."

Declan was smiling at her.

"What?"

"'We'?" he said with a chuckle.

It rankled. "I have no intention of sitting around like a target. There has to be *something* I can do."

"Stay alive?"

She shivered. "That's at the top of my list," she assured him. "I know you have a whole team of people but I am an asset. I'm organized and I have great research skills. Maybe there's something in Lansing's past that I can dig up."

"I have a vehicle database," Declan told her. "You can try to identify the car taillights."

"Sounds mind-numbing."

"Right now it's one of the best leads we have. If you can identify the car and we can trace it back to Dr. Lansing, we can probably extinguish the threat to your life."

She rubbed her bare arms. "*Probably*?"

"I'm pretty convinced the guy after you is a pro. Normally they get half up front and half on completion. If we can prevent Lansing from paying out the second half, the pro will probably walk away from the job."

"And how do we find the guy to let him know there won't be any payment on the back end? Even if he does his job?"

She watched as the corners of his mouth turned down. "The only way is to demonstrate that Lansing can't or won't be able to fulfill the contract."

"A public arrest?" she asked.

"That's one possibility."

"Is there another one?" Chasyn wondered.

"I get the killer first."

* * *

It was close to ten by the time they returned to Declan's

fortress of a house in West Palm Beach. Chasyn was a heap
of frazzled energy. Declan offered to make her an omelet but
she wasn't hungry. "I'd like to call my parents and check my
work email," she said.

Declan didn't look up from his task of brewing a mug of
coffee. "Call your parents from the burner phone I gave you
but make it quick, under two minutes. Stay off your email."

"For how long?"

Declan turned and rested one hand behind him as he
leaned against the counter top. He took a sip from the mug.
"I don't know the extent of this guy's tech skills but I'm not
willing to risk his ability to back trace the IPS to this house."

She placed a hand on him. "Then how do I keep in touch
with work?"

"I took care of that."

"How?"

"Once I explained that you have a determined killer after
you, your boss was more than willing to put you on leave until this is resolved."

Chasyn blinked. "An undetermined period of leave will
probably jeopardize my career. The plan is for me to—"

"Plans change."

She pressed her lips together, then let out a frustrated
breath. "Mine don't," she countered. "I could work remotely
until this is all cleared up."

"Too much of a risk."

She was torn between frustration and tears. She'd worked
everything out so precisely. Her life plan was working and
she was proud of that. Hell, she lived for it. Her entire focus

these last years was now slipping away. It made her angry to think all of her effort, all of her time, might be in vain. Damn Lansing! If this dragged on, she could very well find herself without a job and standing at the starting line again. *This sucks*, she thought before saying, "Taking an extended period of time off pushes back my timetable."

Declan offered her an infuriating smile. "Maybe you should lighten up on the timetable thing. Let life happen organically."

"Food should be organic. People should have goals and purpose."

He laughed. "Life is a lot more interesting when you take it as it comes."

"That may work for you, but if I'm working remotely, I can keep up with everything. I prefer a plan."

"Well," he began as his expression grew somber. "Right now, the plan is for you to get killed."

She rubbed her arms. "I'm just saying I can't just sit here and do nothing." Intellectually she knew Declan was only concerned about doing his job, but that didn't stop her from resenting the way he was moving her around like a chess piece. She'd go nuts in about twenty minutes if she didn't find some way to occupy her mind. Chasyn met his eyes and held his gaze.

Declan appeared to blink first. "I'm not saying you should do nothing." He paused to take another sip of coffee. "Call your folks and then meet me in the office. We'll get started on the vehicle identifications."

Chasyn had a tearful and brief conversation with her par-

ents. She was careful to keep the call under the allotted
two minutes and even more careful to keep any hint of her
location out of the conversation. When she was finished,
she went into the bathroom and gently removed the bandage from her forehead. The three stitches were right at her
hairline and barely noticeable, save for the annoying itch.
The bandage at the back of her head was more difficult to
remove because her hair was stuck in the adhesive tape. Several *ouches* later, she sat on the edge of the vanity and opened
the medicine cabinet, positioning the mirror so she could
assess the damage. Again, the wound was healing nicely and
covered mostly by her hair. Chasyn opted not to re-cover
them.

The house was quiet, save for the sound of typing on a
keyboard. She followed the sound and found Declan in his
office. There, he sat at a huge mahogany desk facing the wall.
On top of the desk sat two computers with incredibly large
monitors. There were lateral file cabinets and a credenza,
with one executive chair and two other chairs along the side
wall. A variety of framed documents and a smattering of
photographs decorated the walls. His life in frames included
some military citations and several certificates related to his
current line of work. But she found herself most interested
in the pictures. Based on the hair and clothing styles, the
photos were more than a decade old. Probably older. All
featured the progression of four young boys transitioning
into manhood. It was easy for her to identify Declan, even
as a youngster. Those piercing blue eyes were a dead give-
away. She was fairly sure she recognized Jack from their

brief meetings, which meant the other two were Michael and Conner. Knowing Conner was the baby of the family, she found herself drawn to the images of Michael. He sure didn't look like a murderer—not that she knew what a murderer looked like.

"If you're too tired…" Declan's comment trailed off.

"Not at all," she said as he relinquished his seat and indicated she sit.

The screen was open to the dashboard of a database for automobiles. They were in alphabetical order from Acuras to Volvos. There were roughly fifty manufacturers. "I guess I start with the *A*s, huh?" She placed her hand on the mouse.

Declan came up behind her and placed one hand on her shoulder and the other hand over hers on the mouse. He leaned in, close enough that she could hear and feel the warmth of his breath against her ear before it spilled teasingly down her neck.

Chasyn's mouth went dry and an unexpected lump of desire lodged in her throat. Her skin tingled where he touched her and her whole body tensed.

"Start here," he said in a low, sexy tone as his hand guided hers.

They went through a series of links until a collection of sedans appeared on the screen. "Just hold the left button and move each car around until you see its taillights."

She was still back on *start here*. She was painfully aware of him. His bicep brushed her bare arm and she felt corded muscle against her exposed skin. A series of vivid images flashed in her brain. Declan holding her in his arms. Crushing her against him. Claiming her mouth as his hands wound through her hair. It was sheer lunacy. And yet it was total temptation. All she would have to do is turn in the chair and her fantasy would be reality. Chasyn longed to run her hands across his massive chest. Wondered what it would feel like to strip off his shirt and touch his warm flesh.

Declan's hand moved up from her shoulder, gathered her hair and set it off to one side, fully exposing her neck. Chasyn went perfectly still. Vacillating between expectation and extrication. Maybe her hair was blocking his view of the screen. Maybe there was just an innocent explanation. Maybe she was going to go insane wondering.

* * *

Declan told himself this was a bad idea but his body seemed to be operating without benefit of his intellect. This hadn't been his intention when he'd lifted her hair away from her neck. But the minute he felt the silken strands of her hair his mind flashed an image of it splayed on his pillow. And her skin was warm, almost flushed. He could tell by the erratic pulse at the base of her throat that she was just as curious. He couldn't think of a single reason to stop.

Slowly, he dipped his head and took a tentative taste of her. The minute his mouth closed over the sensitive spot near her collarbone, he heard a small moan pass her lips. He kissed her softly, tracing a line up along her jaw, happily drinking in her floral scent. Declan gently twirled the chair so they were face to face. Her blue-green eyes were hooded and her gaze was fixed on his mouth. Her lips were slightly parted. His body was fully alert. Painfully so.

He reached up and cupped her face in his palms. His thumbs made gentle circles on her flushed cheeks. He was about to break off the contact when she lifted her hands and flattened her palms against his chest. He was fairly certain she could feel the racing of his heart. Any notion of stopping went right out the window.

Declan pulled her from the chair and wrapped his arms around her. Careful of her injury, he laced the fingers of one hand through her hair and tugged gently, forcing her head back. She got up on tiptoe and kissed him. There was nothing tentative about it. Her tongue sought his, her body pressed tightly to him. Before he knew what was happening, her fingers were working the hem of his shirt.

It was magical.

It was thrilling.

It was a mistake.

CHAPTER TEN

Chasyn felt stunned and abandoned when he gently set her aside. Had she misread the situation? The mere thought of rejection brought a flushed warmth to her cheeks. No, she told herself, Declan had started it. He'd been the one to trail tiny kisses along her throat. He'd spun the chair and taken her in his arms. So why the sudden change of heart? She was as confused as she was annoyed.

He'd backed a few feet away from her, his hands rammed into the front pockets of his jeans. Chasyn looked to him for some sort of explanation, but his head was dipped so she couldn't read his expression. His body language, however, practically screamed regret.

When she couldn't stand the silence any longer, she said, "We can forget that just happened."

Declan looked up and met her gaze. "I didn't anticipate your quick response."

That stung a bit. "Don't get overly impressed with yourself. I've been experiencing a dry spell for a while."

His head tilted to one side and he donned a decidedly cocky smile. "Then you're claiming you kissed me like that due to a recent lull in action?"

"*You* kissed *me*," she countered.

He shook his dark head. "I was about to, but you beat me to it." His grin widened. "And I wouldn't have guessed you've been in a dry spell. You were hot and pliant and—"

"Can we skip this postmortem and just agree not to let it happen again?" she asked, trying to keep her tone cool, her gaze steady.

"No," he responded casually.

"Excuse me?"

He shrugged. The motion drew the fabric of his shirt taut against his solid torso. "I liked the way you kissed me."

"Will you please stop saying that? It was a mutual thing."

"And unexpected," he said with a sexy half-smile that reached his eyes. "You're full of surprises, Chasyn."

"No," she said rather emphatically. "I'm not. I live a predictable, organized life. That kiss was a fluke." It was, right? Had to be. She wasn't the type of woman who just kissed a guy for the hell of it. Lord, she even had a no-kiss-on-the-first-date rule. So why him?

"A really incredible fluke."

Realizing he wasn't going to let it go, she changed the subject. "If it's all the same to you, I've got a few zillion cars to look at." She stepped back and sat in the chair. When Declan made a move toward her, she held up one hand. "I'm fine on my own."

"Scared I might touch you again?" he teased.

Honesty was her best choice here. "No. I'm scared I might touch you again and I'd like to avoid that complication." She didn't have the nerve to look at him as she made her admission. She only knew that all this talk of kissing and touching had caused a lump in the pit of her stomach. And was it any wonder? The man was handsome as sin, sexy as hell and clearly available. What woman with a pulse wouldn't be attracted to him? *So what*, she thought with determination. *SO I find him attractive. That doesn't mean I have to act on that attraction.* Except being in his arms, feeling his mouth on her, were two of the most incredible sensations she'd ever experienced.

* * *

Declan left her in the office as she clicked from car to car, seeking the elusive taillight design. He felt his brow furrow as he went to the coffee maker to brew a new mug. In all his years in business, he'd never once kissed a client. Had never wanted to. But Chasyn was different. Having her was an ever present thought in his mind—more vivid now since he'd had the experience of having her body pressed against his. The feel of her breasts against his body; the way her palms flattened against his chest; the floral scent of her skin. To say his interest was piqued was an understatement.

"You, my man, are playing with fire," he acknowledged in a whisper before he took a sip from the mug.

Not only was this interaction piss poor timing since she had a professional killer on her tail; it was her. Or rather the kind of woman she was. Declan had made a habit of dating tall, striking brunettes who were in it for the short haul. No drama, no complications, and definitely no strings attached. He liked it like that. But Chasyn was a whole different kind of enticement. For some unknown reason, he was drawn to the petite blonde with the clear blue-green eyes and the killer body. And his interest wasn't limited to the physical. She was smart and strong. An impressive package. The kind of package you took home to meet the family.

And that wasn't part of his skill set.

His cell chirped and he retrieved it from his pocket. "Kavanaugh."

"It's Ziggy," his computer whiz said on a rush of breath. "I've scoured every financial institution within a hundred-mile radius and I can't find a safe deposit box in Mary Jolsten's name. Want me to widen the search?"

Declan sighed. "Might as well. Based on what her ex said, Mary probably had some sort of incriminating evidence against Dr. Lansing. Hopefully it will be something the cops can use to arrest him and end the threat to Chasyn."

"Oh, and I called in a favor at the state crime lab so I have a copy of the DNA report on Mary Jolsten's fetus. Now all we need is a sample from Lansing for comparison," Ziggy reported.

"Any word from the surveillance teams yet?" Declan asked.

"Yeah," she answered with a derisive snort. "Lansing is one freaky dude. According to Joey and Sam, Lansing leaves his office carrying his empty water bottles with him. And he must be storing them at home because an examination of his trash came up empty."

"He's a forensic psychiatrist. He knows better than to toss

anything with his DNA on it. We need to come up with a way to get the doctor to lower his guard."

"Think his wife would help?" Ziggy asked. "I mean, Dr. Lansing has been all over the news as a person of interest since Mary's murder. Surely his wife must have suspicions."

"So far, at least publicly, she's standing by her man," Declan said on a sigh. "Listen, can you do a quick background on a couple from Boca Raton named Wellington?"

"A new suspect?"

"I just want to confirm Mary's ex's story."

"Speaking of which." She went silent but Declan could hear the clicks of her fingers sailing across a keyboard. "William Jolsten has two vehicles registered in his name. A Suburban and an F-150. The Suburban is green and the truck is white."

"Yeah, we can probably cross him off the suspect list."

"You sound tired," Ziggy said. "Adam and Tom are on their way over to guard your perimeter so you and Chasyn can get some sleep."

"Thanks, Ziggy. I'll touch base in the morning."

"'Night, boss."

* * *

Chasyn's eyes burned as she clicked her way through sedan makes and models after sedan makes and models. She'd had no idea taillights could come in so many shapes and sizes. Some wrapped around the trunk, some were oval, others were rectangles. She felt like she was searching for a needle in a stack of needles and she'd only gone from Acura to Buick. And she was only looking at current year models. She was discouraged and tired. Leaning back in the chair, she wiped at her dry eyes and stifled a yawn. Hearing footfalls, she turned to see Declan return.

"Any luck?" he asked.

"Nope. Nothing yet."

"Maybe you should call it a night and pick this up in the morning."

She glanced at the clock on the bar of the monitor. "It's almost two a.m.," she said with surprise. "No wonder my eyes feel like sandpaper."

"Go to bed, Chasyn. It's been a long day."

She left him in the office and walked through the family room to the back hallway where the guest suite was located. Chasyn was so tired she had a knot between her tense shoulders, so she opted for a hot shower before bed.

Gathering up her toiletries, she went into the bathroom, undressed, pinned her hair up, and stepped beneath the warm spray. She allowed the showerhead to massage her tense muscles while her mind wandered back to the kiss she'd shared with Declan. *Stupid, stupid mistake.* "Wonderful, wonderful kiss," she whispered. She closed her eyes and conjured the memory of his hot mouth on her bare skin. On the way his tongue sparred with hers. And the feel of his arousal pressed against her belly. A low groan escaped her lips as she braced her hands against the tiled wall. Just the memory of the kiss had her weak in the knees.

And weak in the head. There were so many reasons why

this was a bad idea. First and foremost, she had a determined killer on her trail. Secondly, no matter how interested she was in Declan, he wasn't part of her plan. She'd long ago promised herself that she wouldn't even entertain a serious relationship until after her thirtieth birthday. Of course when she'd made that rule, she hadn't considered a man like Declan. Not that Declan was serious relationship material. After all, there had to be a reason why he was still single. A choice. And who could blame him? With his looks and charm, he could probably find a willing female at every turn. And all his crap about things happening organically was just another way of saying *temporary*. Chasyn could never be fulfilled being someone's transitory plaything. No, she wanted what her parents had—a partnership for life. A few children. Things men like Declan avoided like the plague.

But maybe there was some wiggle room in her life plan. Maybe there was a place for a temporary relationship with Declan. Something just for fun and giggles. No strings attached. It was both an appealing and frightening thought.

She stepped from the shower, dried off and slipped on a pair of pink pajama pants and a floral print camisole. The place on her palm where she'd been cut by the glass during the shooting at her apartment building was a non-issue. The stitches itched, but everything seemed to be healing nicely. And if she did her hair just right, she could cover the injuries completely.

As she slipped beneath the covers, she listened for sounds. She heard nothing so she assumed Declan had also gone to bed. To that big bed in the master bedroom with plenty of room for two. Chasyn rolled on her side, punched down the pillow and fell into a fitful sleep.

She awakened several hours later to the sound of a bird and the scent of coffee. Knowing she had to go back to the monotonous chore of searching through taillights, she rose slowly and without much enthusiasm. Going to the closet, she reached into her suitcase and selected a pair of white capris and an aqua handkerchief top with lacey straps.

After brushing her hair and her teeth, she applied a small amount of makeup and slipped on a pair of ballet flats. Before she put the burner phone in her pocket, she tried her parents' number. There was no answer. They were probably out grocery shopping or possibly at a doctor's appointment. Chasyn put the cell away. Because the kiss was still fresh in her mind, she dawdled a bit before heading to the kitchen.

Declan was seated at the table with his laptop open, a steaming mug in his hand.

"Good morning," she said.

"Morning," he greeted her. "Coffee?"

"I'll get it," she insisted. She went to the Keurig and selected a hazelnut flavored pod of coffee, then took down a mug and waited the eight seconds for the coffee to brew. She joined Declan at the table. He smelled of soap and his black hair was still slightly damp. As usual, he was wearing a black T-shirt and black jeans. "What are you doing?"

"Reading what Ziggy found out about the Wellingtons—the family Mary was pulling the adoption scam on."

"Poor couple," she mused. "They must have been devastated when Mary and her baby were murdered."

"It gets worse," Declan said. "They've been down this road before. Three years ago they supported a girl from Indiana during her pregnancy but the girl backed out once the baby was born. And that was after almost ten years of infertility treatments."

"How shitty for them. Poor people want a child so badly that they'd risk heartache a second time. That's extremely brave of them. I'm not sure if I wanted something that badly whether I would be strong enough to try again. Can I make breakfast?" she offered.

"My fridge is pretty bare," he replied.

"Let me take a look," she said as she got up and went to survey the contents. Eggs, butter, milk, sriracha, mustard, and an assortment of takeout containers. "You eat like a frat boy."

"I cook like one, too."

While Declan continued to work at the table, Chasyn scrambled some eggs and added a touch of sriracha to give them a little kick. She found plates in the cabinet next to the microwave and plated the food. Grabbing utensils from the drawer next to the sink, she carried the plates to the table. "Take a break," she said as she waited for him to move the computer out of the way.

"Great eggs," he said after the initial bite.

"Thank you."

"I wouldn't have pegged you as the chef-y type."

Tilting her head, she regarded him for a few seconds. "I'm not chef-y; I'm competent in the kitchen and I like to cook."

"Doesn't it get in the way of your career goal? I thought work was your sole focus until you hit thirty."

She sensed a touch of censure in his tone. "It is, but I still have to eat."

"That's what ChowCab was invented for. You call in your order from your favorite restaurant, they pick it up and deliver it for the very reasonable price of three ninety-nine."

"It's not the same," she said dismissively. "There's something very satisfying about creating a dish from scratch."

"My mother used to make everything from scratch," he said in a subdued tone.

"Was she a good cook?"

He nodded. "She made peach cobbler to die for."

"I'm not much of a baker. Too much exact measuring."

"For you?" he said with an arched brow and amusement in his eyes. "I would think someone who makes lists for everything would like the concept of exactness."

"Lists keep me on track," she said defensively. "I'll be right back," she excused herself and went into her bedroom to retrieve her legal pad. Then she rejoined Declan at the table. "What if Mary didn't have a safe deposit box? What if she had a storage rental instead?" She tapped where she had written *storage unit?*

"That's a possibility. Good thinking," he said as he took out his phone and sent Ziggy a text to check out local rental places.

"Thank you," she said. "It makes sense. A small unit is pretty cheap, so she could have paid cash, leaving no financial trail to trace back to her."

"Right."

"I assume it would be close to her apartment or maybe

the restaurant," Chasyn speculated. "And given Mary's past, there's no telling what might be in there."

"Don't get ahead of yourself. First we have to determine if she had a storage unit."

Chasyn ignored the last few bites of egg on her plate. "I guess it's time for me to go hunt taillights again," she said without enthusiasm.

"I know it's boring, but it's the best lead we have."

She started to clear the dishes but Declan reached out and caught her wrist. "You cooked, I'll clean up."

"I don't mind," she said.

He smiled and she felt it in the pit of her stomach. "You just don't want to wade through a litany of sedans."

"True."

"Welcome to my world," he said.

She stood silently for a few seconds, waiting until he let go of her wrist. Her skin tingled at the memory of his touch. *Keep your distance*, she silently chanted.

Once she was back in the office, she tried her parents again and still got no answer. It was starting to bug her. Normally, they left her a message or sent a text of their daily plans so she knew where they were almost every moment of the day. Being out of contact made her uneasy.

Abandoning her lingering misgivings, she navigated her way back to the automobile database and started clicking her way through sedan after sedan. A few came kind of close, but nothing matched. Until nearly three hours later, when she reached the Ford Taurus. It was almost perfect. Almost. "Declan!"

He was at her side in a moment. "Did you find it?"

"Maybe." She pointed toward the screen. "This has the same shape but there's no border around the headlight. But it does have lettering below the taillight that looks very familiar."

"Hang on," he said as he reached around her and pulled up another database. "This has photos of that sedan going back ten years. You've been looking at the current year models. Maybe we need an earlier model year."

Chasyn went back several years until she found the exact match. "That's it!" she exclaimed. "A 2013 Taurus SEL."

Declan gently squeezed her shoulders. "Great job. Now we have something with legs."

"Does Dr. Lansing own a 2013 Taurus?" she asked.

Declan shook his head. "No, but he could have borrowed one or rented one. We'll extend our search to family and friends and contact various rental agencies."

Relief washed over her. "If we can find the car, the state's attorney can convince a grand jury and get an indictment. Then they can arrest that bastard, get his DNA, prove he killed Mary, and link him to Kasey's murder."

"Don't get ahead of yourself. We have to find the car first."

"I have faith in you," she said, undeterred in her excitement. She took the phone out of her pocket.

"Who are you calling?"

"My parents. They'll be thrilled with this news."

"You're being a little premature," he warned.

Chasyn held the phone to her ear and listened as it rang and rang. "This is weird. They've been out for hours."

"Is that unusual?"

Chasyn nodded. "They normally schedule their errands

around going out to lunch. I haven't been able to reach them since last night. Maybe they sent me a text or left me a voice-mail."

"Using your phone is too risky," Declan said. "But maybe Ziggy can find a way around that."

Chasyn followed him into the kitchen. He called Ziggy and explained the situation. Declan put the phone on speaker and placed it in the center of the table.

"What's the password for your phone?" Ziggy asked Chasyn.

"Nineteen-eighty-nine."

"Hang on."

Chasyn could hear clicks and it felt like forever before Ziggy came back on the line. "We have a problem," she said.

"What?" Chasyn practically yelled as panic gripped her.

"There's an incoming call from your parents' landline at one-fifty-seven this morning," Ziggy explained.

"My parents are never awake that late."

She heard Ziggy let out a breath. "There's a voicemail."

"Can I hear it?" Chasyn asked.

"It isn't good," Ziggy hedged.

"Oh god," Chasyn grasped the back of the chair to keep her balance. "Play it."

"Boss?"

"Play it," Declan said.

There was a *beep*, then "Your mother and father are fine for now. No harm will come to them if you meet me at Carlin Park next Tuesday at eleven p.m. No cops. Come alone or they die."

CHAPTER ELEVEN

"Oh God," Chasyn whispered, knees suddenly boneless.

Declan took her by the shoulders and lowered her into the chair. "Ziggy, send Gavin over to Chasyn's parents' house to check it out."

"What if he's watching?" Chasyn asked. "I don't want him to think I've involved anyone else. I can't risk my parents' safety."

He squeezed her hand. "Gavin is stealthy. He'll get in and out without anyone knowing."

"There's a spare key under the red flower pot on the back patio," Chasyn said. "The alarm code is oh-five-two-one. And they have a video surveillance system. The recorder is in the den."

"Got it," Ziggy said. "Anything else?"

"No. Let's hope Gavin can recover the recorder. Maybe we can finally get a good look at this guy." Declan was about to end the call when he said, "One more thing. I need you to find a link between Dr. Lansing and a 2013 Ford Taurus."

"I'm on it, boss," Ziggy said before the line went dead.

Chasyn looked up at him, silently wondering how bad this was going to get. Her skin prickled cold, then hot as her heart thudded with dread. She had to swallow twice before she could push out any words. "What are the chances my parents are still alive?"

"Fifty-fifty," Declan answered candidly. "A real pro doesn't usually concern himself with collateral damage, but, in this case, I'm guessing he won't harm them unless and until he gets what he's after."

"Me."

"That's not an option," Declan said flatly. "But we have to go to my office. We're going to demand proof of life."

"What's that?" she asked as she rubbed her arms.

"We'll call your parents' cell phone and tell this bozo that there won't be any meeting unless he provides you with some sort of tangible proof that your parents are alive and well."

"And if he won't?" Her voice cracked from the terror holding her chest like a vise.

"We'll cross that bridge when we come to it." Declan tugged her to her feet. "Come on, he's only given us a seventy-two-hour window. We don't want to waste time."

Chasyn was fairly silent on the drive to the compound in western Palm Beach County. She was paralyzed with guilt. If she had been honest with the police from the get-go, she never would have been involved in the Mary Jolsten case. Kasey probably wouldn't have testified, so she wouldn't be dead, and her parents definitely wouldn't be being held by a professional killer. How had this gotten so crazy?

Once they were inside the hangar, Chasyn followed Declan into the partitioned off office part of the building. Ziggy greeted her with a tentative smile. Beyond her, there were a half dozen computer screens scrolling code and symbols against a black background.

"Is the phone ready?" he asked.

Ziggy produced Chasyn's cell phone. "I downloaded the content and wiped it clean," she explained. "The only numbers in there are for her parents. No other identifying information."

"Why did you have to reset my phone?" Chasyn asked.

"We're going to head to a neutral location and then you'll send our killer a text asking for proof of life. He may be sophisticated enough to hack your phone so we don't want there to be anything he can grab and use as further leverage."

"But won't he be able to track my phone?" Chasyn asked.

"We'll only turn it on for a few minutes for you to send the text, then we shut it off," Declan explained.

"If he's got the equipment, he might be able to track a tower ping, but you'll be long gone before he can do a triangulation," Ziggy added.

"Then what?" Chasyn asked.

"Ziggy can monitor your phone by hacking your account. When he replies to the request for proof of life, we'll know it without having to turn the phone back on," Declan said.

"That's how I got the first voicemail," Ziggy added. "Oh, and you got a text from a Mr. Becker."

"Kasey's father?" Chasyn asked. She couldn't recall him ever texting in the past.

"He wants to send you a check for his daughter's portion

of the rent but he hasn't been able to reach you and doesn't know where to send the money."

Chasyn sighed. "He shouldn't be worried about that right now. He just buried his daughter, for god's sake. Besides, I don't know if I can even go back home. Not after the killer trashed the place. My apartment feels violated."

"You can call him or text him from the burner phone," Declan suggested.

"I'd like that," Chasyn said. "He's got to be hurting and he's always been so kind to me. I still feel badly for missing Kasey's funeral."

"You were in the hospital," Declan reminded her. "I'm sure he understands. Let's take care of contacting the guy who's holding your parents."

"Where to?" she asked.

Declan led her to the SUV he'd used for transportation before. "We'll just drive to a random spot and send the text." As he spoke he checked the power button on her personal cell phone just as a precaution.

"Why am I using my cell instead of the burner phone to talk to the killer?" she asked.

"He'll recognize the number, which increases the odds of his cooperation."

Chasyn let out a breath. "I'm really worried."

Declan reached over and patted her thigh. "I know. But you're going to have to trust me on this one."

Anger was a hard knot of acid in her stomach. "I'd like to take one of your guns over to Dr. Lansing's office and force him to tell me where my parents are."

"That is an appealing option," Declan agreed. "But in my experience, professional killers work fairly autonomously from their employers. Chances are Lansing doesn't know exactly where they're being held."

"But he probably knows they're being used to lure me to Carlin Park, right?"

"Lured, yes. Carlin Park, probably not. That gives him plausible deniability if things go south."

She shivered. "Why wait three days for the meeting?" she asked.

"Possibly to give Lansing time to set up an alibi."

She raked her hand through her hair. "This is getting overly complicated. Maybe we should call in the police."

"Too dangerous," Declan assured her. "Right now, we have to play by his rules and hope he makes a mistake."

"And if he doesn't?"

"Then we adjust," he said with less confidence than she would have liked.

Declan kept his hand on her thigh as they drove north on I-95, until they reached Bathtub Beach in Martin County. He pulled into the public lot and parked. Because it was still snowbird season, the lot was near capacity. The minute she exited the car, she smelled the ocean carried on the breeze coming off the surf.

She followed Declan to the boardwalk that traversed the dunes. They walked halfway down the wooden path to where the walkway turned into a ramp that led out onto the pale sand. The beach was dotted with brightly colored umbrellas and chairs. People of all ages, shapes, and sizes were represented. Bathtub Beach got its name from a natural coral formation in the shape of a bathtub. Shallow water made the enclosed space a magnet for small children and the grandparents they visited. A large lifeguard tower stood off to one side, manned by two guards in bright red trunks with orange buoys strapped over their shoulders. The rip current caution flag was flapping in the breeze but that didn't deter many of the swimmers.

"I'm going to turn it on now," Declan said over the sound of the waves lapping at the sand. "Text as fast as you can and let him know you want proof of life by tomorrow morning or you won't meet him."

"Tomorrow morning?" she practically scoffed. "I want to know that they're okay right now!"

"Trust me. Giving him twenty-four hours guarantees your parents stay alive for that long."

Chasyn sent the text, then powered off the phone and handed it back to Declan. "Now what?" she asked.

"We wait for his reply."

Chasyn pursed her lips. "Waiting around is going to make me crazy."

"Then we'll have to keep you busy," he said as he placed his hand at the small of her back.

Through the thin fabric of her shirt, she felt the warm play of his fingers as he guided her back to the car. She chalked it up to hypersensitivity due to incredible stress. Acknowledging, even to herself, that there might be a different reason she was so tuned to his every touch wasn't something she could cope with just then.

She was completely overwhelmed. Responsibility weighed on her; then there was the anger. She longed to go to Lansing and beat him into submission. A fantasy not based in reality, but still, she just knew he was the key to this whole mess. Then there was her attraction to Declan. It had to be some sort of syndrome. He was her lifeline and that had to be why she was so aware of him. Maybe it was some sort of variation on the Stockholm Syndrome. Not that he was her captor, but he was in control of her life.

That notion rankled. Chasyn wasn't accustomed to someone else being in control. It was a foreign concept and one she didn't care for at all. Normally, she solved her problems by creating a detailed pro-con list and rationally evaluating any situation. She always gave herself a reasonable timetable in which to solve a problem or make a decision but all that was out the window. None of the life skills that had gotten her to this point were helping.

* * *

Declan's secret fear that she'd cave under the pressure of this new wrinkle was unfounded. Yes, she'd been quiet and introspective on the drive back from Martin County, but after she exited the car, he saw the determination in her eyes and the set of her jaw and knew Chasyn was going to keep it together.

He admired that about her and had to admit that it ran contrary to his initial impression of the woman. At the hospital she'd appeared frail and fragile. But now he knew she had a well of inner strength and he admired that about her. Hell, he admired a lot of things about her, some of which were totally inappropriate. He really had meant to comfort her when he'd patted her thigh during the drive but the truth was, he just liked touching her. In fact, he liked it a lot. Too much, maybe.

Ziggy was still trying to link Dr. Lansing to the Taurus when they returned, and Gavin was waiting for them.

"The parents?" Declan prompted.

Gavin shook his head. "No one has seen them since yesterday afternoon. Car's in the garage and no signs of a struggle in the house."

"That's good, right?" Chasyn asked. "I mean, the part about no struggle?"

"Yes," Declan answered. There were ways to kidnap someone that left no disturbance at the scene but he didn't want to give her cause for concern.

"I spoke to them last night, so he had to have taken them some time after that. Was their bed slept in?"

"Yes," Gavin answered, then shrugged. "Makes sense he'd grab them up in the middle of the night."

Chasyn rubbed her bare arms. "What about the video system?"

"I brought it back with me. Ziggy was just about to connect it."

Chasyn, Ziggy, and the two men went over to a large-screen television in another part of the office area. Ziggy made quick work of connecting the DVR to the television. Almost instantly, the screen came to life with a tic-tac-toe pattern of images from the various cameras.

Chasyn leaned against the corner of the desk. Declan was behind her, Ziggy was to her side, and Gavin hung back behind the group.

"About what time did you call?" Ziggy asked.

Chasyn told her and she fast-forwarded the recording to that time. In the bottom square of the image was the kitchen and her father and mother were seated at the table, passing the phone back and forth. Then the call ended and her mother puttered in the kitchen while her father went into his study.

Ziggy fast-forwarded through the footage until well after her parents had gone to sleep. Chasyn was starting to think this was a pointless activity when she noticed a shadowy figure approaching the house. The picture was dark and grainy, but it was definitely a man, dressed in dark clothing.

He moved to the front door and crouched down while he placed something in the lock. As soon as the door was opened he went to the alarm pad and used alligator clips to override the system. It wasn't until he turned to head for the stairs that the camera picked up his face.

"Pause that," Declan said. "Look familiar?" he asked Chasyn.

"He matches the description the guy from the gun shop gave us. But I've never seen him before in my life."

They advanced the tape and she watched in horror as he crept up to her parents' bedroom and moved immediately to her father's side of the bed. Via moonlight, they saw the intruder pull a gun out of his waistband, he placed it to her father's temple, then gave him a nudge. He woke up and seemed disoriented at first, then based on the expression on his face, he appeared to instantly appreciate the gravity of the situation.

The infrared tape had no sound, but the killer must have said something because her father reached over and shook her mother awake. He forced them from the bed and held them at gunpoint while they hastily dressed. Next, he held the gun to her mother's head and began marching them downstairs. Chasyn felt tears sting her eyes when she saw the terrified expression on her mother's face.

The man led them out of the house and down the driveway. Then a few minutes later the exterior camera caught a glimpse of a champagne-colored minivan speeding past the house.

"Can you zoom in on the plate?" Declan asked Ziggy.

Ziggy tried but the more she enlarged the picture, the more the image pixilated into a blur. "It's just too far away," she said.

Chasyn dabbed at the tears on her cheeks and tried to swallow the lump of emotion choking her. She felt like one big frazzled nerve. Like she wanted to jump out of her skin. "We have to do *something*," she said. "What if we turn the video over to the authorities? Maybe they have special software that can pull up the plate."

"Too risky," Declan told her.

"What's risky about it?" Chasyn asked.

"If the guy even sniffs cops, it will jeopardize your parents' safety. Ziggy, can you make a print of the guy's face and run it through facial recognition?"

"Consider it done, boss."

"What can I do?" Chasyn asked. "I feel so helpless." She saw a look in Declan's eyes and tried to decipher it. Was it pity? Concern? God, what he must think of her. She was practically a basket case at this point and the bad stuff kept piling on. She met his gaze and thought she saw compassion in his expression. Maybe she was only seeing what she wanted to see.

Declan looked at her quietly. "How about a distraction?" he suggested.

Chasyn followed him out to the shooting range and waited while he loaded a handgun for her. As he handed it to her, he said, "Don't forget about the recoil. Plant your feet before you fire."

"This isn't distracting me," she said.

"Concentrate on hitting the target," he countered, setting a pair of headphones on her head, then another pair on his own.

Chasyn conjured up the image of Dr. Lansing. He was six feet tall, with sandy blond hair and a golfer's tan that set off his light eyes. She imagined that face on the paper outline dangling from the line yards in front of her. Carefully and deliberately, she sited the target, took a breath and let it out slowly, then pulled the trigger several times in rapid succession. She pulled off her headphones while Declan reeled in the target.

Nine shots.

Nine hits.

Too bad it was only paper instead of Lansing himself.

CHAPTER TWELVE

Y ou're a quick study," Declan complimented.

Chasyn placed the discharged gun on the stand next to her. "I'm motivated. I'd like to take this gun over to Lansing's house and force him to call off his killer and free my parents. They must be so scared."

Declan drew her into his arms. Her cheek rested against his chest and she could feel and hear the even beat of his heart through the fabric of his shirt. Hooking her fingertips on his waistband she closed her eyes, tuning out everything. Fear, anger, anxiety—even the sound of the birds faded into the distance. Her mind was laser-focused on the security of being wrapped in his embrace. There was something infinitely comforting about the feel of his solid body pressed against hers. She drank in the scent of his woodsy cologne and found a few minutes of solace in his arms.

Eventually Chasyn took a reluctant step back. She could have gladly stayed in that position for hours, but she knew that was a dangerous and fruitless way to think. As soon as she was alone, she'd create a pro-con list on letting her emotions override her intellect when it came to Declan Kavanaugh. She needed to weigh her options for a fling, something she hadn't considered in the past.

But right now, she needed to return Mr. Becker's call, a task she wasn't looking forward to. Not that she wasn't fond of the man; she thought of him as a second father. She was just at a loss for words. Nothing she could say could ease his pain and everything she thought she might offer seemed trite and rehearsed. Still, she didn't want to ignore him.

Declan picked up the gun and secured it. The smell of gunpowder still hung in the air. They returned to the building and as soon as they were inside, Chasyn took the burner phone out of her pocket. "I'm going to return Mr. Becker's call," she told Declan.

As she punched in the phone number, she was vaguely aware of the din of conversation coming from the office area. But her attention was diverted by the sight of Declan walking away. The man had swagger. Broad shoulders, a tapered waist, and with each step the fabric of his jeans stretched and strained against his muscular thighs. It wasn't until she heard Kasey's father's voice on the other end that she snapped back to reality.

"Hi, this is Chasyn," she greeted him.

There was a nanosecond of silence. "How are you doing?" he asked.

Grief made his voice sound cold and distant. "I'm fine. I'm sorry I couldn't be at Kasey's funeral."

"I understand," he replied in an even tone. "Do you know

what's happening with the case?" he asked. "The police aren't telling me much. Only that they have insufficient evidence to take the case to the grand jury at this time. Something about your testimony?"

"I didn't get as good a look as Kasey," she admitted. "But I'm doing everything I can to find evidence against Lansing."

"What can *you* do that the police can't?" he asked.

"I'm not sure yet, but the situation has ballooned and this is very personal to me."

"Not as personal as burying your only child."

Chasyn fought back tears. "I'm so sorry, Mr. Becker."

"Thank you," he said as if by rote. "What are your plans for the apartment?"

She actually hadn't thought that far ahead but she assumed Mr. Becker was concentrating on things like that to keep from thinking about his deceased daughter. "I'm not sure I want to go back."

"Understandable. Perhaps the best thing is to break the lease and pay the penalty."

She thought about the break-in and it sent a shiver down her spine. "That makes sense. I'll contact the leasing office and get the details."

"I've already done that. The pay-off for breaking the lease is twenty-six hundred dollars provided everything is out by the end of the month."

That would give her two weeks to pack up. And cost her a hunk of her savings to pay off the landlord. "I didn't know it would be that expensive."

"Don't worry about the money, Chasyn. I'll send you a check to cover the cost."

"That's very generous, but I can't let you do that." She checked the time and realized she was nearing the two-minute mark.

"I insist," he said. "Kasey would have wanted me to."

Hard to counter the dead daughter argument. "Well, then, thank you."

"I'll send a cashier's check. The landlord mentioned that you haven't been back to the apartment. Where are you staying right now?"

"With a friend," she hedged.

"Give me the address."

She thought for a moment. "Just send it to my job. Keller and Mason," she said, then gave the street address. "I'm sorry, Mr. Becker, but I need to go now. Thank you again, and I'll be in touch."

He started to argue with her, but Chasyn cut him off before the two-minute mark. She felt guilty for being rude to him. He'd been a part of her life for so long and she knew how much he adored Kasey. Her murder must be hitting him hard.

"I so rock!" Chasyn heard Ziggy yell just as she was putting the phone back in her pocket.

Curious, she went to the office and found the whole team staring up at an image on the large monitor. There was a buzz of excitement in the room. Chasyn looked at the face on the screen and instantly noted the similarities. Same hairline. Same squared jaw. Ziggy did rock. She'd found the man who had taken her parents. "Who is he?" she asked.

"Albert Müller," Declan answered. "Wanted by several countries and Interpol and some Middle Eastern Big-Wig who's offering a five hundred thousand-dollar bounty on his head."

"For what?" Chasyn asked.

"He's a prime suspect in at least a dozen deaths. German national. Former highly decorated member of the *Bundeswehr*—the German military." Declan stroked his chin. "He's been called in for questioning by no less than five different law enforcement groups, but there's never been enough evidence to tie him definitively to any crime."

"So how come an international criminal is after me and my family?" Chasyn wondered aloud.

"He's a pay-to-play kind of guy," Declan explained. "Someone must be paying big bucks for a pro like Müller."

Her mind was spinning. None of this made any sense. "How does someone find someone like Müller?" Chasyn wondered aloud. "Last time I checked, killers didn't advertise in the Yellow Pages."

"It's easier than you think," Gavin responded. "With the right amount of cash, you can buy your way into a job like this."

"Does Lansing have that kind of money?" she asked.

"His wife does," Declan said. "Except we can't find any trace of any major withdrawals out of her accounts."

"What about credit card statements?" she offered excitedly.

Declan smiled. "Killers don't take Amex."

"No," Chasyn said. "I handled a divorce case a bunch of

years ago, and the husband was hiding assets by overpaying his credit cards. He squirreled away a couple hundred thousand dollars that way and no one was the wiser. The amounts just showed as payment credits."

"On it," Ziggy said as she stood and went back to her computer station.

Declan gave Chasyn a little nod. "Good call."

Chasyn smiled. "I told you I'd be useful."

* * *

Declan's admiration for the woman grew considerably. He knew she was frantic about her parents, yet she was holding it together well. Hell, she was more than holding it together. That little credit card tip might just lead to the break they needed to nail Lansing and end this nightmare.

Of course, that also would mean an end to his…his…He wasn't sure what to call his relationship with Chasyn, other than he knew he felt like more than just her protector. He was far too aware of her. The memory of the smell of her hair when he'd taken her in his arms, and the enticing shape of her body where it molded to his had stayed with him hours later. He might have chalked it up to a reasonable explanation. She was a beautiful woman and he was just reacting to her sensuality. Except that he was as impressed with her mind as he was with her body. This was new territory for him. And it was disconcerting, to say the least.

"Guys?" Ziggy called from the computer area.

Declan and Chasyn walked in together with Gavin right

on their heels. Up on the screen, Ziggy had several credit card statements tiled on the screen.

"So, starting two months ago, Dr. Lansing was overpaying his credit cards just like Chasyn said."

"How much," Declan asked.

"Altogether? Roughly fifty grand. But, he made a two thousand-dollar cash withdrawal the day before the court-house shooting that killed Kasey."

"Can you trace it?" Declan asked Ziggy.

She shook her head. "Can't trace the cash. But he made a second withdrawal of twenty grand two days after the shooting."

Chasyn reached out and wrapped her fingers around his upper arm. There was a flash of excitement in her eyes. "So, he paid the guys in the white SUV two thousand up front and then twenty thousand after Kasey died. Right?" Some of her guilt was assuaged by the knowledge that she was helping make forward progress. It was the first time since Kasey's murder that she had felt anything other than respon-sible. That knowledge shone in her eyes.

"Possibly," Declan hedged. Something about the with-drawals didn't add up. "I'm just not sure why he'd pay twenty grand for a job that was only half completed."

Her hand dropped away and he felt palpable disappoint-ment.

"He did kill the only real witness to Mary's murder in that parking lot."

Chasyn appeared lost as to what to do with her hands now that she wasn't touching him. And Declan, well, he was distracted—a first for him—by her body language. By the way she looked and, scariest of all, by her intelligence.

"Right," Declan said. "Except at the time you and Kasey were shot, neither Lansing nor the police knew you didn't actually see the murder. As far as Lansing was concerned, you were as much a threat as Kasey."

Her shoulders slumped slightly and he could tell she was struggling. Made sense; her parents were in jeopardy, her best friend was dead, and she had a top-flight guy on her tail. Declan sucked in and blew out a breath. If only he could find a way to ease the pain in her stunning eyes…

"I guess he wouldn't have paid the balance on the contract when I didn't die."

"However," Declan added, "there's always a possibility that the second withdrawal was to hire Müller to finish the job."

Chasyn perked up. "Can we take the credit card statements to the police and see if they have enough to arrest him for Kasey's murder?"

"Not enough probable cause," Gavin interjected. "Plus, we'd be playing our hand. Right now, we want Lansing where we can keep an eye on him."

Chasyn let out a long breath. "While you watch Lansing and wait for an elusive sample of his DNA, Müller has my parents. On Tuesday he'll probably try to kill me when I show up at Carlin Park."

"You aren't going to Carlin Park," Declan told her with finality. "There's no way I'll let Müller get that close to you." Even he thought that sounded a little dictatorial. What was it about this woman that made him want to shield her from harm? Yes, that was his job, but this time it felt different. The mere thought that Chasyn could get close to a killer made his stomach cramp.

She turned and caught his gaze. Her expression could only be described as defiant. "There's no way I'm going to jeopardize my parents' safety."

"I'm not going to let him hurt your parents," Declan responded.

"Really?" she challenged. "What's the plan?"

It was his turn to blow out a slow breath. "I'm working on it."

* * *

An hour later, Ziggy informed her that a text had come through on her phone. Gavin had gone to relieve one of the guys staking out Lansing, so only Declan joined them in the computer area. On the screen was a blow-up of a photograph that chilled her to the bone. Her mother and father were strapped to two chairs set in front of a white sheet that looked as if it had been hung as a backdrop. They were secured with zip ties, their mouths covered with duct tape. In her father's lap was that morning's newspaper.

Her mother's eyes were red and swollen, her nose pink above the gray duct tape. Knowing her stoic mother had been reduced to tears tore at Chasyn's heart. When they found this bastard, she was going to rip his face off.

"Look at the floor," Ziggy said as she zoomed in.

"Hardwood," Chasyn said.

"Planking," Declan corrected. "Like on a boat."

"Well, that narrows things down," Chasyn said sarcastically. "You can't throw a pebble around here without hitting a marina."

"So we get him to send a video," Declan suggested. "Let's go."

"Where to?" she asked.

"Lake Worth," he said.

"What's in Lake Worth?" she asked.

"We need to make contact with Müller again," he explained. In reality he was dragging this out to give her more time to process the situation. They could call from the side of I-95, but then he wouldn't have any extra time alone with her.

Chasyn went with him, though she had some misgivings. What if another request for proof of life pissed Müller off? That thought didn't bode well for her parents.

The sun was low in the sky by the time they reached the Lake Worth pier. It was a long pier, dotted with people. Chasyn could hear the gentle crash of waves hitting the pylons as they walked to the end of the pier, past several fishermen. The wind had kicked up a bit, giving her a chill. She was astonished that the relatively short drive had given her something of a boost. Yes, she was worried sick, but knowing Declan had a plan put her frazzled nerves to rest. For now.

"Okay," Declan began as he took out her cell. "Thank him for the photograph but tell him it isn't enough. You want a video of your father speaking as a show of good will, you want your mother released before you'll agree to meet him."

"Do you think he'll go for it?" she asked as she powered up the phone.

"It's worth a try."

On the second ring, a man's voice said, "Hello?"

Just hearing him speak inspired a flood of anger and frustration to surge through her from head to toe. But she knew it was imperative that she follow Declan's instructions if she had any hope of seeing her parents again. "T-This is Chasyn," she began, then cleared her throat. "Thank you for the photograph but it isn't enough."

"You asked for proof of life."

"And you sent a photo with no distinguishing date or frame of reference. I want a video of my father proving my parents are alive and unhurt."

"I never said *unhurt*," the male voice taunted.

Chasyn swallowed her emotions. "Provide me with the tape or we have nothing further to discuss."

There was a prolonged silence, then he uttered the word "Fine." Chasyn powered down the phone and handed it back to Declan. "Now what?" she asked.

"We wait for the tape. Let's get some dinner," he said. "I'm starving and there's a great seafood place about a mile from here."

Until he mentioned food, Chasyn hadn't thought about how long it had been since she'd eaten. She wasn't sure she could eat with the knot of worry lodged in her throat, but she was willing to go with him just because it would be a welcome distraction.

They walked down to a restaurant with ocean views and were immediately seated in a secluded booth near the back of the restaurant. Declan took a seat that gave him an unobstructed view of the comings and goings of their fellow diners.

Chasyn guessed their pleasant waitress was somewhere in her fifties as she appeared and handed Chasyn a tri-fold, laminated menu. The offerings seemed endless. "What's good here?" she asked Declan.

"Everything. If you like salmon, you'll love the grilled filet."

Chasyn closed the voluminous menu and set it aside just as the waitress returned with two glasses of water garnished with lemon wedges. She took out her pad and pencil and asked, "Are we ready to order?"

Chasyn went with the salmon while Declan opted for the mahi-mahi. The smells coming from the kitchen inspired her dormant appetite. "I'm actually hungry."

"You should be," Declan said. "You haven't been eating much for days now."

"It's a little hard to work up an appetite when you have a professional killer on your tail who is holding your parents hostage in exchange for your life." She took a sip of water. "What do you think the odds are that he'll release my mother?"

"Seventy-thirty."

"Seventy percent yes?"

He shook his head. "Sorry. He's kind of got you over a barrel and there's not a lot of benefit for him to relinquish a hostage."

Chasyn tamped down the panic tightening her gut. "I've been thinking…"

"Yes?"

"We need to talk to Lansing."

Declan offered a grim smile. "I don't think he's going to agree to a meet and greet."

"Unless he thinks we have something on him," Chasyn said.

"Like what?"

"Like whatever Mary might have had on him."

"Tough bluff to carry out since we don't know what she had on him."

"He doesn't know that. All we have to do is claim we found her storage area. That should get his intention."

"And the attention of Müller," Declan warned. "Say we do get him to agree to see us. What's to say he won't send Müller instead?"

"Didn't your surveillance team say he went to the same coffee shop every morning?"

"Yes."

"Then I think tomorrow morning we should ambush him there."

Declan smiled. "I like the way you think."

CHAPTER THIRTEEN

The early evening's setting sun painted the sky a tapestry of gold, pinks, and corals. Chasyn's mind was on her parents. She tried not to think about what Müller might be doing to them as she hurried to keep pace with Declan. Tried, but failed. So far, the only clue to their whereabouts was boat planking, which in South Florida wasn't very helpful.

On the drive back to Declan's place she struggled to keep her composure. It wouldn't do anyone any good if she gave in to the tears burning behind her eyes. She had to stay focused, and she rubbed her arms, her gaze on the taillights of the car in front of them. "*Someone* in Lansing's world has to own a 2013 Taurus."

Declan dropped one hand off the wheel and rested it on the console between them. "So far we haven't found the link. Ziggy ran down every registration for every car owned by Lansing, his wife, his office manager and even rental agencies. Nothing."

"But if we can prove Lansing had Kasey killed, then wouldn't Müller walk away since he wouldn't be paid for finishing the job?"

"That's a possibility," Declan reluctantly agreed. "Depends on the terms of the contract."

Chasyn shifted in her seat so she was speaking to his profile. "So far all we can prove is that Lansing hid fifty thousand dollars. He's spent twenty-two of it, which doesn't leave him much for a final payment. Wouldn't someone like Müller be more pricey than that for his, um, *services*?"

"That would be on the low side for someone like Müller," Declan agreed.

"Maybe we should call the cops, or the FBI or Interpol," she suggested. "Wouldn't they launch an intensive manhunt for Müller?"

Declan raked his fingers through his thick hair. "Yes. Which would put your parents in danger. People like Müller cut and run if the job goes south or draws too much unwanted attention. And they don't leave witnesses behind."

A chill slithered down the full length of her spine. "So, our only hope is to force Lansing to call it off?"

"That's one option," Declan said. "If we can prove he paid to have you and Kasey shot, we can have him arrested."

"How will that help?"

"Müller will have no more financial incentive to finish the job."

Chasyn sighed. "Think he'll just cave when we confront him with the credit card scam?"

"If we can get his DNA and show the withdrawals, that's probably enough for the cops to arrest him."

She sat back against the seat. "He's guarding his DNA like it's a state secret."

As he pulled into his driveway, he said, "He'll screw up eventually and my guys are right there waiting on him."

Chasyn followed him inside the secure house. He flipped on lights and went directly to the coffee pot and turned it on. "Coffee?" he asked

"I'd prefer water," she answered, going to the fridge and selecting a bottle from the shelf. It was amazing how comfortable she felt in his home after such a short period of time. It was just as amazing that she was so fixated on the man standing a mere few feet from her. In the midst of danger and chaos, part of her brain processed genuine attraction. It was stupid and ill-timed, but it was there nonetheless.

Okay, so she was attracted to him. What woman wouldn't be? That didn't mean she had to act on it. Chasyn continued her internal monologue. So he was proverbially tall, dark and handsome. So what? She'd dated attractive men before. *Yeah, but they didn't have his particular skill set or his piercing blue eyes.* There was something dangerous about him. Not in a way that made her fearful. No, it was more like he had a way of making her feel safe and protected.

Right. Because that's what he's being paid for.

Chasyn leaned against the counter. No more than three feet separated them. "How much is this costing my parents?" she asked.

Declan turned and met her gaze. "Does it matter?"

She nodded. "I mean they're financially comfortable but hardly in the same league as, say, Kasey's father."

"Don't worry; I won't bankrupt them," he said, then flashed her a disarming half-smile before his expression grew serious. "I should have anticipated Müller might go after them, so now I have a personal stake in catching the bastard."

"You couldn't know he'd kidnap my parents," she insisted. Just saying it aloud frazzled her nerves. No one could have, but she understood what he was feeling. She hadn't considered that her parents might be in danger. She didn't want him to feel responsible, so she said, "Besides, you had no way of knowing that Lansing had hired someone of his caliber to finish me off." She set her water bottle down and rubbed her bare arms.

Placing his mug on the counter, Declan closed the distance between them in two steps. He was close enough for her to feel the heat coming off his large body. Declan crooked his finger underneath her chin and tilted her head back. Quietly, he regarded her as his warm, coffee-scented breath washed over her face.

It felt as if the room closed in. Like there was nothing in the world but his handsome face and enticing closeness. All she had to do was reach out and wrap her arms around him and pull him to her. She felt a taut rope of desire stretch between them. As the seconds ticked by, the sensation only grew. Chasyn noticed the pulse at the base of his throat. It was calm and even, whereas she could feel her own pulse pounding in her ears. When it became unbearable, she reached out and flattened her palms against his chest. Only then did she feel his heart racing beneath her touch.

"I swore to myself I wouldn't do this," he said softly as his head dipped closer to hers. "But I *really* want to kiss you right now."

His hands brushed her shoulders, then tentatively ran through her hair. "I don't want to hurt you."

"I don't think a kiss will hurt," she said in a breathy tone she barely recognized.

"I was talking about your stitches," he clarified.

"Oh." Chasyn dropped her hands to his waist and slipped her fingers beneath his belt and pulled him against her. "My stitches are a non-issue."

"Good," he said with his mouth just millimeters from hers.

Gently, Declan kissed her. His mouth was hot and his hands began a slow exploration of her back. His fingers lingered on each vertebrae as his tongue engaged with hers and the kiss deepened.

Chasyn literally felt weak in the knees. But raw need propelled her to do some exploring of her own. With her hands nearly trapped between them, she ran her nails gently over his chest, then lower to trace the outline of his muscled core. She felt him shudder slightly when she reached the waistband of his jeans. His kiss became more urgent when she tugged on his shirt and was treated to the feel of solid, bare flesh beneath her exploring hands.

Declan's hands had reached her butt and he pressed her closer, so that she could feel the extent of his arousal. Then he reached for the hem of her top and slid his hands up from her waist. His palms rested on the sides of her bra while his thumbs fanned out to find her nipples. It took only one brush of his thumbs to make them erect and Chasyn moaned against his mouth. Her head was spinning and her body was on fire.

Declan responded to her groan of pleasure by breaking off the kiss and running a path of tender nibbles down her throat, lingering on her exposed collarbone. All the while he continued to explore her breasts. She ran her hands over his back, enjoying the solid feel of his heated skin.

His mouth dipped lower just as his cell phone chirped.

"Seriously?" he groused as he slowly disengaged and took out his phone. "Kavanaugh," he said gruffly.

The desire in Chasyn's belly didn't subside when he took a step away from her. His expression grew pensive as he listened to whoever was on the other end. He let out a few grunts and the occasional "uh-huh" but ended the call as abruptly as it had started.

When he was finished with the call, he didn't reach for her. Chasyn felt self-conscious and discretely straightened her clothes. *Guess the moment's over*, she thought as she looked at his deeply furrowed brow. "What's wrong?"

"We have to ride out to the compound," he said. "You have a video from Müller."

* * *

Declan mentally berated himself as he sped down the back

roads of unincorporated Palm Beach County. He was supposed to protect her, not seduce her. *Especially* not someone like her. She was a happily-ever-after girl and he was a temporary guy. Of course, knowing that and keeping his hands off her seemed to be a challenge. Chasyn was soft and sweet and pliant and hot. A combination he'd never come up against before. He could still taste her skin and smell the faint floral perfume she wore. It was as distracting as the memory of feeling the weight of her breast in his hand. If he didn't stop replaying that in his mind, he'd probably get hard again, so he forced himself to keep his full attention on the road.

Chasyn was unusually quiet during the ride. She was probably trying to figure out where his mind was. That made two of them.

They reached the isolated compound, parked and entered the hangar. Ziggy and Gavin were the only two people in the building. Ziggy uttered an excited greeting, then led them all into the computer station.

"This came in about an hour ago," she explained. She clicked the mouse and the freeze-frame came to life.

Chasyn's father was staring right into the camera lens, his expression strained. He was tied to the same chair with the white backdrop and the plank floor. Based on the size and pixilation of the image, Declan was certain this video had been taken with a cell phone.

"Chase, baby," her father began. "He won't release either of us until you meet him at Carlin Park. Until then, Mommy and I just want you to go to your happy—" The video ended abruptly.

He turned to Chasyn, who was ashen. "Your happy what?"

"Let me think!" she fairly barked. "I don't call my mother 'mommy'. At least not since I was about seven."

"Is this some sort of code?" he pressed. "Did something important happen when you were seven?"

"We moved," she said. "From Fort Lauderdale up to Jensen Beach."

"A good thing?" Declan asked.

She nodded, then her expression brightened. "My happy place!" she exclaimed.

"Fort Lauderdale or Jensen Beach?" he asked.

"Bathtub Beach," she corrected. Müller must be holding them somewhere near there."

"Ziggy," Declan said. "How many marinas are there in a five-mile radius of Bathtub Beach?"

"Twenty-seven," she answered after a speedy trip across her keyboard. "If we pull Joey and Sam off of Lansing, we can probably hit all of them by the morning."

Declan shook his head. "Not both. We need Lansing's DNA. Gavin?" he asked, turning to his friend. "Get a hold of Chuck, Adam, and Joey, and show Müller's picture to every Harbor Master and Marina worker you can find."

"What about us?" Chasyn asked. "I need to find my parents before Müller hurts them."

His better judgment told him to lock her away in his house but he knew she wouldn't go for it. Not when he saw the determined thrust of her chin. "I'll ask the questions, you'll stay locked in the car. Deal?"

"But—"

He placed his finger to her lips. "Non-negotiable."

Her slender shoulders slumped but she nodded her agreement.

* * *

Chasyn was an open nerve as she fidgeted in her seat during the forty-minute drive up to Martin County. Absently, she pressed against the stitches on her forehead, struggling not to itch them even though they were driving her nuts. And that wasn't the only thing getting on her last frazzled nerve. Declan's apparent ease in switching gears was amazing. The minute he'd walked into his office, he had turned back into the personification of professionalism. She still had rubber legs from their brief encounter but he was all calm and collected.

Then there was seeing her father duct taped to a chair. Just the thought of it made her heart hurt. The situation was closing in on her. She was terrified of facing Müller but she was more terrified that he'd kill her mother and father when they were no longer useful. She had no choice but to put her full faith in Declan and his crew.

They pulled off I-95 at the Kanner Highway exit. It was a nondescript section road lined with strip malls and gas stations. Next, they headed east toward the water. Most of the marinas were located on the Intracoastal, though there were some at the inlets. Working off a list generated by Ziggy, Chasyn directed Declan to the first one on the list.

As he pulled the SUV into the lot, he took his nine millimeter out of the console and racked the slide. He drove at a crawl.

"What are we looking for?" she asked softly.

"A white SUV or a 2013 Taurus."

"Right." Chasyn started scanning the sparsely populated parking lot. The sun had set, so it was dark save for a sliver of moonlight. The marina was dimly lit, mostly shadows cast by the lights on the piers in the marina beyond. There was nothing she could see that matched either vehicle. That was disheartening.

Declan parked next to the marina office. "Stay put and keep this close," he said, sliding the gun into her lap.

"What about you?"

He reached across her and took a second weapon out of the glove box. "I'm good," he said with a reassuring smile. "Keep low and if you see anything suspicious, lay on the horn." He took the color photo of Müller with him and locked her inside the car.

"Good tip," she muttered.

Chasyn crouched down in the seat as her eyes darted in every direction. She twisted the rearview mirror so she could have a clear view of the pier areas and watch as Declan went into the Harbor Master's office. She checked her watch. It was just after seven o'clock.

For two minutes, she only had the sound of her own breathing as company. The only people she saw were a young couple sitting on their boat drinking wine. Then Declan returned.

"No luck," he said.

Chasyn let out the breath she'd been holding. "On to the next one," she said.

They repeated this process five times as they meandered up the coast. By the time they reached destination number six, she was starting to think this was a bust of an idea. Especially when they'd received calls from the others that they, too, had been unsuccessful.

"Last one," Declan said as he went through the motions, then got out of the car.

Chasyn checked her watch again. Nine-fifteen.

Her hopes were dashed when she saw Declan come out of the building in under a minute.

"No luck," she confirmed when he slipped behind the wheel.

Declan pulled his gun out of his waistband and set it in his lap. "Perfect luck. Müller is renting slip number seventeen."

"He's here?" she asked with a blend of fear and excitement.

Declan shook his head and grabbed his phone. He quickly called the other teams and told them to hurry to their location.

"Why are we waiting on them?" she demanded. "Can't we just go aboard and check to see if my parents are here?"

"Too risky," he said as he backed the SUV into a spot and cut the lights. "The counter guy said Müller left about an hour ago. He could be back any minute."

"What can we do until then?"

"Watch and wait."

CHAPTER FOURTEEN

For Chasyn, seventeen minutes felt more like seventeen years. She could hear and feel her heart racing in her ears as she kept her eyes trained on the quad-engine boat in Müller's slip. It was white with blue accent stripes, with a triple deck rising up to a captain's perch. Definitely a deep-sea fishing vessel, but from her vantage point, there were no signs of life on board. Which brought a lump of emotion to her throat.

"Finally," she muttered when the last of Declan's men pulled into the parking lot.

"Stay put," he said.

As if choreographed, the whole team disappeared into one of the SUVs. She didn't know what they were discussing, she just wished they'd do it a hell of a lot quicker.

Splitting her attention between the slip and the entrance to the parking lot, Chasyn drummed her fingers against her thigh as her sense of urgency multiplied with each passing second. She was a heartbeat away from just getting out of the car when Declan and his team emerged. Declan came back to the car, opened the door, and slid into the driver's seat.

"What are you waiting for?" she practically yelled.

"Nothing," he said as he racked the slide on his gun. "I'm staying with you while the rest of the guys check out the boat."

"Isn't there strength in numbers?" she challenged.

He tossed her a disarming smile. "My job is to protect *you*. Müller could come back at any second. I'm not leaving you out here alone."

She could tell by his coiled body language that he wasn't accustomed to being sidelined from the action. Chasyn watched as the group, all dressed in black and armed to the hilt, crept down the boardwalk toward the slip. Every few seconds, she would turn and look at the marina entrance, terrified that Müller might return and do God only knew what. She realized she'd been holding her breath and forced herself to let go. The tension in the air was as palpable as the pulse drumming in her ears.

She heard nothing but the faint lapping of the water against the pylons and the occasional distant sound of a bell on one of the channel buoys. The air was thick with the scent of the inlet water and her growing anxiety.

"What if they aren't here?" she asked, just to break the tension.

Declan reached over and patted her knee. "Have faith. If they aren't here, we'll keep look— Shit!"

Chasyn's head whipped around to see what had caused

Declan's sudden curse. A dark van was pulling into the parking lot. Müller was behind the wheel. In one move, Declan pushed her toward the floorboards, then leapt from the SUV. Chasyn heard the pop, then a ping, then the sound of tires squealing. She poked her head up enough to see Müller ram his car into reverse and gun it. He backed into the street, cutting off oncoming traffic.

Declan jumped behind the wheel, started the car and said, "Get on the radio and tell the others we've got eyes on Müller."

Chasyn grabbed the communication device from the console. "Declan and I are chasing Müller. He's in a dark van heading north on A-1-A."

There was a slight pause, then a crackle, then Gavin's voice came back. "We have your parents."

Chasyn squeezed her eyes shut. "Thank God. Are they okay? Can I speak to my mother—"

"Sorry." Declan closed his hand around her fingers. "We need to keep the channel open."

"You'll catch him, right?" Müller was several car lengths ahead of them and moderately heavy traffic prevented them from getting any closer, although Declan was an excellent driver and weaved between slower cars, trying to close the gap. Chasyn thought for a minute. "What do we do if we catch him?"

Declan wove his way through the traffic; ahead of them Müller was doing the same. "First we get him. Then I beat the crap out of him. Then we turn him over to the authorities."

Sounded excellent to Chasyn. "Try not to get us killed in the process. You may be doing the speed limit but you're weaving like a maniac." She held tight to the strap above her door as the SUV picked up speed.

"I'm chasing a maniac," he said calmly.

Declan had gotten within three cars of Müller when he jerked into the left lane, then made a quick left, nearly slamming into oncoming traffic in the process. They couldn't follow him for a few seconds, until traffic cleared the intersection. As soon as they turned, Chasyn could see the flashing red lights at a railroad crossing up ahead. Scanning the line of cars in front of them, they could see that Müller was third in line at the crossing.

"He's trapped," she said excitedly.

No sooner had she said it than Müller darted to the left and slalomed around the downed safety bars. An instant after, the train crossed the tracks. Declan slammed his palm on the steering wheel. "Damn it!"

He held out his hand for the walkie-talkie thing. Chasyn forgot she'd been clutching it during the harrowing ride.

He put the SUV in park as the slow-moving freight train rumbled down the tracks. "Gavin?"

"Did you get him?"

Declan sighed and she could just make out the strained vein at the side of his neck by the light coming off the dashboard instruments. "No. But he's in a black van, first three of the plate are K-6-6. How are the parents."

"Shaken. A few bumps and bruises."

Chasyn's heart sank. "Take me to them."

Declan shook his head. "Have Tom take the parents to the house in Fort Myers."

"But I want to see them!" Chasyn protested.

He turned to her. "Too dangerous. The best course of action is to put them somewhere out of Müller 's reach."

"But I want to see them first," she insisted.

"No," he said with finality. "You're just going to have to trust me for a little bit longer."

* * *

She hadn't spoken to him with more than single syllable responses in the time it had taken them to return to his house. Chasyn was physically tired, but her mind raced with possibilities. Sitting at the table, pen poised over her legal pad, she made herself a list:

1. How is Lansing paying Müller?
2. Mary…storage unit?
3. White SUV at courthouse?
4. Black van Müller was driving?
5. 2013 Taurus?
6. Mary's adoption scam?
7. Lansing's credit card cash hiding system?
8. Lansing's DNA?

"What are you doing?" Declan asked when he pulled up the chair next to hers and slid the pad over so he could read her notes. "You forgot something."

"What?"

"Why three different weapons?" he asked. "There were nine-mil casings at the courthouse and 30.06 projectiles at your apartment building. And Mary was killed with a hunting knife."

She thought for a second. "I'm assuming a knife was used on Mary because it was an up close and personal killing. Not to mention people would have heard gunfire outside the restaurant."

"I'll give you that," he said with a slight nod. "But a handgun and a rifle? That's just odd."

"And the witnesses said there were two people in the white SUV that shot at Kasey and me. Would Müller use an accomplice?"

Declan pensively stroked the shadow of stubble on his jawline. "Unlikely. It makes more sense that Lansing hired someone local for the hit at the courthouse and when that went south, he hired Müller."

"How did he manage that?" Chasyn asked. He shrugged his broad shoulders. "Lansing is a forensic psychiatrist. I'm guessing he's crossed paths with a few killers in his time. Maybe he called in a favor."

"He's been consulting for over a decade," Chasyn explained. "I could go to my office and use our database to cross-reference him with what cases he's been involved in. Besides, I have to pick up my check from Mr. Becker so I can take care of my apartment lease before too much time passes."

"How much time is your boss willing to give you off work?"

She half-grunted a humorless laugh. "I called him briefly from the burner phone and after the shooting at my apartment, he doesn't want me back until"—she made air quotes—"I no longer pose a threat to the office."

"Do you have a key?" he asked.

"Sure," she said. "But it's almost midnight."

"No time like the present," he suggested, scooting his chair back. "Unless you're too tired."

"Too tired to figure out why someone wants me dead?"

"Point," he acknowledged with a sexy half-smile.

They both stood and Declan casually guided her toward the door. Her nerve endings ignited at the sensation of his splayed fingertips. The warmth spread through her body as they stepped out into the cool night air.

It was a relatively quick drive to the four-story glass building off Blue Heron Boulevard that housed the Law Offices of Keller & Mason. Declan pulled into a spot in front of the double doors etched with gold lettering. Before they stepped out into the otherwise vacant lot, Declan retrieved a gun from the glove box and tucked it into the waistband of his jeans.

"Are you always armed?" she asked as he hurried her to the door.

"Müller is still out there," he said as he stood behind her while she slipped her key in the lock and opened the door. A loud beep sounded every few seconds until Chasyn disabled the alarm. She waited for the door to close, relocked it, then reset the alarm.

She went to the round reception desk and leaned over the

smooth mahogany top to reach for her messages. Not that she was going to do much with them; retrieving them was more out of habit than anything else. There were only three pink message slips and an envelope from Mr. Becker—the apartment cancellation fee, no doubt. It was sweet of him to take care of it given that she now needed to move and she wasn't getting paid leave time so every penny was welcome.

Just the thought of finding a new apartment was daunting. Sadness settled over her. A move would be a huge change with Kasey gone.

"What's wrong?" Declan asked. His deep voice echoed in the two-story atrium of the reception area.

Chasyn blew out a breath and held up the envelope. "Kasey's dad sent me the money to pay off the lease at my apartment, so that made me think of her and…"

Declan gently turned her around; his hands bracketed her hips. She tucked the envelope in her back pocket and reached out to bracket her hands at his waist. Her intent had been to push him away, but the instant she felt corded muscle, her intentions melted away. Instead, she snaked her hands around his body and pressed her cheek against his chest.

"I still can't believe she's really dead," she said as she gathered strength from his embrace. It didn't hurt that he was gently stroking her back. Or that she could feel the outline of his thighs where they pressed against hers.

Chasyn squeezed her eyes shut. Her brain was all over the place. This whole situation was turning her organized, logical mind to mush. One minute she was feeling despair and the next desire. It made no sense. Well, no *logical* sense. She needed to concentrate and that wasn't possible when she was drinking in his scent.

Stepping out of his embrace, she plastered a smile on her face and said, "This way," as she led him to the elevator. Once inside, she pressed the button for the second floor. With a soft *ding*, they were welcomed to the dimly lit area.

Declan followed her to the third office on the left, across from a massive law library. Chasyn flipped the wall switches and the fluorescent bulbs flickered to life. Hers was a modest office with a functional desk, a credenza, and two chairs. On top of the credenza were a few framed photographs. The only adornment on the walls was her diploma and a nondescript painting of a beach scene that added color to her otherwise sand-colored office.

"You spend hours in here?" he asked.

"It's not huge, but it's fine for me. Not everyone has the space for a hangar and a gun range." She smiled as she slipped behind her desk and fired up her computer. "There's a mini-fridge in the credenza, help yourself to some water or whatever." In no time, she logged into the database and began her search while Declan settled into one of the chairs opposite her desk.

Chasyn was acutely aware of his presence and struggled to keep her mind on the task at hand. Not easy because she could see him looking around her office above the top of the monitor. She watched as his attention settled on the pictures on her credenza.

"Europe?" he asked, nodding toward the picture on her credenza.

"Kasey and I spent six weeks traveling around after graduation," she explained. "A graduation gift from Mr. Becker."

"Generous guy," he responded vaguely as he continued to catalogue her stuff.

Chasyn was into the database and quickly put in the search parameters. "He is that. He also sent Kasey and me to Hawaii for our high school graduation gift."

"I'm jealous. I never had rich friends in high school or college."

"You went to college?" she asked, then felt completely embarrassed because it came out sounding so incredulous.

He smiled. "Yes. I got my degree in criminal justice then did a six-year stint in the Army."

"Is that where you learned all your, um, *skills*?"

"I was a quick study," he replied evasively. "How's the search coming?"

Chasyn glanced back at the monitor. "Lansing has been an expert witness in sixty-six trials in the last eleven years."

"All for the defense?"

She shook her head. "Roughly about seventy percent of the time. He also works with the State's Attorney's office."

"Can you print a list of cases?" he asked. "Ziggy can run backgrounds on all the participants and try to figure out if any of them could be Lansing's link to Müller."

She pressed three keys, frowned at the screen, and then stood. "The printer is off. I'll be right back."

Chasyn went into the adjacent room and switched on the machine. Then she returned to her office and re-sent the information to the printer. After collecting the pages, she grabbed an accordion folder from the shelf and slipped them inside before powering down the printer and returning to her office. "All set," she said.

She reversed her actions as they left the building: shutting off lights and resetting the alarm. Chasyn had the file tucked under her arm and was shielding a yawn when she reached the car. She glanced down at her watch. It was nearly two a.m. No wonder she was tired.

As soon as they were belted in and Declan had pulled out his gun and placed it in the cupholder in the console, he started the engine, and she asked, "Where are my parents and when can I talk to them?"

"I'll arrange a call in the morning," he promised as he steered out onto Blue Heron.

The road was all but deserted this time of night, save for the occasional vehicle stopping into one of the many gas stations that dotted each corner. As they drove toward I-95, overhead lighting strobed through the car.

"My folks must be frantic," she commented. "Did Müller hurt them?"

"Not according to Gavin," he said with a reassuring pat on her knee. "Shaken up a bit, but otherwise fine."

As they veered off to the on ramp, a bright glare illuminated the car from behind. Chasyn turned to see a white SUV coming up fast. "Declan, I—"

"I see them," he said, his voice calm but crisp. "Hang on."

Chasyn grabbed the overhead strap with one arm but remained twisted in her seat trying to get a look at whoever was chasing them onto the highway. Unfortunately, Florida didn't require front license plates, but she did take note of the name of the rental company logo on the vanity plate. All the while Declan was increasing his speed and gunning it down the interstate. The white SUV stayed with them. The road was empty save their two vehicles, and Declan was flooring his car.

Her heart was pounding in her chest and she kept her eyes glued to their pursuers. The highway lights made it just barely possible to detect the occupants of the vehicle. "There're two men in the car," she announced breathlessly.

"Neither one is Müller," Declan replied.

"He sent minions?" she asked.

Before he could answer, their back window shattered.

CHAPTER FIFTEEN

Stay down!" Declan yelled and revved the engine, knuckles white on the steering wheel.

Chasyn did as instructed, terrified that another bullet would come piercing through the car at any second.

They swerved back and forth. "He's coming up on your side!" Declan's voice was grim. "Hold on, I'll try to bump him."

No sooner had he spoken than Chasyn felt a sharp jerk, followed by the sound of metal against metal. Their SUV bounced back toward the left and Declan cursed loudly as he took one hand off the wheel and pulled his gun from the console.

A second shot wiped out the window above her head, then burrowed into the GPS display. The small screen went dark and acrid smoke sizzled from the bullet hole.

Chasyn crouched into a fetal position, her hands protecting her head. Declan fired three shots in rapid succession. She could smell and taste the gunpowder and her ears rang from the sound.

"Got him," Declan said excitedly.

Cautiously, Chasyn lifted her head and saw the white SUV veer onto the shoulder, then slammed into the jersey wall of a construction zone at full speed. The SUV went airborne, landing several yards ahead of them like an upside down turtle, its wheels spinning.

Declan slowed the car and eased close to the abbreviated shoulder in the construction zone. "Son of a bitch," he said.

Chasyn followed his line of sight and saw a man running into the strip of woods lining the interstate. "Can you catch him?" she asked.

"I'm not leaving you alone," he answered. "Call 9-1-1 from the prepaid I gave you while I check on the other guy."

Chasyn reported the incident but kept her eyes locked on Declan. He leapt over the cement barrier with ease, then went to the overturned vehicle. He crouched beside the driver's side window and reached inside. After a few moments he rejoined her.

"He's dead," he said flatly.

"Did you shoot him?"

He shook his head. "He wasn't wearing a seatbelt."

"Who is he?" she asked.

"We'll have to wait for the cops—"

Approaching sirens silenced him. Flashing lights and a strobe of red came rushing up.

Declan leaned close and said, "We'll answer their questions but don't volunteer anything. The last thing I want or need is the local cops screwing with my investigation."

"But what if they can help?" she argued. "Maybe they can find the connection to Lansing."

"Have you forgotten Detective Burrows and the State's Attorney both blame you for being less than honest with them before the grand jury proceedings? This is one of those situations where you can't trust anyone but me. Okay?"

Chasyn blew out a breath then nodded.

The first officer on the scene was a tall, lanky man in his mid-twenties. The plate above his crisp uniform shirt read WILSON. He had a powerful flashlight tucked in his armpit as he approached. "Ma'am," he greeted her. "Are you hurt?"

"No, but the guy in the other car is…"

The officer asked about Declan's possible injuries, then went over the wall and checked the overturned van. As he did so two more police cars arrived, along with an ambulance and a firetruck that was quickly used to barricade the accident site.

Deputy Wilson gave out instructions and assignments to the first responders before he started back to where she and Declan stood.

Reaching into the breast pocket of his shirt, he retrieved a small pad and a pencil. "Let's move over toward the wall," he suggested. "I'll need full names and addresses," he said.

They complied and he asked, "Are you sure neither one of you require medical attention?"

"I'm sure," Chasyn said. Declan echoed the same sentiment.

"Okay, then," Wilson began, pencil poised. "Your name, ma'am?"

"Chasyn Summers."

"And you, sir?"

"Declan Kavanaugh."

Wilson went on to ask a litany of basic questions: like address, employment, contact information and basic background. Then he got to the point. "Which one of you was driving?"

"I was," Declan said. "We were on the interstate when the SUV came up on us. They fired a shot that took out my back windshield. Then they tried to run us off the road. At that point, I took out my weapon and returned fire. The white car swerved, hit the wall, and landed on the roof. I saw one man run from the vehicle."

"Which way?" Wilson asked.

"West. Into the tree line and then probably to one of the businesses on Congress."

Wilson looked up from his notes. "Did you see him run all the way to Congress Avenue?"

Declan shook his head. "No, but that's the only thing that makes sense. He's on foot and probably desperate to contact someone to get him out of the area. Best place to do that is one of the convenience stores or gas stations along Congress."

Using the microphone clipped to his shoulder, Wilson called for a K-9 unit to begin a search for the runner. Then he asked, "Where is your gun now, Mr. Kavanaugh?"

"Console of my vehicle," Declan responded.

Again, Wilson dispatched one of the half-dozen or so on-scene deputies to recover the gun. "Do you have any idea why you were chased and shot at?"

"Dr. Lansing," Chasyn said.

Wilson looked at her for a moment, then asked, "The Mary Jolsten case?"

Chasyn nodded. Declan placed his arm around her shoulders and pulled her against his side as he slowly recounted the events leading up to the night's shootout. He never mentioned Müller and she found that odd. Almost as odd as the fact that as he was speaking, she was more focused on the feel of his well-muscled, warm body than the peppering of questions from the deputy. Exhaustion settled over her as the minutes stretched into nearly an hour.

"We're going to have to take you to the station," Wilson announced after returning from his patrol car.

"Is that really necessary?" Declan countered. His grasp on her upper arm tightened. "Miss Summers is tired and so am I. We'll come in later today."

"I'm sorry, Mr. Kavanaugh, I checked in and but Detective Burrows is waiting for you."

"May I get my tote out of the car?" Chasyn asked.

"You can retrieve your personal belongings and then I'll take you in."

They strode to the car together and Chasyn asked in a whisper, "Why did you leave Müller out of the story?"

"Because Müller wasn't the guy who ran from the car. That guy was too stocky. I don't want the police going off on a wild goose chase for Müller when they can be of some assistance finding the driver who was shooting at us."

"But isn't Müller the most dangerous one of all?"

"And the hardest to catch. The guy is a professional and he hasn't evaded capture all these years because he's stupid."

"And you think you can catch him?"

Declan gave her a squeeze. "Actually, I do."

* * *

By the time Gavin and Tom had picked them up from the sheriff's office, provided them with a replacement car, and they'd driven back to Declan's place, the sun was coming up. Every muscle in her body ached with fatigue. It took some doing, but she dragged herself inside and immediately took a seat at the table. Even the guestroom seemed like an insurmountable distance to travel.

Declan immediately started a fresh pot of coffee.

"You drink too much of that stuff," she chastised him.

"I have to get the taste of the sheriff's rot-gut coffee out of my mouth," he joked. "You look whipped."

"Then I look better than I feel," she teased.

"You always look good," Declan said, his voice just a fraction deeper than normal.

The unexpected compliment settled in the pit of her stomach. "Then you have pretty low standards."

"Actually," he began as he joined her at the table with a mug of coffee for him and a bottle of water for her, "I have very high standards."

"Is that why you've never married?" she asked, then immediately wished she could reclaim the inappropriate question.

He smiled, then took a sip. "My line of work isn't very conducive for a relationship, let alone marriage."

She forced a smile but inside she was sad to hear the finality of his words. Which, she realized, was completely silly and foolish. He was her temporary bodyguard, emphasis on *temporary*. His attachments shouldn't be any of her concern. But in the deep recesses of her mind, they were. She took a drink of water and tried to swallow the lump of disappointment in her throat. *You are being an idiot*, she mentally chided herself. And how and why had she gotten to this pointless train of thought? She had no choice but to give him her trust, but only a fool would give him her heart to boot.

The door buzzer sounded and she gave a little start.

"Calm down," Declan said. "It's just Gavin with some bagels."

Declan buzzed him through and in a matter of seconds he was walking in the front door with a large white bag. The minute Chasyn smelled the baked goods she practically salivated. Until that moment, she'd had no idea she was even hungry.

After Gavin left, Declan grabbed a couple of plates and knives, setting out the bagels and an assortment of flavored cream cheeses. Chasyn wasted no time slathering her bagel with salmon spread, then took a healthy bite. They ate in relative silence; apparently he was as hungry as she was. Once he was finished, Declan said, "You have enough time to take a shower before we leave."

"Leave for where?"

"It's time to pay a visit to Dr. Lansing. I want to get to him before the detectives let him know what happened last night."

"Give me five minutes," Chasyn said as she made a dash for the guest room. She showered in record time and didn't bother to dry her hair. She selected a simple cotton print shift dress and a pair of flat sandals from her belongings. She was switching her stuff from her tote to a smaller cross bag when she came across the accordion file they'd gathered a few hours earlier.

When she returned to the kitchen, a barechested Declan was rubbing a towel over his hair. Chasyn very nearly dropped the file, along with her jaw. God, but the man had an incredible body. He was deeply tanned and sculpted, with a patch of hair that tapered from his chest to the waistband of his jeans like some big arrow tempting her to explore.

Like her brain needed any more temptation. Hell, her mouth was dry, her pulse had quickened and she was battling the nearly overwhelming desire to toss him down on the couch and have her way with him. When he caught her gawking at him, she lowered her gaze and felt her cheeks warm. Thankfully he couldn't read minds.

"I-I have the cases Landry worked on," she said in a breathy, sultry voice that had to belong to someone else. She cleared her throat and looked up. "What do you want me to do with them?" *Or with you?*

"We'll fax them to Ziggy and she can get started."

He grinned as if he knew what she'd been thinking. Impossible, but disarming. He let the towel drape around his shoulders as he raked his fingers through his damp hair. "Let me get a shirt and we're out of here."

He was back in a few minutes wearing a blue T-shirt that mirrored the color of his eyes. Paired with his dark jeans, the combination made him look fabulous, which didn't do much to quell Chasyn's inappropriate sexual fantasies. Obviously sleep deprivation had lowered her immunity to the situation.

"Ready?" he asked.

"Very," she replied without meeting his gaze.

She followed him out to a dark green Ford Explorer. Like the black SUV and the Hummer, it was equipped with all sorts of tech and communications toys. "I'm sorry your car got shot up last night," Chasyn said as she hauled herself into the high passenger seat.

Declan slid inside and fastened his seatbelt. "Cars can be fixed," he replied casually. "I'm just glad the guy was a lousy shot."

"How long do you think it will be before the police identify him?"

"He didn't have any ID on him, so they'll probably run his prints later today. If he has any kind of a record, the identification should pop pretty quickly."

"And then it will just be a matter of linking him to Dr. Lansing and this whole nightmare will be over," she said with excitement.

"You're forgetting Müller."

Her spirits fell. "Can't the FBI or Interpol hunt him down?"

"They haven't been successful yet."

She angled in the wide seat so she was looking at his

handsome profile. She tugged at the snug seatbelt, then asked, "What about the boat where he held my parents? He has to have left some sort of trail for them to follow."

"We're following it," Declan assured her. "Adam is all over it."

"Oh, what about that call to my parents?" she reminded him.

He took one hand off the wheel, fished his phone out of his pocket and said, "Hit speed dial seven."

Chasyn did and an unfamiliar male voice answered on the first ring. "Hello?"

"May I speak to Mr. or Mrs. Summers?" she asked.

"Chasyn?" the male voice inquired.

"Yes."

"Hang on."

"Sweetie, is that you?" her mother asked in a very chipper tone.

"Mom," she said on a breath of relief. "How are you?"

"I'm beating your father at gin. But that isn't important. How are you?"

Baffled. "Fine." She opted not to share the details of the shooting with her mother. No sense in getting her all upset. "Did Müller hurt you or dad?"

"A few bumps and bruises, but nothing major. Don't you worry about us. You have enough on your plate right now. All things considered, we came out of the situation relatively unscathed."

"Mom, this isn't *Murder, She Wrote*. That man was dangerous."

"We know that, but Mr. Kavanaugh's people were on top of it."

Chasyn spent a few more minutes speaking with her mother, then had an equally surreal conversation with her dad. The two of them sounded as if they were on vacation instead of squirrelled away in some safe house. She ended the call and held out the phone for Declan. For a brief instant during the transfer, their fingers brushed and Chasyn experienced a quick tingle.

"Sometimes I think they're both nuts," she muttered.

"They're in a very posh place and well-guarded," Decan assured her.

"In Fort Myers?"

He shook his head. "The less you know the better."

Declan steered the Explorer through downtown West Palm Beach, then parked in the lot across from City Place. After he'd cut the engine, he turned and held her gaze. "Joey and Sam are set up across the street from the café. We'll wait here until we get word that Lansing has arrived."

"Then we just walk up to him and demand to know why he killed Mary and Kasey and is hell bent on killing me?" she asked.

"Something like that," Declan replied.

"How long do we have to wait?"

Declan checked his watch. "Lansing usually stops in around nine."

"That's a half hour from now!"

CHAPTER SIXTEEN

Declan placed a tentative kiss on her open lips, but within seconds there was nothing tentative about the way his mouth explored hers. No hint of tenderness or restraint. Just pure, unadulterated passion. Chasyn savored every second of it. She explored the chiseled angles of his face with her fingertips while his tongue teased hers. The flicker in her stomach sparked to flame when he ran his hands along her sides, lingering near the swell of her breasts.

Chasyn's hands dropped to the broad expanse of his shoulders and she dug her fingernails in as he pulled her lower lip between her teeth, then began to kiss his way down her throat. Her head fell back, giving him unfettered access to her neck as her body turned into a taut rope of desire. Everywhere he kissed, her skin burned. She drank in the scent of his woodsy cologne as he nibbled and teased her collarbone. With her pulse pounding in her ears and her heart beating erratically, Chasyn got lost in the pleasurable sensations surging through her. She wanted more. No, *needed* more.

Then that little voice in her head reared its ugly head. *What are you doing?*

Making out with a guy in a parking lot. And not just any guy—the man who held her life in his hands. At least temporarily. The man who could make her weak in the knees with just a few well-placed kisses.

Gently, she placed her palms on his chest and pushed away, ignoring the sense of regret that accompanied the action. "This is a bad idea," she managed over the lump of raw need lodged in her throat.

He tilted his head to the side and regarded her with a sexy half-smile. "It was working for me."

"I'm sure it was," she said as she straightened her disheveled clothing. "But it isn't what I want."

"Liar," he said without accusation. "Or did you think I didn't notice the way you were looking at me a little while ago?"

Chasyn attempted to fight off the urge to blush. "You were the one walking around without a shirt."

"Well, if it makes you feel more comfortable, feel free to walk around my house without a shirt, too. I won't mind."

She gave him a sidelong glance. "Very magnanimous of you."

His expression grew more serious. "What can I say? I'm attracted to you and you're attracted to me and we're consenting adults."

"I never said I was attracted to you," she protested, though her words sounded insincere even to her own ears.

His smile broadened. "You're a lousy liar. Do you think I haven't noticed the way you look at me? Did you think I wouldn't respond to that?"

"You're supposed to be my bodyguard, not my lover," she lamely protested.

Her shrugged. "I can multitask."

Maybe he had a point. Maybe there was nothing wrong with a harmless fling. Only something told her it wouldn't be a casual fling. *Could she handle a no-strings-attached relationship with this man?* What was the alternative? Walking away? That thought filled her with sadness and a sense of loss. It all came down to what she was willing to sacrifice. Clearly they had different goals, so there was no future in Declan Kavanaugh for her. On the other hand, she was still two years away from her master plan's timetable for meeting Mr. Right. Maybe Declan could be a temporary diversion. Yes. Just someone to date until she was ready to move on with her life plan. The only flaw in her thinking was the *what if*? What if her heart got involved? She'd be setting herself up for some serious heartbreak. But taking one look at his handsome face, she decided it might just be worth it.

* * *

You pushed too far, jackass.

Declan pressed his back against the seat and stretched his legs as far as the car's interior would allow. His erection was subsiding even though he could still taste the heat of her pliant mouth on his lips. Not only had his behavior been unprofessional, it was totally out of character. He wasn't the kind of guy who dragged women over consoles to kiss them senseless. But Chasyn wasn't just any woman. She was a client—a client with the most intriguing blend of strength and vulnerability. And it didn't hurt that she had a body that inspired a multitude of fantasies.

As his breathing steadied, he reached for his phone.

"Sam here."

"Any sign of him?" Declan asked one of the two operatives he had surveilling Dr. Lansing.

"Parking on Clematis Street now," Sam said. "I've got eyes on him."

"We'll be right there," Declan said, then ended the call. He turned to Chasyn. "Ready?"

"For what?" she asked. "Lansing will never talk to me."

"You're not going in," Declan stated. "I'll leave you in the surveillance car with Joey while I go see the good doctor."

"Can you punch him or something?" she asked.

"Why?" he inquired with a snicker as they got out of the car.

"If he bleeds on you, we get his DNA."

"And I get an assault charge," he pointed out. "No, this little chat is just meant to rattle his cage."

"In the hopes of?"

"Throwing him off his game," Declan said. "I want to see his reaction when I tell him one of his two prospective killers died last night."

"Which will prove what?"

"We'll see."

The late March sun had already coaxed the temperatures into the low seventies. Pleasant enough for the two-second walk to where Joey and Sam had parked their nondescript panel van across from Lansing's favorite coffee spot. Declan was mildly distracted by Chasyn's reflection as they passed windows along the busy street. He'd never seen her in a dress and he had to admit, she had great legs. For a petite woman, she was perfectly proportioned. She wasn't tan, but her skin glowed like she'd just had a healthy kiss from the sun. Her blond hair reflected golden highlights from the sun. She wore a minimum of makeup, which he liked. And no lipstick. He'd kissed that off her in the car. Chasyn was a natural beauty and that was refreshing in an area rife with breast implants, Botox, and collagen injections.

Staying on the opposite side of the street from the café, Declan and Chasyn slipped inside the cramped van. Only the driver's and passenger seats were in place; the rest of the seating had been removed to make way for video and sound recording equipment. Everyone exchanged pleasantries, then Declan asked, "Is he inside?"

"Waiting on his order," Sam said after looking through a pair of binoculars. "When he comes out, he always sits at the small table to the left of the door. Latte in one hand, bottle of water in the other. The guy is predictable."

"This shouldn't take long," Declan said as he moved toward the door.

He crossed the street just as Dr. Lansing was coming out of the café. He was easy enough to spot. He was in his mid-fifties, lean, and dressed in a designer polo shirt, khaki pants, and tasseled loafers. Lansing's wedding band glinted in the sunlight as he moved to take his seat at the small wrought-iron table.

Without hesitation, Declan fell into the seat across from the startled doctor. "Morning."

"This table is taken," the doctor returned irritably.

"I'm not staying," Declan promised him. "I just want to ask you if you'd heard the news?"

"News?"

"Your paid assassins blew it last night. One of them is dead and it's only a matter of time before the police identify the driver and link him back to you."

No surprise registered in the doctor's narrowed green eyes. "I can assure you, I have no idea what you're talking about."

"Sure you do," Declan returned conversationally. "We both know you killed Mary Jolsten and had Kasey Becker gunned down. What isn't going to happen is killing Chasyn Summers." Declan leaned closer to the doctor. "If so much as a hair on her head is harmed, they won't even be able to identify you with dental records."

"I'm not going to sit here and be threatened," the other man huffed indignantly.

"What are you going to do? Call the cops?"

Lansing scowled. "Who the hell are you?"

"I'm the guy who's going to make sure you spend the rest of your life in jail."

"With what proof?" he countered smugly. "The police haven't been able to link me to any murder."

"Yet," Declan said. "But that was before I killed one of your flunkies last night. By this afternoon, the cops should have an ID and then it's just a matter of time before I find the link between you and the dead guy."

Lansing stood. "I hate to disappoint you, Mr.—"

"Kavanaugh. Declan Kavanaugh."

"Well, Mr. Kavanaugh, no one will be able to link me to anything."

"Right. Because you covered your tracks too well?"

Lansing gathered up his two beverages. "No. Because I'm smarter than you are."

* * *

"He's a smug son of a bitch," Declan announced when he returned to the panel van.

Chasyn nodded. "Always was. Condescending, too. Did you learn anything?"

"He's very confident that the duo from last night can't be traced back to him." Declan told Joey and Sam to stay on the doctor. "I don't care what you have to do, but get your hands on that coffee cup or that water bottle. I want to bury this bastard."

"What now?" Chasyn asked as they dashed back to the parking lot where they'd left the Explorer.

"Time to push Ziggy into overdrive."

Chasyn stifled a yawn. "I feel like we have a bunch of puzzle pieces that don't fit into the puzzle."

"Me, too. There has to be something else to this that we're not seeing."

"Like how and why Lansing hired two different hit men to kill me. If all the intelligence on someone like Müller says he doesn't work with minions, then the two guys from last night were working on their own. Why the overlap?"

Declan was quiet for a minute. "Lansing is a pretty thorough guy. Maybe he was just hedging his bet."

"But isn't that dangerous? I mean the more people involved, the better chance of getting caught, right?"

"He seemed pretty sure that he was untouchable," Declan told her. A minute later, he glanced over at her. "You look exhausted."

"I'm a little tired." God, was that ever an understatement. She was so tired her body actually hurt.

"There's a sleep room at the hangar. Why don't you try to get some rest while Ziggy and I work on a few things?"

"I can't sleep while you work."

Declan reached out and patted her bare knee. Her skin tingled from his touch. "I need you to work on Lansing's past cases and you're too exhausted to do that right now. A few hours of sleep will do you some good."

"What about you?" she asked. "You were up all night, too."

"I'm used to it and I have a serious caffeine addiction that helps me get over the hump."

"You'll rot your insides with all that coffee," she warned.

"I'm tough," he said as he put the Explorer into drive. Not long after, he pulled into the hangar and cut the engine.

Gavin, Chuck, Adam, and Ziggy were gathered around an industrial coffee maker, the kind Chasyn had only seen in diners and restaurants. Without asking, Declan went to the adjacent fridge and took out a bottle of water and passed it to her. She took a long drink and waited for the others to fill their mugs with coffee.

Once everyone was gathered, Declan had the floor. "Several things," he began. "First, I want to know the minute the cops get an ID on the dead guy from last night. Then I want to know everything about the white SUV down to the VIN number and the mileage. Then I want whatever information you can get"—he looked at Ziggy—"on the names in the cases Chasyn printed at her office."

Chuck spoke up. "I've already talked to my contact at the police lab. He'll call me as soon as they run the guy's prints."

Adam added, "I've got a lead on the SUV. I'm just waiting for the rental place to open for business."

Ziggy said, "I've already started on the searches on Chasyn's list. There are a lot of names in the transcripts—witnesses and experts—so it won't be quick." She took a sip from her mug. "While I'm waiting, I'm still going through Mary's and Lansing's financials. I decided to go back a few months to see if anything pops."

"Good idea," Declan said. He turned to Chasyn. "Come with me. I'll take you to the bunk room."

She felt a little guilty that she'd be napping like a toddler while the rest of the group was hard at work. But she was having a hard time keeping her eyes open. Declan led her into a small room with a pair of cots and one rickety table with a lamp on it.

"It isn't the Ritz…"

"It's fine," she insisted. "Just a twenty-minute power nap and I'll be as good as new." She lay down on the cot but Declan remained, leaning against the doorjamb. "What?" she asked.

"Just making sure you go to sleep."

"I *can't* go to sleep with you watching me. It's creepy."

"I like watching you."

Chasyn lifted her head off the pillow. "I'm too tired to spar with you right now. Maybe later."

Declan chuckled, then left the room. Chasyn took just two coffee-scented breaths before she fell into a deep sleep.

* * *

When she roused, she checked her watch and bolted upright. She'd been asleep for nearly six hours. She sat up, ran her fingers through her hair, careful to avoid the annoyingly itchy stitches, then reached into her purse for a breath mint. Following the sounds of muffled voices, she made her way back down to the first floor.

Chasyn was self-conscious about her long nap but if any of them noticed, it wasn't apparent. Everyone greeted her as if it was normal to sleep half the day away. "May I have some coffee?" she asked.

"You never drink coffee," Declan said.

"I'm making an exception this time. Why did you let me sleep so long?"

"Because you're sleep deprived. I just made a fresh pot," Declan said. "Help yourself."

Chasyn went to the machine and poured herself a small mug of coffee. One sip and she nearly choked on its strength. These people didn't fool around. But she valiantly drank it down, needing the caffeine boost to clear her head.

"Anything new?" she asked.

"Does the name Armando Velez mean anything to you?"

Declan asked as he led her to Ziggy's wide world of computer monitors.

There was an unflattering mug shot up on one of the screens of a scruffy brown-skinned man with black hair and brown eyes. Very weathered looking. "I've never seen him before. Why?"

"He's the dead guy from last night," Declan explained.

"He looks homeless," she offered.

"He was. Has a long list of priors but they're all for penny ante stuff. Trespassing, loitering, drunk in public."

"So why was he shooting at us?"

"He was the passenger," Declan said. "No traces of gunpowder on his hands. So he definitely wasn't the shooter."

"How do we find the shooter?" Chasyn asked.

"I'm on that," Chuck said. "I'm heading out now to see some of the people he's been arrested with in the past and to hit a couple of shelters to see who he used to hang with."

"What about the white SUV?" she asked. "Anything to link it back to Lansing?"

"It was stolen three weeks ago from a rental lot in Lake Worth."

"Then we basically have nothing," she said on a sigh.

"Not true. We have a few more pieces of the puzzle," Declan countered. "And we're not finished digging."

Chasyn blew out a breath of frustration. "Only we don't know what the puzzle looks like."

"But we will," Declan assured her.

"We need a miracle," Chasyn said.

CHAPTER SEVENTEEN

As if on cue, Ziggy came rushing out of the computer lab. "I think I found something," she said excitedly. "Come take a look at this." She led them back to her area. All the screens were compiling data or displaying information and images.

Declan and Chasyn waited while she pulled a bank statement up on the larger, main screen mounted on the vast wall. "Nice going," Declan said.

Chasyn scanned the data until she spotted an intriguing entry. "A 354-dollar debit card transaction to Store-All in Delray Beach made four months prior to her death."

"I did a little digging," Ziggy said. "That company has a small unit they rent for 59 dollars a month if you prepay six months up front."

"I think we need to take a look inside. What's the address?" Declan asked.

Ziggy wrote it down on a small sheet of paper and handed it to him.

"Aren't those places secured?" Chasyn inquired. "I don't think the management will just let us stroll in and browse. And we don't have a key."

"Minor details," Declan remarked with a lazy grin. "Grab your purse."

Chasyn retrieved her bag from the bunk room and joined Declan at the Explorer. "Do you have a strategy?' she asked as she hoisted herself into the seat.

"Always," he assured her. "We'll stop on the way to the storage place for some food. I need to refuel."

"Do you eat all your meals out?"

He shrugged. "Pretty much."

"I love to cook," she said. "It relieves stress."

"Are you any good?"

"Maybe I'll just show you. All I would need is a quick trip to a grocery store."

Declan merged the car onto I-95 and increased his speed. "And a trip to Bed, Bath and Beyond. My kitchen is stocked with the bare minimum in cookware."

"I have everything under the sun back at our apartment," she said. She felt a pang of grief stab at her heart. "I mean *my* apartment." Chasyn tugged on the seatbelt to relieve some of the pressure. "I have to buy out my lease and get my stuff moved. I guess I have to find a new apartment first."

"You've got enough on your plate right now," Declan told her. "You can worry about the apartment situation later."

"Says the man who owns his own home."

"You made that sound like a character flaw."

"Sorry," she mumbled. "I didn't mean it that way. I guess

I'm just jealous that you're all settled and my life is a total shit show right now." She rubbed her bare arms even though the car was filled with bright sunlight. Shaking off her uncharacteristic self-pity, she asked, "So what do you think Mary kept in her storage unit?"

"We'll find that out soon enough." A short while later he eased the Explorer down the off-ramp and pulled into a small restaurant adjacent to the interstate.

As soon as Chasyn stepped from the car, her nostrils filled with the most wonderful smells. She found herself practically salivating as she walked with him to the nondescript place. A neon sign above the door said WELCOME, and based on the number of cars in the lot, this little place wasn't much of a secret.

Opening the door for her, Declan ushered Chasyn into a dimly lit, funky room with a bar running down its right side and small tables crammed along its left. There was a kitchen behind the bar and a small group of men and women manned the various stations.

"Two?" a pleasant hostess wearing jeans and a shirt with the restaurant's logo asked.

"Yes," Declan said.

Chasyn placed the young woman somewhere in her late teens to early twenties. The hostess grabbed two voluminous menus and said, "Follow me."

They were directed to a small table near the rear of the room. Declan asked Chasyn to squeeze into the bench seat while he took the chair. The hostess handed them menus and a loose page of daily specials.

"How did you find this place?" she asked over the low buzz of other diners' conversations.

Declan placed the menu aside and held on to the list of specials. "Jack turned me on to it," he said. "He tried a case in West Palm for three weeks and ate here every day. I joined him once and got hooked on the food."

Chasyn perused the menu. It was a fascinating salute to Caribbean fare with some interesting pairings, like tuna over a bed of spicy seasonal fruit. She felt oddly normal just sitting in a restaurant, selecting an entrée. This felt almost like a date. Correction: a *first* date. She had a fluttering in the pit of her stomach and there was a palpable thread of tension connecting them. Or maybe that was just in her mind. Maybe she was just indulging in a fantasy. Still, it was intriguing to wonder what it would be like if he'd actually asked her out. If they were just two people on the cusp of getting to know one another.

He would definitely be the kind of man she would notice. Who couldn't? There was something implicitly sensual about those ice-blue eyes set against his tanned skin. It didn't take her mind long to conjure the memory of him shirtless in the kitchen. Doing so caused a flip-flop in her belly. Heaven help her. She was strongly attracted to him on many levels, but his attraction seemed to be limited to the physical. That wasn't her style but the alternative was grim. Maybe she should accept him on his terms. Maybe not for the long haul, but for however long it lasted. She could get him out of her system and then go back to her carefully thought-out life plan. Somewhere in the dark recesses of her mind, a question lingered. *Was Declan Kavanaugh really the kind of man she could get out of her system?*

"Have you made a choice?" he asked.

I'm working on it. "Yes."

The waitress arrived, took their drink orders—Chasyn really needed a glass of wine—then scurried off toward the bar. In a flash, she was back with a beer for Declan and a glass of merlot for her. She stood tableside, pen poised above her pad. "Are you ready to order?"

"I'll have the tuna," Chasyn responded with a smile, then folded the menu and handed it to her.

Declan selected the grilled mahi-mahi with plantains on the side. Then he relaxed in his seat and brought a frosty bottle of beer to his lips. They were magnificent lips, she thought as she took a healthy sip of her wine.

"What do you do for fun?" she asked.

"Life is fun," he answered easily. "I have a career I enjoy. Every day is different so I'm not tied down to anything. I really can't complain. You?"

"I run."

"From killers?"

She shook her head. "I run on the beach every morning. I like to watch the sunrise."

"I wouldn't have pegged you as the athletic type."

Chasyn tilted her head and regarded him for a moment. "I'm not a gym rat but I do try to stay fit."

"I just meant that you don't have that gaunt runner's look. You have great curves."

She almost choked on her drink. "You have to stop saying suggestive things to me."

"Why?"

She pursed her lips for a second. "Because! Because we're having a professional relationship and we shouldn't complicate it by, by…"

"Sleeping together?" he said easily, reaching across to gently brush the back of her hand.

The touch was a jolt she felt from the top of her head to the ends of her toes. This man had some sort of magical powers. One steamy look and her bones turned to mush. And her brain…well, that part of her anatomy was fixated on his physical attributes. And there were many.

She was horrified when she felt her cheeks warm. Thank God the light was low in the restaurant. She pulled her hand away. It was hard to think—hell, it was hard to breathe when he was touching her. She had to regain some modicum of control. "We shouldn't even be kissing."

"It's a prelude to the sleeping together part," he explained as casually as if he were giving her directions to the closest service station.

Chasyn ran her fingertip around the rim of her nearly empty glass, trying in vain to get the visual of them tangled in his sheets out of her brain. "You make it sound like a foregone conclusion."

"You won't get any resistance from me," he said in a deep, sensual tone. "I can tell you get all hot and bothered when I kiss you."

"Now you just sound arrogant."

"Arrogant maybe, but not wrong. But I'm not going to push you, Chasyn. I'm just letting you know that I'm interested. *Very* interested."

The way he said it made her toes curl. She was in big, big trouble with this man.

* * *

They reached Store-All a few minutes before six. Inside the single-story office they were greeted by a young man in an orange shirt with the storage logo emblazed on the front. "Can I help you folks?"

Declan stepped forward with authority. "My sister's storage bill is about to come due and I want to extend her rental for another six months," he said as he took a credit card out of his wallet.

"Name?" the clerk said as he stepped to a computer terminal.

"Mary Jolsten." Declan impressed the clerk by rattling off the dead woman's date of birth, phone number, and driver's license number.

"Unit 104," the clerk said with a nod.

"Right," Declan agreed. "Oh, and she's lost her key to the unit."

The man looked up and frowned. "There's an additional hundred-dollar fee for replacements."

"Not a problem," Declan assured him. "Just add it to the bill."

"I'll need some ID," the clerk said.

Declan pulled out his driver's license and passed it over the Formica counter.

The clerk looked at it and then looked back at Declan. "Your last name isn't Jolsten."

"My sister's married name," he explained easily.

The clerk thought for a moment, then seemed to accept the lame deception. Chasyn was awed by how easily Declan lied when the situation called for it. When she lied, red blotches appeared on her throat.

In no time, they left the office, key in hand. Declan drove slowly around a long row of units, then turned and drove partway up the second row before they reached 104. The building was concrete under a layer of beige paint. The garage-style door for each unit was painted the same bright orange as the young man's shirt.

Key in hand, Declan grabbed the lock on the door and twisted the key until she heard an audible *click*. Reaching down, he grabbed the handle at the base of the door and rolled it up on its tracks. At the same time, an overhead fluorescent light within flickered to life.

It was a small unit, maybe five-by-eight, practically empty save for a few boxes, an assemble-it-yourself plywood-veneered desk, and an expensive mountain bike.

"Where do we start?" she asked.

"The boxes," Declan answered, moving into the musty-smelling room toward where five boxes were stacked in a single tower against the back wall. He placed one at her feet, then selected the next one for himself.

Chasyn's box contained a pile of loose photographs. "Mary, the early years," she said as she began picking through the images. Still, there could be something of importance in the three or so inches of photos, so she kept digging.

"I've got books," Declan said. He took down a second box and peeled it open. "I've got more books."

Chasyn finished looking at the photographs and shoved the box aside with her foot. She had started for the next box in the stack when Declan grabbed her arm. "Let me get that for you," he said.

She moved back and he took down the box and laid it at her feet. Chasyn was about to bend to open the flaps when she felt him come up behind her. She straightened immediately. Too late. He was already lifting her hair off her neck. The sensation of cool air was instantly replaced by the feel of his hot mouth nuzzling her neck. Instead of breaking away, she reached around and gripped his thigh as he slowly explored the side of her throat. He moaned against her skin and his hand snaked around her waist.

Declan's fingers were flat against her belly and he pulled her gently so that she could feel every hard inch of him against her back. His hand moved higher, until he cupped her breast. He tested its weight, then his thumb began to tease her nipple erect. An exquisite kind of need was building inside of her. It was urgent to the point of desperation. Her pulse was pounding and she felt helpless to do anything more than dig her nails into the fabric of his jeans.

Using her free hand, she removed his hand from her breast and did a quick spin. Getting up on tiptoes, she planted her mouth on his. There was nothing slow or tentative about the mingling of their tongues. He tasted faintly of beer.

Chasyn ran her palms up over his chest, then laced her fingers behind his neck and dragged him closer. Declan's hands skimmed her sides, pausing briefly at her waist before reaching around and cupping her bottom. He pressed her to him and there was no mistaking the feel of his erection. His quick response made her feel powerful, and desire pulsated through every nerve in her body.

She lowered her hands and began to explore the expanse of his body. She was emboldened when he let out a little gasp when her fingertips dipped beneath his waistband. Chasyn's probe went further, until she managed a whisper-light pass across his boxers and the outline of his rigid penis.

Before she realized what was happening, Declan swooped her up in his arms and carried her to the desk. Still kissing her, he laid her down gently, then reached up her dress and made quick work of slipping off her thong. She heard the sound of his belt buckle and then his zipper. He reached up and covered her breast with one hand as he positioned himself between her legs.

Chasyn's mind was mush. All she could think about was the promise of satisfaction. She wanted it now. She reached for his hips but when she did, he caught both her hands in his and said, "Wait," into her mouth.

Chasyn didn't want to wait. She wanted the fullness of him inside of her. She was teetering on the brink of climax and they hadn't even had sex yet. Ignoring his instruction, she reached for him again. This time, he captured her wrists in one hand and lifted them above her head. She was half-on, half-off the desk and practically immobile. And she was out of her mind with desire. She broke off the kiss and breathlessly said, "Now."

Declan just offered a hooded, sexy smile and began kissing her neck as he moved close enough so that she could just feel him brush against her moistness. He was driving her absolutely crazy and she arched against him as her fingers raked through his hair. "Declan?" she practically purred.

Still holding her wrists, he thrust into her, filling her. Three more thrusts and Chasyn's body shivered as an intense climax rolled through her entire body. Declan followed suit and then practically collapsed on top of her.

A million thoughts raced through her head, but the most pressing was her need for air. "You're crushing me," she said.

"Sorry," Declan said, standing. "That was incredible," he complimented as he redressed.

Chasyn reclaimed her thong and straightened her clothing. "Incredibly stupid."

"I used protection," he argued.

She looked up into his eyes. "I wasn't talking about that. I was talking about the suddenness of it."

"You're complaining because I gave you a quick, mind-blowing orgasm?"

She sighed. "No. I just mean I haven't really thought this through. Having a sexual relationship with you has complications."

"Such as?"

"First, there's my parents."

"You tell your parents about your lovers?"

"No. Not that it would be a very long story but thanks for making me feel like the Whore of Babylon."

"Then what's the problem?"

"They're paying you to protect me, not fuck me."

"You're overthinking this."

She crossed her arms in front of her. "I like to weigh the consequences of my actions *before* I take them. But with you I seem to be acting first and thinking second."

Declan bent down and kissed her temple. "You need to embrace your inner spontaneity. We had hot sex in a storage unit. That's a first for me."

"Good to know you can cross that off your bucket list. Can we just finish going through the last two boxes?"

"Sure," he replied easily.

Chasyn half-heartedly wanted to slap the smug smile off his face. Of course, the other half of her wanted to drag him back to the desk for round two. She was a mess. Instead of dwelling on it, she went over to the next box and discovered a collection of porcelain figurines wrapped in bubble wrap. She opened them all but didn't find anything secreted away. "This was pointless," she grumbled. "There's nothing here that sheds any light on her relationship with Lansing."

He winked at her. "It was still worth the trip."

"The desk," she said.

"Was amazing," he finished.

Chasyn walked back to the desk and opened the top drawer. Empty. She tried the second one: same result. But she hit pay dirt in the bottom drawer. Reaching inside, she retrieved the sleeve. "A DVD."

"Of what, I wonder?" Declan asked.

"I doubt it's Christmas with the family," Chasyn said. "But there's nothing written on the disc."

"Think it might be a sex tape?" he asked.

"Or it could be a video of Lansing and Mary together. Pictures tell a thousand words."

Chasyn slipped the disc into her purse. "I only want three words—'Lansing did it.'"

CHAPTER EIGHTEEN

They left the storage locker and headed back to Declan's to look at the DVD's contents. It was early evening and the sun was already setting. While it was a very comfortable seventy-five degrees, the minute the sun went down, so would the temperature. But Chasyn didn't need to worry about getting a chill. Her body was still warm from their passionate love-making. Not that she'd ever admit it to Declan, but hands down it had been the best sex of her life. And she didn't want to admit to herself that it was special for more reasons than just spontaneity. She snuck a quick glance at his handsome profile. She didn't see anything but perfection and a lazy smile.

A slight pain stabbed at her heart. Declan met every item on her checklist save for two. If she wanted him, she'd have to accept his terms. Just a temporary thing until it burned itself out. A fling might be okay, maybe. If she could just get over her fear that she wouldn't be able to keep her heart separate. Conversely, she had never been so attracted to a man in her life and she certainly didn't want to walk away. As soon as this situation was resolved, there would be no reason for her to continue a relationship—such as it was—with Declan. And that was the ticking clock. As soon as they had proof that Lansing was behind the murders, there really was no reason for their paths to cross again. Unless Declan called her for the occasional booty call. She cringed inwardly at the thought. She wasn't the booty call type. She needed more of a connection than just being some guy's convenient bed buddy. Of course, she'd thought that way before she'd met Declan. If she didn't want to say good-bye, then she'd have to accept him on his terms.

Hardly the end of the world. Sex with him was mind-blowing and she enjoyed his intelligence and his sense of humor. Hell, she even envied his sense of spontaneity. Chasyn raked her fingers through her hair and struggled to keep from scratching her stitches. God, it would be good to have them removed. They served no purpose now except to remind her of how close she'd come to death on the courthouse steps over a week ago.

"I'm starved," he said as he eased the car off I-95.

"We ate three hours ago," she reminded him.

"I'm a growing boy," he teased. "Like Chinese?"

"Sure," she answered, though she was still full of tuna and spicy fruit.

Declan pulled into a small strip mall, parked and cut the engine. "C'mon."

Sliding down from the high seat of the Explorer, Chasyn adjusted the hem of her dress and followed him to the storefront advertising free egg rolls with the purchase of any dinner. Once inside, she drank in the pleasant smells of the food wafting forward from the kitchen. She still wasn't really hungry, but she couldn't resist the lure of the food. She settled on an order of pot stickers, which earned her a frown from Declan.

"Is that all you're going to eat?" Declan asked.

She nodded. "It's my usual order."

Declan went on to place a large order for himself, and in a short period of time the counterman was passing them a giant bag full of containers. Food in hand, they returned to the Explorer and drove the few miles to Declan's place. Once inside, Declan laid the food out in the middle of the table, then retrieved plates, utensils, and enameled chopsticks before joining her.

"Want an egg roll?" he offered.

"Sure," she teased. "With a side of duct tape so I can attach it directly to my hips."

He laughed. "Trust me, there's nothing wrong with your hips."

Chasyn felt her cheeks warm. "If I keep eating like this without getting any exercise, I'll blow up like a balloon."

"You can go for a run tomorrow if you'd like."

"Really?" she asked with measured excitement. "What about Müller?"

"You can run at the compound. It's totally secure."

"Is it?" she queried. "I mean isn't Müller some sort of long-distance shooter? What if he's perched somewhere just waiting to catch me alone?"

Declan stilled his chopsticks. "There isn't any place he could use as a perch within a thousand yards of the compound and Adam checks all the vehicles for tracking devices."

"He could climb a tree."

Declan tossed out a disarming smile that reached his ice-blue eyes. "Too dangerous. He'd have to hide his car, then climb a tree while carrying his weapon. He'd have no way of guaranteeing a clean shot at you. Then there's wind speed and other variables to consider. Too many variables for a professional like Müller."

"Still, the guy who ran from the van last night is still out there."

Declan reached out for her hand. He lifted it to his mouth and placed a lingering kiss on the back of her hand. "Stop worrying so much. I would never put you in a position of danger."

Chasyn sighed. When he touched her and looked into her eyes it was nearly impossible to do anything but believe him. "If you say so," she said, still distracted by his touch.

Declan gave her hand one more kiss before he went back to eating. Chasyn managed to eat three of the six pot stickers before she pushed the container toward the center of the table. While Declan finished eating, she took the DVD out of her purse and carefully balanced it between her thumb and forefinger. "Think it's a sex tape?" she asked.

"If so that might explain why he killed Mary," Declan said as he closed the take-out boxes and placed them in the refrigerator. "If she had a tape of the two of them doing their thing that would go a long way toward proving paternity."

"So would Lansing's DNA," Chasyn groused.

"My guys are on it," he assured her. He came over, took the DVD from her, and placed it into the state-of-the-art media setup.

In no time, Chasyn stood there dumbfounded as the images played out. Dr. Lansing was the star of the show—well that wasn't exactly true. His clothing—or lack thereof—was the real revelation. He was wearing a red teddy with black lace, a matching garter belt, and a thong. Thigh-high stockings gave way to stilettoes. He pranced in front of the camera, stopping like a trained fashion model to strike a pose.

Chasyn was more than a little stunned. Lansing had always seemed like such a stuffed shirt to her. She exchanged glances with Declan, who also seemed to have his interest piqued by this unexpected turn of events. Not only was Lansing a cheater, he was also into playing dress-up in women's undies.

And he wasn't alone. A female voice behind the camera offered suggestions and at times harsh directives. Lansing always answered, "Yes Mistress."

"Seems the good doctor has a wild side," Declan commented.

"But did Mary know about it?"

"Easy enough to check," he said as he joined her on the couch. "I'll have Ziggy isolate the female voice on the DVD and then run it past the ex-husband. We should know if it's Mary or not in a matter of minutes."

"Is there anything Ziggy can't do?" she asked.

Declan's phone rang just then. "Hello?" After a brief pause he said, "Now?" then, "We're on our way."

"Our way to where?" she asked.

"Detective Burrows wants to see us," he explained. "Something that can't wait until morning."

Chasyn wanted a shower more than she wanted to spar with the surly detective but Declan was already grabbing his keys.

* * *

The Palm Beach County Sheriff's office was part of a large law enforcement building in the heart of West Palm Beach. The parking lot was nearly empty so they found a space very near the entrance. The air had cooled considerably and Chasyn's shift dress was no match for the chilly breeze that chased her to the building' entrance. It only got worse inside. Air conditioning was streaming out of every ceiling vent, creating frigid down drafts in the waiting area. She sat in a battered chrome and pleather chair while Declan told the desk sergeant they were there to see the detective.

The smell of stale coffee, competing with cherry-scented deodorizing cleanser, filled the air. In the distance, she could hear the faint hum of a vacuum cleaner.

Declan didn't have enough time to sit. He had only taken a couple of steps before a door marked AUTHORIZED PERSONNEL ONLY opened. Detective Burrows, tie loosened and the first button on his white dress shirt opened, greeted them with underwhelming enthusiasm. "Come this way," he said as he held the door open with his foot.

"We're waiting for Jack," Declan said as he passed the detective.

That brought a definite scowl to the balding man's face. "I don't think you need an attorney for this. I'm just going to update you on the investigation."

Just as he said that, Chasyn heard Jack's voice in the vestibule. He caught the edge of the door and joined them.

Chasyn did a little mental comparison of the brothers. Jack was handsome in a polished sort of way. Though they shared the same basic coloring, Declan was at least two inches taller and much broader than his brother. More important, she didn't have the hots for Jack.

"Chasyn." He acknowledged her as he came up behind her in the hallway.

"Hi," she said as she caught a whiff of his citrusy cologne. He was dressed in a pair of khakis and a royal blue dress shirt but no tie. "Sorry you had to come out so late."

He just shrugged. "Duty calls."

"You Kavanaughs are big on duty," she muttered as she followed Declan and the detective into a conference room.

It was a long room with several county maps tacked to one wall. On the other side of the room was a large mobile white board. On the white board were several photographs and documents pinned up in what looked like a random pattern, until her eyes fixed on the crime scene from the courthouse steps. Kasey lay in a heap with a large bloodstain around her head. Chasyn's stomach flip-flopped.

"Is that necessary?" Jack asked. Apparently he had keyed in to her reaction.

"Sorry," Burrows said, then went over and turned the picture around before jabbing a tack into the top of the now hidden photo. "Have a seat," he said, waving his arm toward the seats across from him at the highly polished table.

Chasyn was sandwiched between Kavanaughs. Her attention was still on the white board. There were pictures of the crash scene from the night before as well as photographs of the dead homeless man. The display included clues and information on the murder of Mary Jolsten as well. In the center of the board was an eight-by-ten photo of Dr. Lansing.

"We were able to remove a projectile from your car," Burrows told Declan.

"And?" Jack asked.

"It is a ballistic match to the projectile we recovered from Ms. Becker's brain at autopsy."

Chasyn's stomach churned again.

"What I need from the two of you is a better description of the shooter."

Declan let out a long breath. "It was dark and I was more concentrated on avoiding the gunfire."

"I mostly had my head down," Chasyn said. "When they tried to pull even with us, I only got a quick glimpse of the man."

"Describe him," Burrows commanded.

Chasyn closed her eyes briefly and tried to conjure a clear image. It wasn't easy; she'd been scared out of her mind at the time and between the blinding headlights and the darkness, she had more of an impression than an identification.

"Hispanic, I think. Heavyset. Hair slicked back, maybe into a ponytail."

"About how tall was he?"

She blinked. "He was seated."

"Five-ten or eleven," Declan chimed in. "I saw him run from the car."

"Any distinguishing marks?" the detective asked.

"Yeah," Chasyn said sarcastically. "A really big gun."

"Can you describe the gun?" Burrows asked.

Using her hands, Chasyn spread them about ten inches apart. "Maybe that long, with a nubby kind of thing sticking out of the end."

"Sounds like a Tec-9," Declan said.

"That was what ballistics said," Burrows said. He moved forward so that he could rest his fingertips on the table top and lean closer to her. "Miss Summers, is there somewhere you can go until we get the second perp in custody?"

"He found me on an open stretch of I-95," she argued. "I'm sure he'll find me no matter where I go."

"Where were you coming from?" he asked.

"My office."

Burrows frowned. "He probably had your firm under surveillance in the hopes you'd show eventually. You should make a habit of avoiding places you normally frequent. We can offer you a safe house with patrols passing by on a regular basis."

"Pass, thanks," she said without hesitation. "Mr. Kavanaugh seems to have everything under control."

"That's why you almost got killed last night."

She glared at the detective. "As you said, I made an error in judgment going to my office. I won't do it again."

"Suit yourself."

Jack stood. "Do you have anything else?"

The detective shook his head. "I would like to be apprised of Miss Summers' whereabouts."

"You can get to her through me," Jack said with such finality that the detective didn't press the issue.

"If I get any new information, I'll contact you," Burrows said.

* * *

"You know you can take Burrows up on his offer," Declan said after they pulled out of the parking lot. "I won't take it personally."

"Get locked away in some house in God knows where with the occasional police cruiser driving by? Besides, when I'm with you I can be active in the investigation." *And have great, if temporary, sex.*

"Good to know you have so much faith in me," he said as his hand slipped onto her knee. Using his fingertips, he bunched up the fabric until he was touching her bare skin. He began making maddeningly sensual circles with his thumb, inching up her hemline higher and higher. Chasyn's breath caught in her throat when his fingertips reached her thong. Her body was fully alert and she tensed with need.

"Don't," she said on a rush of breath.

"You're wet."

She reached down and pushed his hand away. "And you're driving."

"I keep telling you I can multitask."

"Well, maybe I don't feel like being a distraction," she told him as she straightened her clothes.

Declan placed his hand back on the wheel. "Sorry if you feel pressured."

"I didn't feel pressured," she assured him. "I just haven't had enough time to process this yet."

He chuckled. "What's there to process?

"I need to make a pro-con list to put this all into perspective."

"Tell you what," he began easily. "You make your list and I'll restrain myself until you've beaten this dead horse."

"That was condescending."

"It wasn't meant to be," he said. "I'm just saying I'm willing to give you time."

"How much?"

"However much you need."

They reached the compound, went through the gate, and parked. Chasyn was a little surprised that Ziggy and Gavin were still in the office. Didn't these people ever sleep?

"How's everyone?" Declan asked.

Gavin was grinning like the Cheshire cat. "I was just about to call you."

"Yes?" Declan prompted.

"Lansing finally made a mistake."

"Really?"

"He went home about an hour ago, and while he was

waiting for the gate to open, he stepped out and tossed a water bottle into a recycling bin." Gavin rubbed his hands together. "Joey and Sam recovered the bottle and they're driving it up to the lab for DNA testing as we speak. We should have the results in about twenty-four hours."

Declan turned to her and said, "This could throw the whole case open. We prove Lansing is the father of Mary's unborn baby and they go before the grand jury. You won't need me anymore."

Wanna bet?

CHAPTER NINETEEN

This is great news, right?" she asked when they were headed back to Declan's place.

She couldn't make out his expression in the dark, but his tone spoke volumes. "Maybe."

Chasyn fidgeted in her seat. She was a jangle of raw nerves and exhaustion. "Is it the money?"

"Something doesn't add up," he confirmed, his tone serious. "Why would Lansing pay an extra fifty grand to his checking account and then only make two withdrawals?"

"How much would it cost to hire those two bozos who fired on us last night?"

He blew out a slow breath. "Two grand sounds about right for an upfront payment. Probably another two grand when the job was completed."

"Then what did he spend the other twenty-eight thousand dollars on?" she asked. "The upfront payment to Müller?"

In the shadows, he shook his head. "Müller wouldn't get out of bed for twenty-eight grand."

"Really?"

"A guy of his caliber?" Declan asked. "He probably goes for more like a hundred thousand as a retainer."

"I know Lansing's wife has a ton of money. Maybe she isn't protecting him from a pregnant girlfriend. Maybe she has an interest in making sure her husband isn't revealed as a cross-dresser and a submissive."

"I agree, however…" Declan's thought trailed off.

"What?"

"Why would Lansing risk killing Mary in a public place, then go to such elaborate measures to kill off the only witnesses?" he asked.

Chasyn pondered the question for a few seconds. "Maybe Lansing couldn't do it again. I mean, he did kill Mary in a very brutal, up-close way. Plus, he knows he's a person of interest in her murder so coming after me could go a long way toward avoiding an indictment."

"When we get the results back from the water bottle, Lansing will be toast."

"What if the DNA doesn't match?" Chasyn asked.

"It'll match," he said with conviction. "Every other man in Mary's life has already been tested. Lansing is the only one who refused to provide a sample."

She tucked one leg under the other. "Which is completely within his rights," she explained. "Without probable cause for a warrant, the police can't compel a buccal swab."

"The police also couldn't keep eyes on him twenty-four-seven," Declan explained. "It was only a matter of time before he screwed up."

"So *exactly* how will this work, assuming it's Lansing's DNA?"

Declan dropped one hand from the wheel and rested it on the console between them. His fingers dangled over and every time they drove over a bump or other imperfection in the roadway, they grazed her thigh. Chasyn tried to ignore it. She wasn't successful. In fact, she was silently wishing for a decent pothole.

"We turn the results over to the state's attorney and the cops and let them take it from there."

"Will that guarantee that the heavyset Hispanic guy will back off?" she asked as a shiver ran the length of her spine.

"Possibly," he hedged.

She raked her hands through her hair. "That isn't very reassuring."

"Don't worry. I'm on it until they find him."

How she longed for the feel of his hand to give her a little reassuring squeeze. Not to mention the wondrous way he felt buried inside her. Geez, she was losing it. Big time. One minute she was telling him she needed space and just a few minutes later she was practically dreaming about having more hot sex with him.

She decided it was time to start her mental pro-con list. At the top of the pro list was her strong physical attraction to Declan. And she was forced to admit that the attraction was more than just physical. Even though it had only been a little more than a week and God knew it had been a stressful week, she found herself on the brink of falling in love with him. Other than the occasional bout of arrogance, she couldn't find a single flaw in the man. He was literally the perfect guy. Only not. He was smart, funny, kind, considerate and her mental list threatened to grow too long to remember. Her intellect warned her off but it was overruled by her emotions. Now there was a new twist in the situation. Now she had to ask herself if she could be in a casual relationship with a man she loved. Man, she needed a legal pad.

Or not.

In reality, all she could think of for the con column was his stated aversion to commitment. Chasyn weighed her options. Well, *option*. Would it really be the end of the world if she continued her liaison with Declan? She'd probably end up nursing a broken heart, but on the plus side if past behavior was any indication of future behavior, she would certainly enjoy her time with him.

"You're quiet," Declan said.

"I'm concentrating on *not* itching these stitches," she fibbed.

"When do they come out?"

"Tomorrow in theory, but I'm afraid to go back to the hospital with Müller and the Hispanic guy out there."

"Either one could be watching the hospital," he agreed. "Want me to call Darby?"

"The vet?" she asked.

"It's either me or her," he suggested. "And Darby is way better at it than I am."

"You know how to remove sutures?" she asked, surprised.

He let out a deep, brief chuckle. "Only my own."

The mere thought of that made her stomach curl. "I'll choose Darby."

Declan took out his cell and gave her a call. Darby would come out this evening to remove her stitches. Good riddance.

* * *

Darby practically floated into the house with Jack hot on her heels. She was carrying a small black satchel and wearing a stunning smile. She was tall by Chasyn's standards. Being only five-two, most people towered over her. *Like Declan.* Guessing Darby was somewhere in her mid-thirties, Chasyn marveled at her flawless skin. She wore a minimal amount of makeup, so she had that fresh, dewy look about her. Oh, and she was dressed in jeans and a T-shirt that hugged her perfect body. Chasyn was starting to feel like a troll.

That wasn't the only thing she noticed. There was an unspoken intimacy between the couple. Jack's eyes followed her every move and he always seemed to be touching her in a casual way. Chasyn was looking at the very picture of love and it filled her with a sense of envy and sorrow.

Darby set her bag on the table and instructed Chasyn to take a seat.

"Front or back first?" she asked.

"Back," Chasyn insisted. "They're making me crazy."

Darby smelled faintly of floral perfume and had a gentle touch. She pulled on a pair of gloves, then took an alcohol swab to the site. It was so cold Chasyn gave an involuntary start.

"Sorry," Darby said.

"No problem," Chasyn assured her. "I just wasn't expecting that."

Darby took some scissors out of the bag along with some long tweezers. In less than five minutes Chasyn no longer felt the itchy tug at the back of her head. Then she switched positions and Darby removed the sutures from her hairline.

"You healed nicely but I can put Steri-strips on the wounds," she offered.

Chasyn shook her head. "I'm over bandages, thanks."

"Then," Darby said with a smile, "this calls for a glass of wine." She turned to Declan. "Please tell me you have more than just beer in that fancy fridge of yours."

Declan went over and tapped the door of the fridge twice. Suddenly the contents became visible. Lord, but the man did like his techno toys.

"Red, white, or rosé?"

Darby looked at Chasyn and asked, "Do you have a preference?"

Chasyn shook her head. "Anything is fine with me."

"Two glasses of white for the ladies," she told Declan.

After pouring the wine into glasses and grabbing two long-neck bottles of beer from the fridge, Declan and his brother joined them at the table. Jack took a long drink then said, "Michael's parole hearing has been reset for next Friday."

Declan scowled. "What do you think his chances are?"

"Conner and Emma are cautiously optimistic," he answered, then turned to Chasyn. "Conner is my brother and Emma is his new bride. She's an attorney up in Purdue. Conner is the sheriff there."

"Where is Purdue?" Chasyn asked.

"North Florida," he answered. "About fifty miles from the prison, so Conner has been able to see Michael on a regular basis. I go up when I can."

Jack asked Declan, "Will you be at the hearing? Michael needs all the support we can give him."

"Wouldn't stay away for the world."

Jack's expression grew serious. "What about your current situation?"

"We're closing in on Lansing and hopefully once he's indicted, Müller will lose interest because there won't be a paycheck in it for him with Lansing under arrest."

Chasyn absently rubbed her arms. "Can all that happen in just over a week?"

"Sure," Declan said confidently. He checked his watch. "We should have the DNA results back from the lab by four or five tomorrow afternoon."

"That coupled with the DVD should give the state's attorney enough probable cause." Chasyn's tense muscles started to relax.

"DVD?" Darby asked.

Chasyn smiled. "Turns out Mary had a video of the good doctor prancing around in women's clothing. Complete with some kinky dominatrix tossed in for good measure."

"Whatever floats your boat," Jack mused. "Have you verified that it's Mary taking the video?"

"My guy is on his way to Tampa tonight to see the ex-husband. He should be able to confirm it's her on the audio."

Jack finished his beer and took Darby's hand. "We'd better get home. I want to tuck Mia in before bedtime."

As soon as they left, Chasyn asked, "They have a daughter?"

"Basically," he said as he got up and took another beer from the fridge.

"What does that mean?"

"Sean Grisom, Darby's husband and Mia's biological father, was an abusive man and a killer. He used Mia as a weapon against the two of them."

"Are they divorced now?"

"Yes."

Chasyn felt her brow furrow. "So how come Jack and Darby haven't married? Especially with a child involved."

"They are getting married," Declan said. "Darby's first wedding was a low-key thing in front of a justice of the peace. She wants a big affair this time around. A whole lot of planning and money for just one day."

"If I didn't already know you were anti-marriage, I'd know it now."

He shrugged and took a long pull on his beer. "Just a huge waste of money with no guarantee that it will last."

So much for her dreams of a magical wedding. She was wavering between ditching her life plan and being with Declan. Compromise was part of any relationship but would that be a compromise or a disaster? Chasyn finished off her wine and stood up. "I'm going to turn in," she said. In reality she just didn't want to listen to him extol the joys of staying single any longer. She'd gotten the message loud and clear and it was chipping away at her heart.

"'Night," he said, raising his bottle in a silent salute.

Their differing philosophies chased her into the guest room. She changed out of her dress, showered, put on a camisole and pair of lounge pants, then slipped beneath the covers. Though she was bone tired, her mind refused sleep. Her thoughts bounced between the memory of their amazing sexual encounter and her own jumbled feelings. *How was it possible to have perfect sex with a guy who wasn't perfect for you?* She wondered. Chasyn kept coming back to the same conclusion. For her, he was perfect. He met all her criteria. Except for the commitment issue. As much as she knew that was a deal breaker, she reluctantly acknowledged that if she wanted to be with him—and she did—it would have to be on his terms. Chasyn wasn't sure she could do it, but the alternative was worse. Walking away from him at this point would be impossible. Mainly because she was falling for him. Hard.

Frustrated by her inability to sleep, she got up and went to the kitchen for a glass of water. No sooner had she crossed the family room threshold than a loud, blaring alarm sounded. Over the deafening sound, she saw Declan's shadowy figure appear from the master suite, gun in hand.

"Jesus," he muttered under his breath as he went to the alarm pad and killed the ear-splitting sound.

"I'm sorry," she said as soon as it was quiet.

Declan stood in the kitchen, wearing nothing but boxer

shorts and his watch. His hair was slightly mussed. He took several steps toward her and she stood perfectly still when she saw the raw desire in his eyes. Only then did she remember that her cami was made of thin, pale pink material that left very little to the imagination.

* * *

Declan stopped just inches from her. She smelled of floral shampoo. He knew the smart thing to do was to turn and head back to his bedroom. But seeing the outline of her nipples through the fabric drained him of his smarts.

Reaching out, he bracketed her arms and looked into her eyes, checking for any sign of censure. That was all he needed. "I can't resist doing this," he said, dipping his head and placing a tentative kiss on her partly open mouth.

Her response was immediate and tangible. Her hands roamed up over his chest before cupping his head and deepening the kiss. She pressed against him. He could feel the taut buds of her erect nipples against his skin and moved quickly to find the hem of her top. He slipped both hands up until he felt the swell of her breasts in his palms. He flicked his thumbs across her nipples, which made her moan against his mouth.

Declan lifted his head and looked into her hooded eyes. "If we keep this up, there will be sex."

She surprised him by responding, "Promise?"

He reached for her hand and led her into his bedroom. They didn't break the kiss during the transition. Declan backed her up to the edge of the bed, then gradually lowered her onto the mattress. Just as he'd imagined, her silken blond hair fanned out on the pillow, creating a golden halo around her exquisite face. Her pale ashes fluttered when her hand moved to the waistband of his boxers.

Declan moved quickly to prevent her from undressing him. "I want this to last," he said.

Conscious of her size, Declan leaned on one side, holding the majority of his weight on his arm. With his free hand, he tugged her camisole free, then dipped his head and closed his mouth over her breast. She groaned and urgently grasped his head with both hands. He flicked the erect bud with his tongue, teasing her mercilessly. Chasyn arched against him and reached again for his boxers.

Again he stopped her, laying her hand on his shoulder as he easily slipped off her pants and thong. Declan lifted his head to take in the sight of her. She was simply perfect. Thin, but not in an anorexic way, with a tiny waist and rounded hips. Her wonderful breasts were full and pert.

His body was fully erect and he wasn't sure how much longer he could wait. There was something about Chasyn that inspired his need for this woman. A craving he'd never known before. He placed a kiss at her throat then trailed lower, tasting her breasts, her stomach…then stopping just below her belly button. He would have ventured further, but he could feel her body tense beneath him.

Declan shed his boxers and lay back on the bed, rolling her on top of him as he did. She braced her hands on his shoulders as he held her by the hips and gently guided himself inside her wetness. He could only pray that he could last.

He reached down between them and found her sweet spot. Applying friction, he watched as her head fell back, then felt her body contract around him. That was all it took for him to reach orgasm.

Declan was slightly out of breath but Chasyn was out of bed. Rather shyly, given what they'd just done, she gathered up her clothing and did her best to cover her nakedness.

"Where are you going in such a hurry?" he asked.

"Back to my room."

"Why?"

She turned and looked at him with a blank expression he couldn't decipher. "Having sex is one thing. Sleeping with you implies *intimacy*."

"Says who?"

"Me," she told him curtly. If she was going to accept his terms, she had to avoid intimacy and focus only on the sex. "And my opinion is the only one that counts right now."

CHAPTER TWENTY

There was a chilly awkwardness between them as Declan silently went about his morning coffee ritual. Pouting. Poor baby. Well, too damned bad. She was willing to explore a relationship with him, but she had to lay down a few conditions of her own. And for all her tossing and turning, this was the best idea that'd come to her.

"Are you going to remain mute all day?" she asked pleasantly.

He joined her at the table. His hair was still slightly damp. His jeans hugged his trim waist and massive thighs and the Carolina blue T-shirt made his incredible eyes sparkle. Expression bland, he took a sip from his mug, then said, "Last night didn't go as I'd planned."

"You planned last night? What were you doing, lying in wait for me to trip the alarm?"

"You know what I mean," he practically scowled. "I didn't mean for you to go racing from the room like we'd just done something worthy of life in prison."

"Look," she began as she took a sip of lukewarm orange juice. "I respect your no-strings-attached lifestyle. But if it's going to work for me, then you have to respect my boundaries, too."

"Which are?"

"So far I've only thought of one, but I'm leaving it open-ended as things progress." She set the empty glass down. "I won't spend the night with you in the same bed."

"That's a little ridiculous; I mean —"

Chasyn held up her hand. "Non-negotiable. Okay?"

"Seems silly," Declan groused. "What if one of us is in the mood for an early bird special?" he asked with an exaggerated lift of his dark brows.

At the mere thought of it, Chasyn's body reacted predictably. A lump of desire clogged her throat and her stomach filled with butterflies. "We'll cross that bridge when we come to it," she answered in a high-pitched, breathy tone.

Which wasn't lost on Dylan. He abandoned his mug and his chair and came over to her, dipping his head to place a passionate kiss on her mouth. It was over almost before it began, leaving Chasyn feeling very unsatisfied when he stepped away.

"What was that for?" she asked when she was sure her voice would no longer sound desperate.

"Spontaneity," he answered simply.

Chasyn got her hackles up. "I was spontaneous last night."

"I know," he replied in a deep, sexy-as-hell tone. "When you give it a chance you're pretty good at it."

"Pretty good?" she challenged. "I was freaking amazing and you know it."

"Whoa," he said, raising his hand. "I was talking about spontaneity, not your performance. Which was, as you say, freaking amazing."

Her ego stroked, Chasyn's flash of temper dissipated quickly. "Before I start blushing like a fool, can we change the subject?"

"Sure."

"I was thinking." She ran her fingertip along the rim of her now-empty glass. "Lansing made those overpayments to his credit card account before he killed Mary. Maybe she was blackmailing him with the DVD."

"We can check," Declan explained. "We'll talk to Ziggy. She can get a time and date stamp off it and Joey should be back from Tampa by now with an ID on the audio portion of the tape from Mary's ex-husband." He checked his watch. "You about ready to head out?"

"Just let me grab my purse," she said.

Chasyn retrieved her purse and made a stop in the bathroom to re-check her hair and makeup. Having the annoying stitches gone was wonderfully freeing, not to mention she looked much better without bandages on her head. With her hair parted on the side, the wound on her forehead was invisible. Same with the one on the back of her head. She'd selected a pair of black jeans and paired them with a blush-colored chiffon sleeveless top with slender halter straps tied behind her neck. She'd pulled her hair into a messy top knot, accentuating her bared shoulders. After dabbing on a bit of perfume and applying some blush-colored gloss to her lips, she returned to the kitchen and reclaimed her wedge sandals from near the doorway.

"You really clean up nicely," he said as he took a step toward her.

She countered with a half-step back. "Rule number two. Don't start something we can't finish."

"I can be quick," he reasoned. "Really quick. So quick you won't even know it happened."

She smiled but retained her distance. "That doesn't sound very satisfying for me. Besides, I—we—have to focus on Lansing right now. Sex can wait."

"Says the woman who *doesn't* have the mother of all erections."

She sighed. "Whining doesn't become you," she said.

"I'm not whining. I'm trying to let you know that you're making me crazy."

"I think a part of you was crazy long before I entered the picture."

He frowned. "I'm hardly crazy. I have laser focus."

"Then laser focus on something other than sex."

"That's a little difficult with you around."

"Buck up, my man," she teased. "Let's go."

* * *

The hangar was a flurry of activity. Everyone was there save for Tom, Sam, and Joey. Declan had Tom and Sam sitting on Dr. Lansing, while Joey was on his way back from seeing William Jolsten in Tampa.

Ziggy was nursing some sort of disgusting-looking kale smoothie. "Did you have a chance to work up those cases Chasyn printed out at her office?" he asked.

Ziggy handed him a flash drive. "Done and cross-referenced by year."

Declan accepted the drive and asked, "Any chance you can burn an extra copy of the DVD for me?"

"Sure, no problem."

"Can you print some stills from the video? Preferably the ones showing Lansing posing at his best?"

Ziggy snickered. "Give me about a half-hour."

"Take your time," he said, then turned and went to reclaim Chasyn, who was chatting easily with Gavin. Declan felt a pang of something as he watched her head fall back when she laughed at something he couldn't hear. Amusement shone in her turquoise eyes and her smile was infectious. It was also directed at his long-time friend. Hence the pang. *You're being a jealous asshole*, he chided himself. He didn't do jealous. At least he never had in the past. Chasyn Summers was throwing him off his game. A system that had worked for him since his late teens.

Pushing the annoying thoughts to the back of his brain, he led Chasyn into his office, then pulled one of the chairs behind the desk so they'd be seated side by side. Technically it wasn't necessary. He could have just swiveled the monitor on his desk, but selfishly he wanted to be close to her. He wiggled the mouse so the machine would awaken, then inserted the flash drive into one of the USB slots.

"What is this?" she asked.

"A database Ziggy created on all of Lansing's court appearances."

She was quiet for a minute, then said, "Wow! She even added witness lists if there was a trial."

"Anything jump out at you?" he asked.

"Yeah." She pointed toward two of the entries. "These were the only cases in which he successfully testified that the defendant was insane at the time of the crime."

"Is that unusual?"

She shook her head. "Insanity is nearly impossible to prove as an affirmative defense."

"Why?"

Chasyn leaned closer to him as she spoke. "There's a two-pronged system. First the defense has to prove that the person was suffering from a mental disease or defect and second—and this is much harder—they have to prove the defendant couldn't distinguish between right and wrong and conform his or her behavior at the exact moment of the crime."

"Now you sound like Jack."

"I am a litigation paralegal," she paused and her expression soured. "Or I was. They'll probably fire me if I keep missing work."

"You can always have a job here."

She looked at him with suspicion in her eyes. "Is a job offer another one of your moments of spontaneity?"

"Yes and no," he told her. "Now when I need legal consultation, I have to go to Jack. It would be nice to have someone around here who spoke legalese." He patted her hand. "Just something for you to think about."

"Speaking of thinking," she began on an expel of breath. "I have to get everything moved out of my apartment and find someplace else to rent."

"Too dangerous," he said with determination.

Chasyn pulled her hand away. "Mr. Becker already paid Kasey's part of the broken lease fee. If I don't get myself out of there by Wednesday I'll owe another month's rent."

"Then we'll hire someone," he decided. "One of those pod places. We have them pack up your stuff and store it until all of this blows over."

"And where am I supposed to stay until then?"

"With me," he replied with a grin he was incapable of suppressing.

"That's very nice but I'm not going to play house with you."

"Forget nice. I've got a secure property. I'm a great shot and I promised your parents I would keep you in my sights at all times."

Leaning back, Chasyn placed her hand on her slender hip. "So this is really about your commitment to your profession?"

"Does it matter?"

Yes. It shouldn't but it did. She didn't want to feel like a responsibility. She wanted to feel…important.

She turned her attention back to the spreadsheet. "I remember this Miami case. It was major headline news a few years ago."

Declan read the name. "Right. The woman who drowned her two children in the pool. Took them out, dried them off, and left them on lounge chairs when she called the cops. She heard voices, right?"

"Postpartum psychosis," she corrected. "Dr. Lansing testified on her behalf."

"And the other case?" he prompted.

"A woman who killed her husband after decades of abuse. Technically it was a Stand Your Ground case since they'd separated. But Lansing was able to convince the judge that even though the wife shot the husband five times in the back, the law still applied because she was suffering from severe PTSD and battered wife syndrome at the time of the killing."

"Lansing must be a very good expert witness."

Chasyn bobbed her head. "You have no idea. For a total bastard, you put him in front of a judge or jury and he can charm the pants off anyone, male or female."

"Maybe he wears a good luck teddy under his suit," Declan joked.

"Thanks," she said with a little laugh. "Now that's an image I will never get out of my brain. Can I check something?" She scooted closer to him so she could reach the keyboard and the mouse.

Declan tried not to notice that the swell of her breast was against his bicep. Tried and failed. Instead he just sat perfectly still and drank in the scent of her perfume and fantasized about unpinning her hair and allowing it to cascade down her bared shoulders. Then he noticed the thin strap at the nape of her neck. It was tied in a bow and all he had to do was give it one tug and her shirt would fall free. He was getting hard just imagining it.

* * *

Chasyn made five errors typing in the web address. It wasn't that she was a lousy typist; quite the contrary. She was just distracted by the feel of Declan's warm breath on her neck. Finally she was logged in, using her work account, to the newspaper archives. She found clippings on the website and began to scan them.

"The first case—the one with the postpartum woman—was handled by the Public Defender's office."

Declan asked, "Is that important?"

"The only way an indigent person can afford someone like Lansing is if he did it pro bono."

"He didn't impress me like a pro bono kinda guy."

She shrugged. "He does it to keep up his reputation and for the publicity. The man has never met a reporter he didn't like."

"What about the other case?"

"Looks like the family paid for an attorney and Lansing's fee. According to this article, it made the dead husband's family furious. They thought she should rot in jail."

"The pro bono case," Declan began. "Who were the witnesses?"

"Her shrink. Her priest. Lansing. Her cousin. And her husband."

"She drowned his kids and he stood by her for the trial?"

"Still does. According to a follow-up article, Mr. Martinez visits his wife twice monthly at the hospital." She pulled up a picture of Fernando Martinez. "Hispanic. Heavyset with a ponytail," she said as she stared at the photograph. "Could be the guy who's been shooting at us," she said excitedly.

"Can you check out the cousin?" Declan asked.

She went back to Ziggy's spreadsheet. "Armando Valez. I think we just found the second half of our Tec-9 team."

Declan brushed her hands aside and went into his database to look for a current address for Martinez. He found two possibilities from his most recent drug arrests. Jotting the addresses on a sheet of paper, he tucked it into his pants pocket just as the buzzer on his phone sounded. "Yeah?"

"I just got the DNA results," Ziggy said.

"We'll be right there."

Chasyn followed Declan, nearly jogging to keep pace with him. When they reached Ziggy's computer lair, two DNA sequencing pages were on the main screen. Even to Chasyn's untrained eyes, there didn't seem to be a match. "Mary wasn't pregnant with Lansing's baby?" she said in an incredulous whisper.

"Can't tell," Ziggy explained. Her fingers flew across the keyboard and a single page report popped up. "According to the lab doing the test, the sequences don't match for a very good reason."

"Which is?" Chasyn asked.

"The sample we submitted was from a woman."

CHAPTER TWENTY-ONE

That cagey bastard," Declan muttered as he began to pace in the small confines of the area.

Chasyn, along with the others, stood quietly by as Declan finished prowling his thoughts. *A woman's DNA?* That made no sense. Lansing liked to dress in women's underwear, but that was as far as it went.

Declan opened his phone, pressed the home button, dialed, then placed it on speaker and held it out away from his chiseled face.

"Hey, boss," she recognized Sam's voice and slight southern accent. "Lansing is at his office, and—"

"Did either you or Joey actually see Lansing drink from the water bottle you collected?"

"Um…no, he carried it from the car and then tossed it. Why?"

Declan blew out a breath and raked his hand through his thick ebony hair. "Lansing slipped in a decoy." He explained the results of the DNA testing. "He knows we're watching and he's taking countermeasures."

"Maybe he knows we aren't the only ones watching," Sam said.

"The cops?" Declan asked.

"Uh-huh. A team comes and goes. They're about as subtle as an earthquake."

"That's probably what spooked Lansing."

"Well, it wasn't us," Sam protested. "We're invisible."

Declan was pensive for a moment, then said, "I think it's time we shook Lansing's cage."

"What do you want me to do?" Sam asked.

"You and Joey stay on him. I want to know about the women in his life."

After he ended the call, Chasyn asked, "What are you going to do to get Lansing's attention?"

"Ziggy, got those stills from the DVD ready?"

She nodded. "Want me to blast them up on Facebook or something?"

"Do we have Lansing's personal email address?"

"Of course," Ziggy answered as though slightly affronted by the question.

Chasyn followed Declan and Ziggy back into the computer area after instructing the others to start working on Lansing's female acquaintances along with the search for Fernando Martinez. Ziggy took her place behind the keyboard.

"What do you want me to send?" she asked.

"Bounce the email off—"

Ziggy waved a dismissive hand over her head, then started typing. "Bounce it off a bunch of servers before it gets to him, yeah, yeah, I know. I'm the expert, remember?" Her grin was evil as her fingers flew over the keyboard. "It will take him until the next ice age to backtrack this IP address. Does he have that kind of tech ability?"

"No," Chasyn said with conviction. "Kasey used to complain that it took him forever to master Power Point to supplement his testimony." She felt that now-familiar tug at her heart when she thought of her friend. And she experienced something new as well. Just thinking about Lansing filled her with silent rage. He'd killed Mary and his own unborn child, which was bad enough. But killing Kasey and kidnapping her parents was personal to her and she wanted to see the man spend the rest of his days in some dank prison being some guy's bitch.

"Send an email with picture number five attached. It's the most salacious one of the lot. Tell him to be at the Lake Worth pier at midnight or I'll send the DVD to channel five news."

"Are you crazy?" Chasyn asked. "That's way too dangerous, to meet a killer on a deserted pier in the middle of the night."

He tilted his dark head and offered her an annoyingly sexy half-smile. "I've got this. And I won't be alone."

"Can I come?" she asked. She didn't relish the idea of the clandestine meeting but she couldn't let Declan go without her.

He shrugged. "You can wait in the car with my team."

Chasyn was relieved. She didn't really want to go out in the dead of night, to a dangerous place, to meet the man trying to kill her. She was good for Declan and the others to go without her on this one. "Can I at least listen in? I can't wait to hear what he has to say about that picture."

"I'll wear a wire," Declan said. "You can listen in from a distance where I know you'll be safe. We still have no clue where Martinez is and Müller is still a wild card."

Declan spent the next hour working out the logistics of the meeting. She'd be in the car with Gavin while Declan went out on the pier. Ziggy was tracking the GPS on Lansing's cell phone, so they'd have an idea of his approximate arrival time.

All Chasyn could think of was how risky the whole operation was for Declan. With potentially three killers—Martinez, Müller and Lansing—on the loose, her mind conjured all sorts of scenarios where this could go badly. Fast. The mere thought of Declan being hurt, or worse, settled uncomfortably in the pit of her stomach. It hurt to breath as panic began to well inside her. Hastily, she excused herself and went out to the gun range before she had a full-fledged panic attack in front of everyone.

Bracing her hands on her knees, she bent over and took in some deep breaths of warm, fresh air. Her heart rate began to return to normal and the tightness in her belly relaxed.

"You okay?" Declan asked as he came up behind her.

"No," she admitted as she stood. "I have a bad feeling about this."

"Well, don't," Declan said in a reassuring tone "I know what I'm doing."

"Do you?" she challenged as she turned to meet his gaze. "What happens if Lansing decides to have you killed? Have you thought about that?"

He bracketed her shoulders in his hands. "Lansing doesn't want me dead yet. Not until he knows what I know. And he's sure I haven't shared his tawdry photos with anyone. You said it yourself, the man *is* his reputation."

She tried not to think about his hands on her body but that was proving to be a difficult task. What she really wanted was for him to hold her against him; there was safety in his embrace. Her gaze dropped to his mouth as silence stretched between them. Instantly she was imagining the feel of his lips on hers, longing for the taste of him.

As if reading her thoughts, Declan's hand slowly glided up her shoulder until he hooked his thumb under her chin. She looked up at him through her lashes. "Please?"

"Please what?" he teased.

She took a step closer so they were mere inches apart. "Please kiss me."

"Isn't that breaking one of your rules?"

"God, you're annoying," she said as she got up on tiptoe, reached for him with great urgency, and pulled him to her.

The feel of his solid body against hers only increased the wonderful sensation of his tongue tantalizing every nerve ending in her body. His large hand cupped her cheek as he expertly explored the recesses of her mouth. There was nothing tentative or restrained about the kiss or her body's immediate response. Desire danced along her spine as his fingers raked through her hair.

He tasted like coffee and temptation. It was a heady mix that made her want to tear off her clothes and have magical sex right there in the sunshine. She moaned just thinking about it.

Declan lifted his head. "Since we can't have sex, I need to shoot something."

"We can't?" she asked, ever hopeful.

"You said so. I'm just going with the flow. So now who's the annoying one?"

She seductively raked her nails along his chest, down to his waistband before he grabbed her wrist and held it gently. "I'm not annoying," she protested.

"And I'm not made of stone. I'm working here, remember?"

"I remember you own the place," she answered as she attempted—and failed—to reignite his passion.

Declan set her aside. "Don't tempt me," he warned. "There are a few things I still have to get done before we go back to my place."

Chasyn knew exactly what she wanted to do once they got there. She could be patient. Sorta. "I have a question…"

"Yes?"

"Why didn't the police search Mary's storage unit?"

He stroked his chin. "I'm guessing they didn't dig too deeply into Mary's life because she was the victim and they had two witnesses to the murder. One *actual* witness."

"I know, I know. I never should have lied to the police but I did it for a good reason. Shouldn't we send them a copy of the DVD?"

"We will. Eventually," he said, absently holding a lock of her hair between two fingers. "For now, I think that they're focused on finding Martinez. I hope we get lucky before they find him."

"Why? Shouldn't we be sharing *everything*?"

Declan shrugged. "I'd like a word with Mr. Martinez before he's given the opportunity to refuse to answer questions."

"You think he'll talk to you if you find him first?"

Declan smiled. "I can be very persuasive."

The back door opened and Gavin stuck his head out and cleared his throat loudly before saying, "Declan?"

"Yeah?"

Gavin was grinning when he said, "Ziggy is ready for you."

"Wipe that smile off your face before I deck you," Declan said as he led Chasyn back inside the building and to Ziggy's area.

She was standing there with a cross body bag over one shoulder and keys in her hand. "I've made all the arrangements. They'll be there to pack in an hour."

Declan turned to Chasyn. "Do you need anything else from your apartment?"

She was flummoxed for a second. "Wait! You're packing up my apartment?"

"You said it had to be done," Declan answered simply. "Ziggy will supervise the packing and she'll bring back anything you don't want to go into storage."

Stunned, Chasyn needed a moment to collect her thoughts. *Geez but these people move fast.* "There's a pink duffle bag in my closet with my running gear."

"Pink?" Declan mocked.

She shot him a sidelong glance. "Were you expecting cammo?"

"Good point. Anything else?"

"So long as I can use your washer and dryer, I'm good."

Declan held out his hand and asked, "Key?"

Chasyn went to her purse and retrieved her keys, then removed her apartment key to give to Ziggy. She took out her checkbook and wrote a check for her portion of the lease termination fee, added Mr. Becker's check and turned everything over to Ziggy. "Thank you for doing this," Chasyn said.

"Maybe the movers will be hot," she mused. "I can always hope. And if they're butt ugly, I'll have my laptop with me."

"Good to know you've got all your bases covered," Declan said. "Make sure you—"

"Aren't followed," Ziggy finished as if it was a mantra.

***

Declan stood at the range, loading his Glock. Chasyn was still inside, finishing the salad she'd ordered for a late lunch. He was wound tighter than a drum anticipating his meeting with Lansing. But there was more to it. He could still feel the memory of her kiss. Hell, just acknowledging it made his body swell with need. She was under his skin. He thought about her when he was with her and when she was out of sight. No woman had ever had that effect on him and he wasn't sure he liked it. Declan wasn't sure of anything. Not since she'd stormed into his life. *Damn it.*

He stepped up to the platform and took aim at the paper target. He quickly emptied the clip, reloaded and fired again. When he turned to reload the gun, he found Chasyn standing by the back door. Sunlight glinted off her blond hair, making it shimmer where tendrils fell from her top knot. Her face was oval, with high cheekbones that accentuated the unique shade of her eyes. Chasyn had a long, delectable neck that he longed to nibble.

Get a grip.

"I think the target is dead," she said jokingly as she pointed to the tattered remnants of a paper human head and torso.

"Interested?" he asked, then smiled when he watched the look of delight in her eyes. "I mean, would you like another lesson in shooting?"

"Sure."

Declan yanked the pulley, replaced the target with a fresh one, then reeled it back into position. Loading the gun, he waited for her to take up her position at the platform, then moved in behind her. Mistake, big mistake. He could feel the roundness of her cute little butt as he wrapped his arms around her and handed her the gun. He covered her hands with his and leaned close to ask, "Do you remember how to remove the safety?"

Her fingers twitched slightly before tripping the lever. He felt and heard her breathing become a tad more shallow. Declan loved knowing he had that effect on her. It mirrored what he experienced whenever she was in close proximity.

Breathing in the floral scent of her skin, Declan said, "Aim and fire."

CHAPTER TWENTY-TWO

Mesmerized, Chasyn watched Gavin wire Declan for sound and video. The microphone was a teeny, tiny flesh-colored insert that disappeared as soon as Declan placed it in his ear. The video camera looked like the buttons on Declan's black shirt. It just snapped in place, then they all turned their attention to the laptop on the desk.

"Check, one, two, three," Declan said as he stepped away from the group.

The audio was clear and the video was crisp. Still, Chasyn wasn't convinced that a meeting with Lansing was the best idea in the world. Any number of things could go wrong. After all, the man had stabbed the mother of his child. That had been a grisly, up-close way to kill someone and it had taken one cold bastard to do that to Mary. Just imagining something happening to Declan caused a tightness in her chest. Not surprising, since they had spent the late afternoon making love, then ordering in Chinese.

After showering, Chasyn had dressed in a pair of black yoga pants and a nude and black wicking hoodie she wore when she ran in cooler temperatures. She put on her running shoes then joined Declan in the living room. As usual, he was dressed in stealthy black jeans and a button-down shirt. It wasn't until she watched the attachment of the video camera that she understood why he'd chosen the more formal shirt. He looked dark and dangerous, especially with the holster on his belt with the dull black stock of his gun protruding.

She tried to tell herself that this was his job. His element. Truth was, she no longer thought of him as a bodyguard. He was more like a partner helping her sort out a horrible situation.

That realization caused conflicting emotions to bang around in her head. Chasyn thought back to her pro-con list and acknowledged she was still grappling with the same issue. It all came down to one simple question—could she settle? Could she be happy knowing the relationship wasn't leading anywhere? That was the only real issue. It wasn't like she could demand that he change his position on relationships. If she wanted to continue seeing him, she'd have to be the one to change. Easier said than done. Declan was so busy protecting her from killers that he probably didn't even notice that no one was protecting her heart from him.

Declan checked his watch. "Ready?" he asked her.

"I still think this is too big of a risk," Chasyn argued for the umpteenth time.

He cupped her cheek. "I've got this."

Chasyn's nerves chased her into the Explorer. Declan was driving while Gavin fiddled with the laptop in the backseat. Behind them a second SUV carried Chuck and Adam, who were going to position themselves on the beach just in case. "What do you think Lansing will tell you? He won't connect the picture with the murders, so he won't admit his involvement in that." She pointed out as they merged onto I-95 South.

"I'll demand that he call off Martinez and Müller and in return I give him my copy of the DVD. Given the conditions of returning the DVD, he'll know I know about his involvement in the murders for hire."

"But if he does that, isn't that tantamount to admitting he killed Mary and had Kasey killed, too?" she asked. "He's too smart to implicate himself in either crime."

"We'll see," was Declan's vague reply.

Declan's phone rang and he connected through the car's Bluetooth speaker. "Hi Ziggy, whatcha got?"

"Lansing is on the move. His phone is pinging off the tower just north of Jupiter."

"Thanks. That gives us plenty of time to set up." Declan took the Lake Worth exit and headed east. "Let me know when he gets closer."

"Will do," she said, then ended the connection.

Declan reached the parking lot adjacent to the Lake Worth fishing pier. It was a moonless night and other than a few lights from Benny's on the Beach restaurant, the area was eerily dark. Chasyn felt trepidation build in the pit of her stomach. It was so dark one couldn't see the end of the long pier. She knew that there was a restaurant at the entrance to the pier, then a series of benches bolted on the planking that continued far out above the surf.

She stepped from the car to breathe in the fresh ocean air while Declan and Gavin did one final electronics check. Chuck and Adam went ahead to take up their positions by the pilings. Her pulse was racing. Absently she rubbed the fear-induced goose bumps on her arms.

Gavin got back in the car while Declan came around to where she stood. "Come here," he said softly.

She needed no encouragement to step into his embrace. He stroked her cheek with his knuckle as his other hand snaked around her waist. "I wish you would rethink this," she said.

Declan placed a tender kiss on her forehead. "I want you back in the car. I don't want you exposed in the open." He nudged her toward the open door. "You'll be able to hear and watch everything."

Reluctantly, Chasyn slipped into the passenger seat and Declan closed the door, then walked the distance leading to the pier with a copy of the DVD in his hand. In a matter of seconds, he was little more than a shadow and blended into the night. "I wish I could see him," she murmured.

Gavin passed her a pair of binoculars. "Try these NVGs. Night vision."

Chasyn held them up and suddenly the world had a green tinge but she could easily make out Declan as he reached the pier.

"Testing," came Declan's voice over the computer Gavin had in his lap.

"Loud and clear," Gavin responded into a small microphone that was built into his headset. "How do I sound?"

"Like you're in my ear," Declan answered.

All the high-tech stuff was new and interesting, but it didn't detract from her growing sense of apprehension. Lowering the binoculars, she looked around the nearly deserted parking lot. The windows of the Explorer were heavily tinted, so Lansing could park right beside them and not know their vehicle was occupied. Gavin closed the laptop, apparently to kill the display until Lansing was away from the parking lot.

Ziggy called to say Lansing's phone was pinging off the Lake Worth tower. Chasyn's heart beat irregularly and her palms began to sweat. "I don't think I'm cut out for surveillance," she told Gavin. "What if Lansing has a knife? What if he has a *gun*?"

"Declan's a pro," Gavin assured her. "He'll cover his *as*…bases."

Chasyn let out a little half-laugh. "You can say 'ass', Gavin. I'm not the cursing police."

"No, but you're my boss's, um…" his voice trailed off.

She was an *um*, all right.

"Car's pulling in," he said as headlights brightened the parking area. A champagne-colored Mercedes parked in the rear of the lot, several spaces away from a beat-up pickup truck. Gavin grabbed the binoculars from her. "It's Lansing."

Reflexively, Chasyn crouched down in her seat and held her breath until Lansing passed. Once he was about ten yards away, Gavin gave Declan the heads-up.

"I see him coming," Declan said.

Gavin angled the laptop so she could see the video feed. Instead, she opted to retrieve the binoculars. She readjusted the focus and observed Lansing walking leisurely to where Declan leaned against the metal railing by the first bench. She glanced over her shoulder and watched Lansing's approach from Declan's perspective. The closer he got, the more anxious she felt. Unease enveloped her as she watched Lansing move closer to Declan.

In a sudden, furtive motion, Declan spun the smaller man by the arm, pinning him against the railing.

"Ouch!" Lansing complained.

Declan proceeded to pat the man down. Apparently satisfied, he released Lansing's arm and took a step back.

"Was that really necessary?" Lansing asked in a snooty tone as he adjusted his golf sweater with its designer logo on the right breast.

"You have a history with knives," Declan replied.

"Allegedly," Lansing corrected. "So, I take it you found Mary's DVD?"

"Yes," Declan said, handing over the disc. "This is a copy, just to prove to you I have it."

"I'm not paying for a copy," Lansing said.

Declan laughed. "I don't want your money."

"What do you want?"

"I want Martinez and Müller."

"I don't know what you're talking about," Lansing lied effortlessly. "I don't know anyone by those names."

"If you think the press hounded you when you became

a person of interest in Mary's murder, wait until they get a hold of your lingerie show. So, let's start again. How do I get to Martinez and Müller?"

"I have no idea."

Declan gave the man a none-too-gentle shove. "Stop dicking around."

"Or what?" Lansing asked. "You'll beat it out of me?"

"Don't tempt me," Declan responded angrily. "What I want is for you to call them off Chasyn Summers. And I want it done tonight."

"I'd love to oblige you, but I'm afraid I'm not in control of Mr. Martinez."

"Channel Five is going to have a field day when I hand the video over. I can just see the crawlers and special bulletins now."

Chasyn set aside the binoculars and turned to the screen. Something was wrong. Lansing was totally calm and collected. He didn't seem the least bit concerned about Declan's threat or his posture. In fact, he was wearing a bland expression, almost as if Declan was boring him.

The mic crackled to life. It was Chuck. "I've got a heavy-set male coming up the walkway from the south. Dark hoodie. Cargo shorts. Hands in pockets."

"Is it Martinez?" Chasyn asked, rattled.

Gavin asked, "You got eyes on his face?"

"Negative," Chuck said.

"Declan, you may be getting company," Gavin warned.

On the screen, she watched as Declan drew his gun and held it off to his side. It was hard to see because of the limited camera angle, but Chasyn was growing more and more anxious with each passing nanosecond. Guns, darkness, and a secluded place weren't a good mix.

"Let's go," Declan said, grabbing Lansing by the arm and steering him off the pier.

"Why the hurry?" Lansing asked. "We haven't concluded our business. I want that video."

"And I want Martinez and Müller."

"Be careful what you wish for," Lansing warned.

A split second later Chasyn heard a series of pops and all hell broke loose. She stared at the images streaming from the camera. It showed Lansing half-crouched in front and to the left of the lens. She could see Declan's outstretched arm, gun trained straight ahead.

"I don't have a clear shot!" Sam yelled.

"I do!" Chuck called just as another shot split the night air.

"Shit!" Declan cursed.

"Is he shot?" she demanded of Gavin.

Then she saw Declan pull the trigger over and over, then the sound of another series of shots coming from a distance."

"What's happening?" she asked more forcefully.

"Everyone okay?" Gavin asked via the mic.

"Lansing's down," Declan said, his voice so calm it gave her shivers.

Chasyn couldn't stand not knowing what was going on. Completely defying Declan's instructions, she bounded from the car and ran toward the pier, Gavin hot on her heels. She ignored his calls for her to get back in the car, increasing her pace until she reached the pathway that ran parallel to the ocean. She could hear her labored breathing over the gentle crash of the surf. When she reached the walkway, she stopped short.

Declan was leaning over the motionless body of a large man crumpled on the ground. But the worst of it was seeing the stain on the front of his shirt. She flew in his direction. "Are you shot?"

"It's not my blood. It's Lansing's," he said as he stood. Then he turned to Gavin and said, "Call 9-1-1. Lansing took one to the chest but he's still alive."

"Who is this?" Chasyn asked, indicating the man on the ground.

Declan reached down and pulled the hoodie back off his face. "Martinez."

"Is he dead?"

Declan nodded. "Very." He knelt down again and began to rifle through the man's pockets.

"What are you doing?" she asked.

"Seeing if he has anything on him that will link him to Lansing or Kasey's murder." He pulled out several receipts and a small scrap of paper with the word "Hannah" written on it. Declan examined it, then handed it to her. "Mean anything to you?"

She struggled to make it out in the dim light. "Hannah? No."

"Let me put it back before the cops come. This is going to turn into a clusterfuck."

CHAPTER
TWENTY-THREE

Chasyn rested her head on her arms as she shivered in the hard seat behind the chipped table in the interrogation room. It was so cold she could practically see her breath. Annoyed and exhausted, she wondered what was taking more than six freaking hours.

Detective Burrows returned to the small room, notepad in hand. He took the comfortable, padded cloth chair across from her, moistened his stubby finger, then flipped over a few pages until he came back to the notes he had taken earlier.

"Let's go over this once more, Miss Summers."

She sighed, sat up, and glared at the man. "My story isn't going to change. You have video of the whole incident."

"Do you know you can be charged with interfering with an official investigation for not turning that DVD over to us when you found it?"

"You've been investigating two murders, not Lansing's

proclivities for lingerie. Declan was only using it as leverage to try to find Martinez and…"

"And?" the detective prompted.

Remembering Declan's warning that she not say anything about Müller just yet, she said, "And now he's dead."

"He was the link to Lansing and the shooting at the courthouse. Now he's dead and we're back to square one." The detective didn't even try to mask his contempt. "The gun we recovered at the scene was the same one used in your shooting and Miss Becker's death." He paused and let out a disgusted breath. "What were you doing out at the pier with Declan and his crew?"

It was her turn to be disgusted. "Am I under arrest?" she asked.

"No."

"Then I'm done answering questions. If you have anything else you want to discuss you can contact my attorney, Jack Kavanaugh." With that, she stood and practically dared him to stop her.

"If I find out you've been withholding information, I'll put your cute little fanny in jail. You've already cost us the Lansing case."

"Did he die?" she asked, thinking about Müller.

The detective shook his chubby head. "He's in a medically induced coma in grave condition."

"That doesn't sound good."

The detective stood up. "It isn't. And if Lansing dies, so does our investigation into the murders and the attempted murder on you."

"What? Why?"

He stepped over to the door and opened it, leaving his pudgy fingers wrapped around the knob. "Once the suspect dies, we close the case."

* * *

She emerged from the station just as the sunrise painted the sky in pastel shades of pink and orange. Sucking in a deep breath of non-stale air, she was surprised to see Declan leaning casually against his Explorer. He had a convenience store cup of coffee in one hand and a bright smile on his handsome face. He was wearing a PBSO T-shirt. "Shop at the gift store?" she teased, indicating his shirt.

"They confiscated my shirt because it had Lansing's blood all over it," he explained. "But I managed to keep hold of this." He reached into his front pocket and took out a wadded bit of tissue. Carefully, he peeled away the paper and revealed the button camera he'd been wearing at the time of the shootout. "Hopefully it has enough blood on it for a DNA test."

"Aren't the police going to do one?"

"Probably, but we use a private lab and they use the Florida Department of Law Enforcement lab, so their results could take forever. Speaking of which, you were in there so long I thought you were confessing to the Kennedy assassination," he quipped.

"I see you got your car back. How?"

"Vehicle roulette," he said as he placed the cup on the roof of the car. "A few of the guys went back to Lake Worth pier and reclaimed the cars. Then brought this one up to me."

Chasyn stifled a yawn. "The police consider Kasey's case closed. Same with Mary."

"I heard about the ballistics match." His eyes softened. "We can resurrect the cases as soon as we can either get Lansing to talk or find proof of his payments to Martinez and Müller."

"Lansing is in a medically induced coma, so I'm guessing he isn't going to be very chatty. And why did you tell me not to mention Müller to the police?"

He retrieved the cup and opened the passenger door for her. "Because that would just give them more ammunition against you. Since you told that lie to the state's attorney about witnessing Mary's murder, he has a real hard-on to find something to charge you with."

She slipped inside and waited for him to take his place behind the wheel. "The detective already threatened me with that. But didn't you tell me that with Lansing out of the picture Müller would back off?"

"Yes," he said as he started the engine. "But Lansing isn't gone. He has a slim chance at recovery so we continue doing what we're doing."

Tugging on her taut seatbelt, Chasyn said, "My parents aren't made of money and this must be—"

"No charge," Declan cut her off. "I returned their money to them two days ago."

She turned in her seat and spoke to his profile. "Why did you do that? I mean this job has cost you a car and God only knows how much money in labor."

Declan reached out and gave her knee a gentle squeeze. "Things have changed."

"Is this just because we're sleeping together?"

His dark head went back and he let out a hearty laugh. "First off, we don't sleep together. You run away from my bed like you're being chased by the devil. I'm trying to move this along at a pace that is comfortable for you. No pressure. But it would be nice if you spent the night in my arms."

"I explained that," she said in a bit of a huff. She wasn't angry—more like frustrated. "Please tell me you didn't tell my parents about us."

He gave a little half-shrug. "I don't see any reason for me to update them on our relationship. I wasn't specific. I just said this had become personal for me and I wanted them to stay at the safe house until we had the last few pieces of the puzzle."

Relationship? Is that what this was? Some sort of non-committal relationship? Chasyn mentally flogged herself for thinking it was or could be anything more. Still, disappointment engulfed her as she shifted uncomfortably in her seat. Having all these doubts in her mind was giving her a headache. By the time they reached Declan's house, she was utterly exhausted; even her bones felt heavy as she walked into the home.

As was her normal routine, she went to the fridge and retrieved a bottle of water. All the while she could feel Declan's gaze following her every move. It was disconcerting and a tad annoying. When she couldn't stand it any longer, she snapped, "What?!"

That disarming grin appeared, threatening her ability to think logically.

"I was just admiring the view," he said in a low, sexy tone. "You should wear workout clothes more often."

"It's 'athleisure' wear," she corrected, then immediately regretted her childish correction.

"Whatever you call it," he said amiably. "It makes you look hot."

He closed the gap between them and took her in his embrace, trapping her arms between their bodies. She was sandwiched between the cool metal of the fridge and the hard warmth of his body. He gently undid her topknot and her hair cascaded to just past her shoulders. Declan toyed with a lock of her hair, twirling it around his forefinger.

"You have the silkiest hair," he said as he lifted the tendril to his nostrils. She watched him drink in the scent of her shampoo.

She tugged the strands free. "Even my hair is tired," she told him.

"I assumed you'd need to crash." He kissed her forehead, then moved down to her cheek before finally claiming her mouth.

This was a new and different kind of kiss. Yes, his tongue worked skillfully to inspire her impure thoughts, but there was something unique about the subtlety of the kiss. It was gentle and patient, two things she hadn't felt with him before. Usually they were all heat and passion. But this was tender, comforting.

And scary as all hell.

* * *

Later that afternoon, Declan could hear her in the shower, then there was a prolonged period of time when he assumed she was dressing and/or primping. Whatever she was doing was taking a long time. He didn't like the fact that it bothered him so much. All he wanted to do was see her.

And do what? that irritating little voice in his head challenged. Take her into his bed was a given. But lately that had started to feel…complicated. Maybe he needed to sit down and make one of those pro-con lists Chasyn was so famous for. Maybe then he could figure out what had him so tied up in knots.

He'd gone to the pot and drained the last of the coffee into his mug when he heard the *click* of her heels on the bamboo floor. *Cool, calm and collected*, he reminded himself as he turned to face her.

She was wearing a casual maxi dress that gracefully fell to where her pink painted toenails peeked out from strappy black sandals. There was embroidery on the bodice of the black dress and a second band of stitching around her tiny waist. Very impressive, but then she turned to move some items out of one purse to another and he got a glimpse of the back. It plunged to her waist, held in place by a tassel-trimmed tie that fastened in the back. In a matter of a few seconds, the alluring scent of her floral perfume settled in the air. He had no idea what the fabric was, only that from her thighs down, it was sheer. Taking her to bed was now the forerunning thought in his sex-addled brain.

"Ready?" she asked.

"Very," he replied, hoping she wouldn't notice his budding erection.

Once they reached the car, she asked, "How are we going to get into ICU?"

"Ziggy handled that," he said. "There's a guy in ICU with no known family, so we just tell them we're there to see Mr. Tillman."

"And make a detour into Lansing's room?"

He adjusted the visor to block the sun hanging low in the sky as he headed to St. Mary's Medical Center. "That part we play by ear," he said.

"What about Müller?" she asked with apprehension in her tone.

"Well." He chose his words carefully since he didn't want to spook her. "Everyone but Ziggy is on deck tonight, watching the rooftops and other potential perches since Müller is a LDK."

"LDK?"

"Long-distance killer," he clarified. "Tom has already scoped out the hospital's garage and we don't have to be out in the open at all. So even if Müller shows up, he won't have a shot."

"I guess that's something," she sighed.

* * *

To say her nerves were frazzled was an understatement. As she walked the hallway with Declan she found herself holding her breath every time they passed a strange man. She needed to get a grip on herself. She trusted Declan and his team.

They arrived at the Information Desk and a nice volunteer in her eighties took their driver's licenses and used them to print out visitor passes for ICU. Following the signs, they took the elevator up and waited for it to open on their floor. The air was thick with the scent of disinfectant and she easily traced it to a janitor off to one side mopping the grainy floor.

There was a nurse's station ahead of them, although it was currently unoccupied. To the right was a long hallway and to the left was another hallway as well as a sign that read ICU WAITING AREA. Coming from that direction, she could hear the sounds of a raised voice. Declan placed his hand on her back to guide her down to the waiting area. Unfortunately for her, it meant skin-to-skin contact and she was instantly aware of him as a man. God, this kind of immediate reaction had never happened to her. Her body ached for him. The only problem was her heart ached as well.

"Leave now!" They arrived in time to see a well-dressed, statuesque blonde reading the riot act to a brunette in a tailored suit and sensible pumps.

"Martha, I just thought if you needed anything..." the brunette offered.

"It's Mrs. Lansing to you," the aggressive blonde countered with narrowed blue eyes. "You may have had my husband's loyalty, and a few other things," she added sarcastically. "But you don't belong here. He's my husband."

"Yes, ma'am," the mousey brunette said, suddenly turning redfaced when she noticed Declan and Chasyn in the doorway. "I'll go back to the office."

"Don't bother," the aggressive blonde said. "You're fired. I want you out by tomorrow afternoon."

The brunette looked like she wanted to argue but thought better of it. Chasyn felt for her and wondered why she and Mrs. Lansing were at such odds. The brunette practically slinked out of the room.

"What are you looking at?" the blonde challenged Declan. "Haven't you ever seen a wife fire her husband's loyal-to-a-fault secretary before?"

"Not in a hospital waiting area," he answered evenly.

Martha Lansing waved a dismissive hand at them. "I'd prefer to be alone."

"Well. We're here to visit a family member, so you'll just have to adjust."

She glared at Declan. "Careful with your tone, young man. I've donated enough money to this hospital to have considerable influence. I can have you removed to another location with a single phone call."

Declan steered Chasyn toward the door. "That won't be necessary. We'll give you your privacy."

They were about twenty feet down the corridor before Chasyn whispered, "Why did we leave without finding out Lansing's condition?"

"Spontaneity," he said, as if that was all the information she needed.

"What was spontaneous about a verbal cat fight?"

Declan pressed the button to call the elevator. "Martha's acting like he's already dead, so I'm guessing they didn't get good news. But the brunette intrigues me. Has to be Lansing's secretary, Tara Ryan."

"I've spoken to her on the phone," Chasyn said. "I didn't picture her as the Della Street type."

"But she impressed me as the kind of person who would do anything for the good doctor. Like leave her DNA on a water bottle."

"I'm still not following."

"We've never taken a hard look at Tara or Martha. Lansing had to have help with his plan. He had the money to pay Martinez but someone else must have funded Müller. And Martha is a very rich woman."

CHAPTER TWENTY-FOUR

W hat if she isn't there?" Chasyn asked as they headed for Dr. Lansing's office.

"She will be; you heard Lansing's wife. She has to clear out by tomorrow," he reasoned as he veered off the exit at 45th Street.

She crossed her legs and enjoyed the billowy feel of her dress against her thighs. She would have enjoyed Declan's touch much more, but she was starting to notice him pulling back. It wasn't anything he said or did; she'd just sensed some sort of subtle change. Probably the prelude to *'gee, it's been fun, but...'* It wasn't one specific thing; it was more like a combination of small things. Like he hadn't reached for her, hadn't even made a halfhearted attempt at seduction and he seemed preoccupied. Maybe she'd been too transparent, maybe he was realizing that even though she was trying, the no-hope-of-commitment thing just wasn't up her alley.

They drove into the parking lot in front of a two-story

stucco building. The first floor was an optician's office; Lansing's office was on the second floor. She could see lights and patients in the first-floor office.

Stepping from the Explorer, she hurried to the door, always mindful that Müller could be lurking around somewhere. She hated being perpetually afraid. It was getting old. Fast.

Declan joined her in the small elevator. She was keenly aware of him. His impressive body, his handsome face, the stern set of his jaw. And the fact that he wasn't looking at her. Either he was deep in thought or distancing himself; she had no clue.

Once the elevator jerked to a halt, he placed his hand at the small of her back and led her out onto the carpeted hallway. The sensation of his hand against her bare skin was as enticing as it was confusing.

Lansing's office was the first door on the left. A light was visible both through the etched glass on the door and under the crack where the door met the carpet. The hallway smelled faintly of fresh paint.

Declan knocked twice, then turned the knob.

When they walked in, Tara was startled, freezing in place with several books in her hand above a box resting on her desk. There was another box on the floor, already packed and ready to cart away.

"I'm sorry, but the office is closed," she said in a soft but professional tone.

He stepped up and extended his hand. "Declan Kavanaugh," he said, shaking her hand.

"Wait," she said, withdrawing her hand. "Aren't you the one who…who…"

"I was with the doctor when he was shot, but I didn't hurt him," Declan explained. "In fact, I'm pretty sure I was the intended target. That's why I went to the hospital."

"So what do you want from me?"

"I want to find out why Dr. Lansing ended up shot on that pier."

She pursed her lips, then said, "Aren't you the man who's been trying to blame Dr. Lansing for that Jolsten woman's murder?"

"No. I've simply been trying to find out what really happened."

As if just noticing Chasyn was in the room, Tara's eyes grew hostile. "Then you're that woman who lied about Dr. Lansing."

"I corrected myself," Chasyn insisted. "I told the police that I couldn't identify Dr. Lansing as the killer."

"He wouldn't kill anyone," Tara insisted. "The man is a saint. I should know. I've been working for him for the past twenty years."

"Then why did his wife fire you?"

Her expression was a blend of sorrow and resentment. "She's a petty woman who has always thought the doctor and I were involved."

"Were you?" Declan asked.

Tara shook her head but not a hair on her lacquered head dislodged. "He was my boss and my friend. He even helped me with my daughter. Paid for private school, then for her college. He treats Hannah like she was his own."

Chasyn's ears perked right up. "Hannah is your daughter?"

"Yes, why?"

"It's just a pretty name," Chasyn lied. "Speaking of names, did Dr. Lansing know a man named Albert Müller?"

Tara thought for a moment, then said, "Not that I know of."

"Are you sure?"

Tara placed the books in the open box, then placed her fists on her hips. "Of course I'm sure. Nothing happens in this office without me knowing about it. I think it's time for the two of you to leave."

"Thank you for your time," Declan said, then he escorted Chasyn from the office and back into the freshly painted hallway.

* * *

"I need everything you have on Lansing's wife," Declan said as soon as they arrived at the hangar. "Someone is paying Müller's bill and she's the one with deep pockets."

"Why would she want me killed?" Chasyn asked.

Declan reached out and absently touched her shoulder. "You saw her at the hospital. She's one controlling bitch. Then Tara said she was the jealous type, so it could make sense that she's the one cleaning up Lansing's mess."

Ziggy pulled up layered screens stacked on one another. "Well, right off the bat I can tell you she spends more money on Worth Avenue in a month than you pay me all year. Her credit cards must be smoking."

"What about recent withdrawals?" Declan asked.

Chasyn watched in awe as Ziggy managed to hack into the woman's accounts in fewer keystrokes than she used to open her email. "Nothing in the past three months," Ziggy said.

"Keep looking," Declan instructed. "Oh, and Chuck, I need a complete history on Hannah Ryan. ASAP."

"Consider it done," the other man said.

"What can I do?" Chasyn asked.

"Cook dinner."

She blinked. "What?"

"There's an app on my phone for Publix. Order whatever you want to make whatever you want and we'll pick up the order on the way back to my place." He handed over his phone.

"Oh, I almost forgot," Ziggy said. "Mr. Becker has left you two voicemails. He wants you to call him back."

"I will," Chasyn promised.

Less than an hour later, they collected their groceries and headed back to Declan's house. "So, tell me again why your whole team is working their fannies off and I'm cooking your dinner."

"I'm hungry. You said you liked to cook, so I thought I'd kill two birds with one stone. My team is very capable and they are experts at having meals delivered. They'll call me if anything needs my attention. So what's for dinner?"

"Chicken piccata over fettuccini and a salad."

"Fancy."

"Easy," she promised him as they reached the house. "I'll have it on the table in under an hour."

There's no simple way to navigate someone else's kitchen. Especially when that someone is a man with few kitchen gadgets. She ended up pounding her chicken breasts between wax paper with one of his hammers. Maybe she should have had Ziggy bring her the tools from her kitchen along with her pink duffle. Right, like there was any long-term possibility to their liaison.

She heard the shower and found it distracting. He was just a few steps away, gloriously naked. Closing her eyes, she imagined every perfect inch of him. And very nearly burned her chicken.

While the pot of water was coming to a boil, Chasyn made the salad and placed it on the table with an assortment of dressings she found in the fridge. Once she heard the shower stop, she dropped the fresh pasta and glanced at the clock on the microwave mounted above the stove.

Declan appeared before the fettuccini was cooked. He was wearing jeans and a Carolina blue T-shirt that brought out the color of his eyes. His hair was still slightly damp and he smelled of soap and woodsy cologne.

"Smells great in here," he complimented as he came over to peer into the pans.

Chasyn started to uncork a bottle of white wine when he took it from her. For a fraction of a second, their fingers brushed and Chasyn's nerve endings tingled.

"I can open a bottle of wine," she said. "I'm supposed to be the cook. Your job is to sit and enjoy."

He handed her the opened wine. She took two glasses down from the cupboard and poured one for herself, then looked to him. "Wine or beer?"

"Wine. A decent home-cooked meal is cause for celebration."

She handed him his glass, then used the remainder of the wine to deglaze the pan. He walked to the perfectly set table and even though her back was to him, she could feel Declan's eyes on her.

After she added the juice of two lemons, she whisked in the butter and sprinkled capers into the sauce. The pasta was ready, so she plated the meal and carried it to the table. "Enjoy."

"I am," he said in a low tone.

"So all I have to do is cook and you'll flirt with me?" she asked.

"All you have to do is breathe and I'll flirt with you."

Her stomach filled with anticipation and she'd yet to take her first bite of food. "You've been weird today."

"I've been distracted."

"By?"

"Obviously, Lansing arranged for Martinez to be at the pier. Why would he kill me without getting his hands on the DVD first?"

"Maybe he thought it was the only copy."

Declan shook his head. "I told him I still had the original and he didn't so much as blink. I watched the tape of our meeting several times this afternoon and I noticed something else."

"What?"

"He reacted when I mentioned Martinez but not when I said Müller."

"Maybe he doesn't know the true identity of the back-up assassin."

Declan chased the last bit of food around his plate. "That's a possibility. Or, his wife is the one pulling the strings. Maybe she resents his working. She all but accused his secretary of being Lansing's mistress. And I'm guessing she must know about his lingerie thing. Mary's death made his affair with her public. What if she doesn't care about his reputation; she just wants him under her thumb? Remember, they did get female DNA off that water bottle."

"So his wife, who comes from a prestigious Palm Beach family and has oodles of money, hired an international assassin?"

"I'm just saying it's a possibility."

His phone rang then and it was Ziggy with an address for Hannah.

When he hung up, he said, "Dinner was amazing. Let's take a drive over to Hannah's place to see what she knows about the Lansings."

"Give me a few minutes to clean up and—"

"You cooked. I'll clean up."

"Thanks. I'll go freshen my face." Chasyn left the room as if she was being chased. She had no idea how Declan would describe their dinner, but to her it had sure felt like a first date. Or maybe she was just reading too much into it. Good God, her mind had all sorts of thoughts zinging around. Was making him dinner too domestic? Would he see it as step one in her setting a trap for him? Or was she just deluding herself into thinking that he was as confused as she was? Knowing Declan, probably not.

* * *

Hannah Ryan lived in a high-rise condo in Juno Beach. It was a pricey place with a guard at the gate. Chasyn thought they'd be stopped right there, but the guard made a call and passed them through.

They parked in a slot marked VISITORS and exited the Explorer. The sun was setting behind them so Chasyn felt the cool air on her exposed back and wished she had changed. Too late to worry about that now. As they walked toward the entrance, she noticed a car parked with a paper temporary tag. "Isn't that a Taurus?" she asked.

"Yes. A new one."

"What parking spot is this?" she asked.

"Six-eleven." Declan repeated from memory.

"Isn't that Hannah Ryan's condo?"

"Yes."

"Well," Chasyn thought aloud. "Isn't it odd that she owns a brand new Taurus when we've been looking for a Taurus from the beginning?"

"Let's add that to the list of things to ask Ms. Ryan."

After checking the board mounted in the entry hall, they took the elevator up to the sixth floor. Declan rang the bell and almost simultaneously the door opened.

Like her mother, Hannah was a brunette. She was tall and thin and dressed in a Bohemian skirt and top ensemble paired with huge hoop earrings. Based on the puffiness around her brown eyes, Chasyn suspected she'd been crying.

"Miss Ryan?" Declan asked.

"Come in," she said, opening the door wide.

"Thank you for seeing us," Chasyn said when they were offered seats on one of two white sofas in the combination living room-dining room area of the condo. Just beyond her there were huge windows with breathtaking views of the dunes and the ocean. On the mantel above the fireplace, a cinnamon-scented candle was burning.

"My mother warned me you might be coming by," she said. "Do you want some tea?"

They said "no" in unison.

"It's terrible what Mrs. Lansing did to my mom. She's been Dr. Lansing's right hand nearly my whole life."

"And you and the doctor were close?" Chasyn asked, nodding slightly in the direction of a photo collage on the wall.

"He was like my father. My real dad bailed when I was a toddler."

"I noticed you have a new car," Declan said.

She smiled. "Thanks to Dr. Lansing."

"He bought you the car?"

Hannah nodded. "It was crazy generous considering all I had to do was loan him my old car for a few hours. When he returned it, he said it was time I got a new one."

"Was your old car a Taurus also?"

"Yes. A 2013, dark green one. Why do you ask?"

CHAPTER TWENTY-FIVE

Several hours after they returned home, Chasyn was making the walk from Declan's bedroom to the guestroom. Yes, it had happened again and it was magical. Chasyn had a happy body and a troubled heart. Especially when Declan didn't offer a single protest when she said she was going back to her room. *But really*, she wondered, *what did you expect? The guy has been one-hundred-percent up front with you from the get-go*.

Now, in the wee hours of the morning, she sat on the bed with a pad and pen in her hands. "Pro side," she whispered to herself as she wrote. "Tall, dark, handsome, funny, intelligent, sexy as hell. Great in bed." On the con side, she wrote *temporary*. Then she went back to the pro side and slowly wrote *I'm in love with him*.

Somehow putting it on paper made it real and scary. It was a wonderful secret that she couldn't share with anyone. God, her heart hurt.

But, she determined as she got out of bed, there wasn't a blasted thing she could do about it, so she would not wallow in self-pity. She'd gone into this with her eyes open. It wasn't like Declan had made false promises. To the contrary. She was the fool who'd allowed herself to fall for a man who could never love her back.

By the time she dressed in jeans and a simple aqua T-shirt, Declan was already at the table, sipping coffee with his phone to his ear. He acknowledged her with a smile.

She returned the gesture and went and poured herself a cup of coffee. As usual, it was strong to the point of being bitter. Chasyn managed to drink about half a cup before switching to bottled water.

"Are they sure?" he asked into the phone. "Great. What about Martha Lansing? Anything?"

Declan spoke for a few more minutes, asking about Lansing's condition at the hospital and any new information on Müller. When he was finished, he said, "The DNA off the button camera is a match to the fetal DNA in Mary Jolsten's case. Lansing is definitely the father."

Chasyn let out a breath. "So they can arrest him?"

Declan took a drink from his mug. "Not necessarily. The DNA proves he fathered Mary's child."

"And since the voice match came back to Mary, the DVD proves she was probably running a scam on him."

"All circumstantial," he said. "I called Detective Burrows and told him about Hannah and her Taurus. If they can track down the one she traded in and you can positively identify the taillights, that's more circumstantial evidence."

"What about Kasey's murder?"

"Ziggy thinks Lansing paid Martinez two grand from his credit card account."

"And the other withdrawal?" she pressed. "Was that for Müller?"

He shook his head. "It was what he gave Hannah to buy her new car."

"So we can kind of prove that Lansing killed Mary and with the Tec-9 match on Martinez's gun, we can prove he shot Kasey, but we don't have enough to prove Lansing was the mastermind behind it all?"

He reached out and patted her hand. "Just because a case is circumstantial, doesn't mean it won't be prosecuted. You know that."

"I also know that Martha Lansing will hire the best attorney in south Florida to defend her husband. If he even lives. Any word on his condition?"

"Upgraded to critical but stable."

"Good," she said, withdrawing her hand so she wasn't distracted by the feel of his touch. "I want him to get perfectly healthy so he can live a long life behind bars. Kasey was an amazing person."

"I'm sure she was."

"Speaking of which, Mr. Becker has been leaving messages for me. Can I call him from the burner phone?"

Declan's brow furrowed. "What does he want with you?"

Her head tilted slightly and she gave him a mildly stern look. "He's been a part of my life since I was a kid. Maybe he just wants to talk to me because he misses Kasey. I am his only real link to her now."

She retrieved the phone from her purse and dialed the number by rote. She walked back into the kitchen area while the line rang. It eventually went to voicemail, so she left a message and promised to call him later in the afternoon. After ending the call, she continued to pace.

"You're wound up," Declan said.

"I want to go for a run," she told him. "Preferably on the beach."

He sighed heavily. "Sorry, but you'll have to settle for laps around the gun range."

"What about spontaneity?" she challenged. "If you didn't even know I wanted to run on the beach how could Müller?"

"No."

"Anyone ever tell you you're no fun?"

He reached out and got her around the waist and pulled her close. Since he was seated, they didn't have that awkwardness of having to adjust for their height difference. For a change, he had to tilt his head back in order to maintain eye contact. "Want me to show you how much fun I can be?"

She meant to push him away. Keeping up the pretext that she was okay with their arrangement just wasn't working. But his fluttery kisses along her collarbone were. Instead of pushing him away, she cradled the back of his head as she bent down to kiss his lips. It was instant pleasure as his tongue sparred with hers. A taut coil of need formed in her belly as his hand closed over her breast. With his thumb teasing the bud erect, she moaned against his mouth. Her mind was spinning as the warmth of desire washed over her entire body.

She needed to tell him to stop. She wanted to tell him she

loved him. Just lay it all out there. But she didn't have the nerve. Realizing that made it possible for her to step away from his embrace.

"Point made," she said as soon as she was sure her voice would be steady.

He gave her a sexy grin. "We can go into the bedroom and I can continue to make my point."

"Or we could go to the beach and run off this…"

"Desire?" he prompted with a satisfied smile.

Chasyn was afraid she'd blush, but luckily, she was spared the outbreak of red blotches on her neck and face. "I really need some exercise"

His grin was positively smug.

"Not *that* kind of exercise," she corrected.

"Then we'll hit the range after I make a few more calls."

"I'll get my stuff," she said. Again she rushed from the room. Mainly because she was too tempted to take him up on his offer. His outrageous flirting was making a mockery of her resolve. Chasyn still hadn't figured out how to handle the situation; she just knew that jumping into his bed was probably not the best way to retain her perspective.

* * *

It was a cool day, even for March, with a strong onshore wind that had the palm fronds swaying in all directions. The sky was mostly cloudy, and a few sprinkles fell from quickly passing gray storm clouds.

While Declan and his team huddled together, Chasyn

took the opportunity to call Mr. Becker again. This time he answered.

"It's Chasyn," she said. "I'm sorry I've been a bit hard to reach."

"Where are you, my dear? You sound like you're calling from a tunnel."

"I'm with a...friend. How are things in Atlanta?"

"Lonely," he said with sadness. "I miss Kasey's daily calls."

"I miss her, too." Chasyn said. "The man who shot her was killed last night."

"I know. Detective Burrows called me earlier today and filled me in on the investigation. Or rather the probable lack thereof if that Lansing fellow doesn't recover."

Hoping to lift his spirits, she told him, "They upgraded his condition. I mean, Lansing is still in critical condition but he's stable."

"Burrows said you were there when Martinez and Lansing were shot. Honey, what are you doing?"

"I'm trying to make sure Lansing is held accountable for Kasey's death."

"As am I," Mr. Becker said. "But putting yourself in dangerous situations isn't a good idea."

"I'm being careful," she promised him.

"I have a few things I thought you might want."

"Things?"

"I've been going through pictures and some of Kasey's little trinkets and I thought you might like some of them."

"That's very sweet of you, but—"

"No 'but' about it," Mr. Becker cut in. "Just tell me where to send them and I'll have my secretary overnight them to you."

"Um," she hesitated as she walked over to Declan and cupped her hand over the microphone. "Can Mr. Becker, Kasey's dad, send me something here?"

Declan shrugged. "Sure." He reached out and scribbled the address on a slip of paper.

Chasyn read off the address and spoke with Mr. Becker for a few more minutes before hanging up and rejoining the group.

"So we're nowhere?" Declan asked, clearly frustrated.

"If Martha Lansing paid money to hire a hit man, she did it with petty cash out of her house," Ziggy explained. "I've gone over her records going back five years and I can't find so much as a decimal point out of place."

"What about all the corporations and non-profits she's associated with?" Chasyn asked. "Could she have somehow funneled money out of one of those to pay Müller?"

"It will take me a bit to get all those records," Ziggy said.

"And Chuck," Declan said in an uncharacteristically stern tone. "You've always been able to find people. Find Müller before he comes after Chasyn again."

With that he pivoted and went back to his office with Chasyn close behind. He practically slammed the door on her. "What's wrong with you?" she asked.

"I'm tired of chasing a ghost," he growled.

"So you take it out on everyone around you?"

She watched as his shoulders relaxed a bit. Declan sat behind his desk and raked his hands through his hair. "You're right. I was an ass. I'm just irritated as hell."

"After you apologize to your staff, let's run off some of that frustration."

"God knows I have to do something," he said, his tone not as biting as before.

"I always feel better when I burn off some stress. As soon as you apologize to everyone, come run with me."

He looked up at her with a devilish look in his eyes. "Or we could just lock the door and—"

She cut him off by shaking her head. "Anyone ever tell you you have a one-track mind?"

"Perhaps. But when it comes to you, I can't help myself."

Chasyn laughed. "You're one of the most controlled men I've ever met."

"I seem to cave whenever I smell your shampoo."

"I'll change shampoos," she said. "Get a move on."

* * *

Declan knew this wasn't run-of-the-mill frustration. He'd had difficult cases before. The only difference was, he wasn't involved with those clients. *Involved.* It seemed like the wrong word to describe the jumble of feelings he couldn't seem to reconcile. He thought about Chasyn night and day. He knew and cherished every inch of her glorious body. Every little sound she uttered when they made love.

Made love?

Where the hell did that come from? He wasn't a *make love* kinda guy. For him sex had always been a pleasant diversion. A period of no-strings enjoyment. He genuinely liked women. But he'd never liked one woman the way he fixated on Chasyn. This was getting complicated and he didn't do complicated. *Right?*

The few seconds of inner dialogue chased him back into the main area of the hangar. He quietly and sincerely apologized for taking his bad mood out on all of them. As expected, everyone shrugged it off. Everyone except Gavin, who took him aside.

"You are in trouble," he said in a near whisper since Chasyn, already changed into her running gear, was just a mere twenty feet away in Ziggy's area.

"I said I was sorry," Declan repeated.

Gavin waved his hand. "Not that, my friend. I'm talking about the girl."

"Chasyn?"

Gavin put his arm around Declan's shoulders. "How long have we been friends?"

"Forever."

"Then I'm going to give you some sage advice. Chasyn isn't like your typical playthings. Either cut her loose or admit you're in love with her."

Declan stiffened. "Who said I was in love with her?"

"You."

"Me?"

"It's evident to every one of us. Your eyes track that woman wherever she goes. You can barely keep your hands off her. I saw you kiss her the other day and it wasn't any peck on the cheek, either."

He shook off Gavin's arm. "Thanks for the advice."

Gavin smiled. "I'm only speaking the truth."

"No, your imagination is playing tricks on you."

"Are you trying to tell me you aren't having sex with her?"

"I'm not telling you one way or another," Declan replied.

"Chasyn and I are going to run the range. Spread the word so no one shoots us."

"Think about what I said." Gavin got in the parting shot before walking away.

Declan dressed and joined Chasyn in the garage part of the hangar for some warm-up. She was very flexible, but then he knew that from having her in his bed. He berated himself for going there. He had to stop focusing on her or he'd start thinking Gavin's warning had merit.

After ten minutes of bending and stretching, they walked back through the building and out the back door. The sun peeked out of the clouds on occasion and they'd be running into the wind.

"Ready?" he asked.

"Yep," she said as she took off without warning.

It was an easy job to catch her. Chasyn's strides were nothing to compare with his. Still, he was impressed by her pace. He got beside her, then turned and ran backward. "Nice day," he teased.

"I hope you trip," she replied sweetly. "Show off."

"I'm not showing off. I'm adjusting the workout to meet my needs."

"How about I blindfold you, too?"

"That would be fun, but—"

He heard the *whiz* of the shot just as he felt the stinging burn at his shoulder. Reflexively, he dove on Chasyn and smashed her into the berm of dirt behind the paper targets flapping in the breeze. He covered her head with his arm and held on as round after round pinged through the air.

CHAPTER TWENTY-SIX

After several moments, Declan rolled off of her and asked, "Are you hit?"

Chasyn tried to speak, but all she could manage was to suck in air.

"Are you hit!" he asked again, then ran his hands and eyes along her body for any signs of injury.

She shook her head, then her gaze fell to his shoulder. There was a growing stain of blood on his upper arm. "You've been shot."

"Just a graze," he insisted as he rolled over onto his back.

She watched the steady rise and fall of his chest with amazement. Not only did she have ringing in her ears from the sounds of the shots, but her pulse was banging in her ears.

"Everyone okay?" Gavin called as he raced from the building, gun drawn.

"We're fine," Declan answered.

"He's not fine," Chasyn corrected. "He's been shot."

Gavin and Chuck appeared and assessed the wound. "Just a scratch," Gavin concluded. "A Band-Aid is all he needs."

Chasyn looked over at the now barechested Declan and checked the injury for herself. There was a red line on his upper arm that looked more like a rope burn than a gun shot, save for the blood. She guessed the heat of the projectile had both injured him and cauterized the wound all at the same time.

"Take her inside," he told Chuck.

"You need to have that cleaned and bandaged," she argued.

"No, I need to study the targets and the berm," he countered. "I want a trajectory so we can track where the shots came from."

"You can do that?" Chasyn asked, surprised.

"Yes. We'll use lasers and a 3-D program Ziggy has on her computer. It shouldn't take too long but I want you safely back inside while we figure this out."

Reluctantly, she allowed Chuck to escort her back. He wasn't leading so much as he was bobbing and weaving. That did little to calm her nerves. Obviously they thought the shooter—in all likelihood Müller—was still in the vicinity.

While Declan and his team compiled measurements, Chasyn took a shower. Thanks to Declan's tackle, all she had was dirt in her hair and smudges on her cheek. It could've been worse. Much worse. She stepped under the flow of the water and allowed her emotions to come to the surface. Hearing the shots, diving to the ground...all of it was enough to unravel her. As the spray of hot water hit her face, she allowed herself to cry. They were tears for Kasey, her parents, herself and the general situation, and she cried until she had no more tears left. She was tired of being afraid. It felt like there was no place on earth she'd be safe from Müller. No place where he couldn't track her down. Odds were that sooner or later his bullet would hit its mark.

A shiver danced along her spine. She didn't want to die.

Once she was clean and cried out, she wrapped her wet hair in a towel and redressed in her jeans and an aqua T-shirt. It took some doing, but she applied makeup until her eyes no longer looked puffy and her lips were freshly glossed. Sucking in a fortifying breath, she stepped from the locker room and nearly ran into Declan.

"I'm sorry," she said. "I didn't know you were waiting."

"Not a problem. We have an idea where Müller was firing from."

"Really?" she asked with renewed excitement.

Declan tossed his towel over his shoulder. "There's an abandoned aluminum warehouse about a half mile from here. That would have given him the range and the angle needed to shoot at us on the range."

"So what now? Do we call the police?"

"No. Chuck, Gavin, Sam, and Tom are all on it."

"Not you?" she asked, surprised since he normally liked to be in on the action.

"I sent Adam and Joey over to my place to pack our stuff."

"Why? Your house is a fortress."

"But it isn't bulletproof. Somehow Müller's found out about me and he knows we're together."

"Should we split up?" she asked. "I could go to a hotel and—"

"I've already made alternate plans."

"Which are?"

Declan reached out and brushed her cheek. "My family has a cabin in Purdue. It's pretty isolated and has surveillance cameras set up all along the only road in. It's a little rustic, but I already spoke to my brother Conner and he's getting the place ready for us."

"What about tonight?" she asked.

"We'll bunk here. I don't want to risk having you out in the open. Then in the morning, we'll head for Purdue."

"What about Müller?"

"We're going to use decoy cars as we leave and that's only if my people don't track him down tonight."

"This is getting crazy," Chasyn said on a rush of breath.

Declan pulled her to him, off to one side to avoid contact with his wound. Luckily he'd been hit in his left arm, so his dominant side wasn't affected. "Try not to worry, sweetheart," he said as he stroked her back.

She rested her cheek against his chest and felt soothed by the even rhythm of his heartbeat. She was still a mishmash of raw emotion and he was cool and level-headed. It took her a second, but her brain suddenly processed the fact that he had called her 'Sweetheart.' Chasyn knew better than to read anything into it. He was just trying to be kind. She stepped away from him and plastered a bright smile on her face. "I trust you."

"Go hang out with Ziggy while I grab a shower."

Chasyn towel dried her hair as best she could, then ran a brush through it before going downstairs. Ziggy was drinking some sort of designer iced coffee and manning her keyboard.

"You okay?" she asked when Chasyn announced herself.

"Yeah," Chasyn answered without much enthusiasm. "Declan is the one who got shot." She rubbed her upper arms just remembering the incident.

Ziggy flipped her wrist. "He's hurt himself much worse."

"Where is everyone?" she asked.

"Hunting," Ziggy replied. "They went to the aluminum storage facility to see what they could find. Who knows? Maybe they'll get lucky."

"You think Müller would shoot at us, then hang around?"

"No," Declan said as he appeared in the office.

Like her, his hair was still damp. He was dressed in his signature black attire—jeans and a tight T-shirt. Despite the situation, she found herself attracted to his raw masculinity. Especially when he was looking at her with those piercing blue eyes rimmed in inky lashes. God, but this man could melt her legs with one look.

"Have you heard from the guys?" he asked Ziggy.

As if on cue the phone rang. Ziggy pressed the speaker button with the eraser end of her pencil. "Go ahead."

"We got lucky and I mean lucky," Gavin said.

"What did you find?" Declan asked.

"Casings in the gutters and a hotel key card. Must have fallen out of his pocket when he was making his getaway. Oh," Gavin paused for a second. "And the guy who owns the convenience shop across the street spotted a black Escalade racing away right after the shots were fired."

"Any idea which way he went?"

"We hit a dead end there. The cops showed up because someone called in a shots fired so we had to scramble off the roof. But we preserved the evidence."

Declan stroked his freshly shaved chin. "Anything unique about the key card?"

"It's got the Hilton logo on it."

Declan turned to Ziggy but she was already ahead of him. In a few seconds, she had a list of Hiltons in the immediate area. "Looks like there's seven in West Palm Beach."

"Send addresses to the guys." Then he said to Gavin, "I'm going to send a picture of Müller to your phone along with the addresses. Split them up so you can cover more ground that way."

"Will do."

"And be careful. Müller is a professional. If you find him, stay on him, but don't try to be a hero." Declan ended the call and began to pace.

"Patience isn't one of his virtues," Ziggy offered.

"So I see," Chasyn agreed. "Can I make you some coffee?" she asked.

Declan grinned at her. "You don't make coffee; you make light brown water."

"You make tar," she countered.

"I like strong coffee."

"Then why don't you make it?" she suggested.

Chasyn followed him to the small kitchen area and took a

bottle of water out of the fridge while he filled the filter with a mound of coffee grounds. They were standing side by side and Chasyn kept her face down as she said, "Thank you for today. I'm so sorry you got hurt."

Declan pulled her into his embrace. "It's nothing but a scratch and you don't have to thank me. I was just doing my—"

"Don't say job. You are doing this pro bono for some unknown reason."

"I've been shot at three times in a little over a week. It's personal to me, so there's no reason why your parents should pay for me to investigate this convoluted mess."

"I'm sorry you got dragged into this," she said as she placed her palms against his chest. Through the thin fabric, she felt the even rhythm of his heart beating. She wasn't so lucky. Her heart raced, a result of being in such close proximity. She felt the outline of his powerful thigh muscles against hers; the outline of his washboard abs where their bodies met.

Without thinking, she dragged her nails down his chest and stopped when she reached his belt. It made her feel powerful when she heard the slight catch in his breath. Chasyn looked up and he instantly captured her mouth. Automatically, she laced her fingers behind his head and savored the minty taste of him. Declan's hands moved to her sides, gently sliding from her waistband to the swell of her breasts. Chasyn's blood pressure rose along with her yearning for him. She wanted to drag him upstairs, rip off his clothes, and have passionate sex with him.

She would have, too, if Declan didn't set her away. "Not interested?" she asked as casually as she could manage.

"Oh, I'm interested," he said immediately. "I'm *very* interested. But I'm also in the middle of tracking an international assassin. A little tough to do when all I want is to take you to bed."

At least the feeling was mutual. "How did he find me here?" she asked.

"My guess is Martha Lansing clued him in. I did—stupidly—give her my name at the hospital last night."

Chasyn felt a chill travel down her spine. "What about Hannah Ryan? I mean, if Martha is willing to kill me then she has just as much motivation to have Hannah killed."

"As soon as they finish searching for Müller's hotel, I'll send someone up to keep an eye on her."

She relaxed a little. Until the phone rang and Ziggy called for them.

"Chuck is on the line," she said. "Go ahead, Chuckster."

"Found him. Sorta."

Declan scowled. "Sorta?"

"It took some doing, but I finally got the desk clerk to admit Müller's been staying here for three days. He's paid through the end of the week but the clerk said he packed up and left three hours ago," Chuck said.

"Shit," Declan muttered. "He bailed right after the shooting. Probably realized he'd left the key card behind."

"The news isn't all bad. He put down a cell number when he registered and listed his license plate number."

"Give it to me," Declan said.

Ziggy was already working the keyboard, entering the number and searching for the owner of the phone. "Trac phone," she said. "Purchased with cash at the Walmart in Jupiter."

"Dead end," Declan sighed. "Hang there, Chuck, just in case he returns."

"Will do."

"How about the license plate?" Declan asked.

"Reported stolen from the Orlando Airport six days ago off a black Escalade."

"This guy is good," Declan said with unadulterated admiration.

Chasyn sipped her water as Declan went into boss mode. He directed most of his team to return to the hangar by nine in the morning, with the exceptions of Joey and Gavin. Joey was to babysit Hannah just in case Martha turned her wrath on the young woman. Gavin was to return with dinner from one of his favorite Cuban places. His last task was to insist that Ziggy go home and get some sleep. She protested but Declan overruled her quickly.

Once they were alone, Declan and Chasyn waited on Gavin.

"We'll leave for Purdue before noon," he said.

"Tell me about it," she asked.

"Very small town in north Florida. I grew up there. Lots of swamps and creeks and canals. Great things to explore when you're a kid."

"Near the beach?" she asked hopefully.

He shook his head. "Dead center of the state. You'll like Conner and Emma."

"Emma is his wife?"

"Right. They're newlyweds. And Conner has a sixteen-year-old daughter from his first disastrous marriage. Samantha."

"But he's happily married now, right?"

"Yes. But it wasn't an easy courtship. My new sister-in-law is Emma McKinley."

Chasyn recognized the name; she just couldn't place it. "Who is?"

"The daughter of the guy who was blamed for the presidential assassination twenty years ago."

"Oh, right. I saw her and her sister on a television special after they uncovered the identity of the real assassin. You have an interesting family," she said.

"Darby, who you met, and Jack went through hell before they got together, too."

"Sometimes you have to go through something extreme to realize how you feel about another person," she suggested.

"A relationship shouldn't be that hard," Declan said flatly. Then he checked his watch and said, "I wonder where Gavin is."

There was a sudden chill in the room.

Deciding a change in topic was in order, she asked, "Will they all be coming up for your brother's hearing on Friday?"

"Yes, we'll be there in force."

"Is there anything I can do?"

"Like what?"

She thought for a minute. "I could write a prepared statement for you to read to the Parole Board. I've done a few of them in the past."

He tipped his head. "Yeah, that would be great." He gave her a sly wink. "I guess I'll have to think of a special way to thank you."

"I'm sure you'll come up with something."

CHAPTER
TWENTY-SEVEN

The delivery from Mr. Becker showed up just after nine. It was a medium-sized box filled with an eclectic collection of memorabilia. The vast majority of its contents were photographs. Chasyn could tell by the paper that they were copies of the originals and she thought of how sweet it was for Mr. Becker to go to so much trouble. She flipped through them, stopping every now and then when a specific memory bubbled to the surface. She came across one that was so special, she pulled it from the stack and placed it in her purse. It was a picture of her and Kasey on the day they graduated from college. It was hard to fathom that Kasey would be dead and she'd be running for her life.

The other items in the box were various trinkets Chasyn had given her friend over the years. Kasey collected Holstein cow figurines, and apparently, Mr. Becker had decided to pass the collection on to her. There were several other items packed in bubble wrap but Declan called for her, so she closed the box and carried it with her.

He directed her to the Hummer, which was already loaded with her suitcase, tote bag, and duffle. There was a large black duffle bag in the back seat along with a garment bag hanging off the hook in the rear. "Can I add this?" she asked.

"Sure," Declan said, gently shoving it past a metal lockbox. "Do you have everything you need?"

"Yes. Clothes, toiletries…Oh, can I get my laptop out of my Prius?"

He shook his head. "We can't take a chance on having your IP address tracked."

"Then, yes, I have everything. You?"

"All set." He turned to the others and said, "Let's head out. You know your routes."

Five of the vehicles started up as Chasyn was buckling her belt. She had a touch of apprehension. Even though all the cars had darkly tinted windows, she was still worried that Müller would guess correctly and turn his high-powered rifle on them. Again.

Declan reached out and touched her bare knee and gave it a reassuring squeeze. "Even if Müller is hanging around, he won't risk shooting up five cars. He'd draw too much attention to himself. And men like Müller do not want attention. That's why he's been so successful to date." His phone rang and he pressed the touchpad on the navigation screen to pull up the call. "What do you have, Ziggy?"

"DNA results."

"And?"

"Lansing is definitely the father of Mary's fetus."

"Any change in his condition?" Chasyn asked.

"I'll call the hospital and see what I can find out."

"Thanks, Ziggy," Chasyn said, then Declan pressed the disconnect button. "That's a point in our favor," she said to Declan as she slipped on her sunglasses. "Maybe the state's attorney can build a decent circumstantial case against Lansing."

"And his wife," Declan added. "We just have to keep digging until we find out how she paid for Müller's services."

He took the Turnpike northwest to I-75. Once they were on the interstate, Chasyn asked him if they could stop and stretch their legs.

"I'd rather wait until we get closer to Purdue."

Chasyn uncrossed and recrossed her legs. "Okay then, can we stop so I can pee?"

"Why didn't you just say so?"

"I was trying to be discreet."

"There's a rest area about ten miles ahead. We'll stop there."

True to his word, Declan eased off the interstate onto a ramp that split into a V, with one direction for cars and the other for trucks and RVs. There was a single-story brick building flanked by picnic tables and just beyond that, a four-pump service station.

"Do you want to get gas while I use the restroom?" she asked. "This thing can't get more than about ten miles to the gallon."

"This *thing* serves its purpose."

"Right," she said with a little laugh. "I forgot the rolling arsenal you have in the back."

He parked, then reached across her and retrieved his Glock from the glove compartment. Declan tucked it in the waistband of his black jeans, then pulled his T-shirt down to cover the bulge. "I'll be right outside the ladies' room," he told her. "That way I can see the parking lot and keep an eye on you at the same time."

"Whatever floats your boat," she said as she unhooked her seatbelt and opened the door. She walked into the archway and directly into the nearly deserted bathroom. The scent of pine deodorizer was strong as she walked in and selected her stall. She could hear and feel the air conditioning blowing down from ceiling vents. Suddenly her cute white halter sun-dress with its pretty rose print didn't seem like such a good choice. It was probably ten degrees cooler this far north.

She used the sole of her wedge sandal to flush the toilet, then washed her hands before checking her reflection. She reapplied rosy lip gloss and made her way back out of the room, glad to feel some sunshine on her chilled skin.

"Want a bottle of water or something?" Declan asked.

"That would be great."

They walked over to a bank of vending machines and De-clan got her a bottle of water and then moved over to get himself a cup of coffee. "Carry this," he said, handing her the steaming cup.

"Why? I mean I don't mind, it just seems like an odd re-quest."

"I want both of my hands free in case anything happens."

She struggled to keep pace with him. "You know when you say things like that you strike fear in my heart." Her pace quickened and she all but bobbed and weaved her way to the car.

"Better you be afraid than dead."

"Point taken."

In no time and without incident, they were back in the car and headed up the interstate. As they drove, Chasyn watched the scenery change from a majority of palm trees and tropical plants to more pine trees and scrub. The sun was beginning to set as Declan took the Purdue exit.

Immediately they were on a two-lane road. He adjusted his speed and they went for what felt like miles before she saw the first sign: PURDUE 5 MILES.

"Five miles from what?" she asked.

"Not a small town girl, I take it."

"I've never had the pleasure." She took a sip of water.

They passed the occasional manufactured home. Some were lovely, with nice yards and flower beds; others were in dire need of repair. Most had a dog or two hanging out in the yard.

Declan slowed the car as they rounded a bend and off to the left was a stunning three-story mansionette. In the curved driveway was a red Mercedes, a green Toyota, a motorcycle up on a trailer and a marked Sherriff's vehicle. The brick home was surrounded by azaleas in full bloom and there were window boxes hanging off the banister of the wraparound porch.

"This is your brother's house?" she asked.

"He married up," Declan joked.

They had barely gotten out of the car when the front door opened and a smaller version of Declan came out onto the porch. He was handsome, with dark hair and the same piercing eyes, so she didn't need to ask if this was Conner. The woman who next exited the house was a willowy blonde in expensive business attire.

Chasyn was suddenly surrounded by the Kavanaugh clan and she hadn't even crossed the threshold.

"I'm Emma."

"Conner, and this is my daughter Sam."

"Who's the kid?" Declan asked, nodding in the direction of the lanky young man hanging back in the foyer.

"Sam's boyfriend David."

"You sure have grown up," Declan said as he wrapped his arms around the young girl and spun her around. She laughed delightedly.

"And that wonderful smell," Emma began, "is Jeanine whipping up her famous Jambalaya and to-die-for cornbread."

She was ushered into the house and they went into an expertly appointed living room. It was bright and airy but one wall was covered in thick milled plastic.

"We're building out," Emma explained. "Adding a suite to the side of the house so Sam has her own space."

"It's going to be totally cool," Sam said excitedly. "I'll have a bedroom and a small office/media area and a huge bathroom."

"Sounds lovely," Chasyn said as Conner placed a cold beer in her hand.

"David's online test is in two hours," Sam said apologetically. "He needs to study before dinner so he's ready for the test. Don't mean to be rude."

"Go ahead, honey," Conner said.

Sam and David left the room and then Chasyn heard heavy footfalls on the steps. "She's lovely," she told Emma and Conner. "Is her boyfriend going to college online?"

"No," Conner said with a twinge of annoyance. "He's getting his GED. He's a smart kid; he just made some dumb mistakes."

"Which can be rectified," Emma said brightly.

"So," Conner said as he took a seat next to his wife. "Tell me about this Müller guy."

Declan brought them up to speed on the case while Chasyn sipped her beer and hoped her stomach wouldn't growl from hunger. The alcohol was going to go right to her head if she wasn't careful.

"So we'll hang at the cabin until after Michael's hearing."

"I went up there today and got the place all ready for you. The fridge is full, so you can just keep a low profile."

"Thanks," Declan said.

A small, frail woman politely interrupted them to announce that dinner was served. Chasyn eventually learned that Jeanine was David's mother. And as the evening wore on, she learned that Emma, too, had been stalked by a killer. She immediately bonded with the other woman and was sorry when Declan said it was time for them to head to the cabin.

"You have a very nice family," she told him as they headed back out onto the darkened roadway.

"I do," he agreed. "I don't know about that whole David-and-Sam-in-the-same-house thing."

"I'm sure Conner and Emma and Jeanine have laid down the law."

"I wouldn't have obeyed that law when I was seventeen."

"Man-whore," she teased.

He laughed and seemed more relaxed than she'd seen him in days. Until the phone rang. Declan pressed the touch pad and answered. "What's up, Ziggy?"

"I think I may have found something on Martha Lansing."

"Shoot."

"Well, she's the chair of the annual Red Cross benefit on Palm Beach and they just had their auction. Sales topped a hundred grand but she hasn't deposited the money in their account yet."

"Excellent work, Ziggy. You're amazing."

"I am," she agreed. "Does this mean you'll be coming back now?"

"No, I've got to stay in Purdue for a few days. I've got a family thing. Hold down the fort for me."

"One more thing."

"Yes?" Declan asked.

"Mr. Becker has called here three times trying to reach Chasyn."

"She can call him from the car," he said.

"Then I'm going back to tracking the money trail. Want me to call Detective Burrows and share this info with him?"

"Go ahead," Declan told her. "If he needs me he might have a hard time getting in touch with me. Cell service can be spotty out here."

"I can handle Burrows. You just take care of our girl."

"Will do. Bye." He glanced briefly at Chasyn and said, "Tap the screen until you get the keypad, then call Mr. Becker."

"Thank you," she said. "I should have called him the moment the box arrived but we left so suddenly."

"Well, hurry up, because once I turn off the main road, the call will probably drop."

Chasyn reached Mr. Becker and said, "Hello and I'm so sorry for my poor manners. Thank you so much for the box of mementoes. Especially the photos."

"You're breaking up, my dear. Where are you?"

"North Florida. I'm sorry, it seems as if I'm losing cell service. I'll call you back when I can."

"Are you still with Mr. Kavanaugh?"

"Yes."

"Good. I just want to make sure you're safe."

"I'm—" the line went dead and the panel asked if she wanted to redial. There was no point. Declan had turned on to an unevenly paved road full of potholes.

Eventually they came upon a small wooden cabin with a stone fireplace on the short end of the rectangle. It looked a little…rustic.

They unloaded the Hummer, including several guns and rifles. The interior of the cabin was better than she'd expected. Well, except for all the taxidermy hanging on the walls. They were just creepy. There was a sofa, two chairs, and a large dining set in the main room. Down a narrow hallway were two bedrooms, each outfitted with twin beds. If she'd had to describe the décor, she would've called it Early American Hunting Lodge. Everything was very masculine, except for the vintage quilts on the beds.

"Which room is for me?" she asked.

"We're sharing that one," he said, pointing to the right.

"Sharing?"

"Don't worry, I'm not breaking your rule. You won't be sleeping in the same bed as me."

She hesitated. "But it is the same room."

"It's also the only room with a security monitor in it and I can't keep an eye on you and monitor outside at the same time."

"But the police know about Martha now."

"Yes. But we don't know if Müller knows his meal ticket is on the brink of being arrested. Until that happens, I'm not taking any chances."

"You have an answer for everything, don't you?"

He smiled. "I try."

Declan turned on the small television perched on the dresser. Like the one in his home, this one had cameras positioned around the property. He went into the great room to start a fire while she dug out a sweater.

When she joined him, he was positioning rifles and guns at every door and window. He did the same thing in the bedrooms. When he was finished, he pulled up his shirt to reveal two guns tucked into his waistband. "You keep this with you at all times, understood?"

She took the gun. It felt heavier than she remembered.

"I put in an extended clip."

"A what?"

"You have extra bullets in the gun," he explained. "If anything, and I mean *anything*, happens, get in the bedroom closet and close the door. If anyone other than me opens it, shoot until you run out of ammo."

CHAPTER
TWENTY-EIGHT

They settled on the sofa. The television was on, tuned to the surveillance channel, and a small fire crackled in the fireplace. There was a table lamp on, but it didn't put out a lot of wattage. If it hadn't been for the guns scattered about, it would have been kind of romantic, Chasyn thought. Except that he didn't do romantic.

"So, do we sit here and name the state capitals?" he teased.

"There has to be something better than that," she insisted.

"How about this," he purred against her ear, then nipped the lobe.

Chasyn's pulse instantly became erratic, fueled by his hot breath against her neck.

Declan dragged her onto his lap; at the same time his hands came to rest on her hips. His mouth found hers and he gently drew her lower lip into his mouth, then ever so slowly allowed it to slip away. His fingers dug into her flesh, pressing her down on his trapped erection.

Chasyn slipped her hand between them and undid his jeans and touched him, gently at first, then with more urgency. All the while his tongue made maddening circles against hers.

Declan reached up and effortlessly unfastened the small hook at the nape of her neck and the top half of her dress fell in a pool around her waist. His mouth dropped first to her throat, then lower to tease her nipple with his nimble tongue.

Her head dropped back and she began to push at his clothing. Declan kissed her parted lips and stood in one fluid motion. He was holding all her weight in one arm and removing his clothing with the other. Next he slipped his hand under her and ripped her thong off in a smooth action. He sat back down on the sofa, holding her just above him.

Chasyn was so ready for him that she guided him inside her in a single, powerful thrust. With her hands on his shoulders, she struggled to put off her orgasm but it was a fruitless effort. After just a few minutes, her body exploded and she rocked in his arms.

Declan wasn't too far behind her, until they sat there spent and sweaty.

Chasyn immediately refastened her dress as she moved away from him. She glanced over and saw the remnants of her panties hooked on the ear of the dead bear rug. Oh well, it had been worth it.

Had it? She wondered. She was addicted to this man. This man who only thought of her as a temporary diversion. This man she loved. Chasyn excused herself and went into the restroom to freshen up. Well, maybe it was more to keep him from seeing the deep hurt in her eyes. What she needed was a good, ugly cry, but that wasn't possible when they were in such close quarters.

She decided a bath would be the next best option. She opened the door and walked to the bedroom to get something from her suitcase. She opted for the most unflattering, unsexy thing she had—a running outfit that was comfortable and not very form fitting. Plus it was warm, which would help when they retired to the chilly bedroom *without* a fireplace.

"I'm taking a bath," she yelled, then slammed the door before he could respond.

* * *

Declan sat on the sofa, sipping fresh, hot coffee he'd just made, watching the surveillance monitors and kicking himself. The way she'd practically flown out of the room rubbed him the wrong way. He would have been content to lie on the sofa for hours, maybe go a second time. Or, simply hold her until she fell asleep with that silken hair spread over his chest. But no. For some reason whenever they had sex he felt her put up a wall the minute it was over. He was doing something wrong but for the life of him, he couldn't figure out what.

He thought back to his conversation with Gavin. Maybe it was different with Chasyn because *she* was different. Different from any woman he had ever known. Not once in his thirty-five years had he felt an inclination to snuggle. Yet that was exactly what he wanted to do with her. Well, one of several things. Gavin was right about her. Chasyn wasn't a temporary fling. There, he'd said it. At least to himself. The huge step would be to tell her. But how? He'd never said "I love you" to a woman. Never. Not once. The mere thought of doing so scared the shit out of him.

She emerged about a half hour later with her hair dried, wearing some shapeless black outfit. Not that it mattered: he had every inch of her body committed to memory.

"There's coffee."

Her nose wrinkled. "I'd be awake all night."

"No bottled water, but there is wine."

"A glass of wine would be nice," she said.

Declan went to the small kitchen, retrieved the wine from the fridge and then got the opener from the small drawer next to the battered and chipped stove. "It's going to have to be a literal glass of wine," he said without turning around. "No wine glasses."

"I'm not a snob," she responded easily.

"No, you aren't," he agreed as he felt some of the tension begin to ebb from his body. When this was all over he'd find some way to tell her how he felt. But until then, he needed to stay focused on Müller. He couldn't afford any distractions.

He had just finished pouring the wine when the electricity went out. He set the glass down and pulled his Glock from his waistband. "C'mon," he said in a near whisper.

"What?" she asked.

Declan was listening intently for any strange sounds. "Where's your gun?"

"In the bedroom."

"Way to keep it on you at all times." He took her by the arm and hurried her down the hallway. He had a bad feeling about this. The power never went out at the cabin. Which meant it was very likely that someone had disconnected the in-ground generator.

"This isn't just a power blip, is it?" she asked with a fear-tinged voice.

"I doubt it. Pick up the gun, go in the closet and remember what I said."

"Declan? Be careful!"

* * *

If she'd thought she was scared when Declan had a hold of her arm, it was nothing like being slouched in the closet with her heart pounding in her chest. Several minutes passed before she heard glass shatter. Then came a non-stop series of shots and she heard wood splinter and more glass breaking. Then an even scarier sound…silence.

She counted to fifty and then cracked the door an inch or so. She could smell gun powder. She wanted to call out for Declan but she was afraid of giving her location away. But she was more afraid of being alone.

Slowly, she crept out of the closet, mindful to stay below the window ledge. Glass crunched beneath her feet as she moved along the hallway. Every so often she'd see a place where a large-caliber bullet had pierced the building. Everything was eerily still save the flames flickering in the dying fire.

The front door was open and the gun Declan had left next to it was gone. His Glock was on the kitchen table. Chasyn hugged the wall until she was in a position to see out the crack between the bullet-ridden door and the front of the property. All she saw were shadows in the darkness.

Several shots rang out and she knew they were coming from the left. With her gun held firmly in both hands, she kept it pointed in front of her as she ventured out of the house. It wasn't smart but it was a better option than leaving Declan out there alone with Müller.

Steadying her breathing, she listened in the quiet for some clue to follow. Then she heard footfalls in the distance. Two sets. Running full out. She headed in that direction, using the tree trunks like barricades as she went deeper into the woods.

She heard two more gunshots. Close. Following the sound, she neared a clearing. Relief washed over her when she saw Declan standing and a man lying on the ground. Declan had his rifle trained on the guy, who had both hands in front of his face.

"Declan?" she called.

"Way to stay in the closet, Chasyn," he replied, a little out of breath.

She ignored his rebuke and went up next to him. Müller was on the ground and had a dark stain on his right shoulder. Just above his head was a pair of discarded night vision goggles. To his right was a nasty-looking rifle.

"Do you want me to go get something to tie him up with?" she asked.

"We'll get him up fir—Jesus!" Declan cried out in pain.

It happened fast but somehow Müller had pulled a knife and buried it in Declan's thigh. Müller was reaching for his rifle when Chasyn raised her gun and fired. She didn't stop squeezing the trigger until she ran out of bullets.

"Well done," Declan said.

Chasyn stared down at the dead man. She only counted two bullet strikes but one of those was in the center of his forehead. "But I fired like a dozen times and I was only three feet away."

"Give me a hand," he said as he draped his arm around her. "Damn it!" he said as he pulled the knife out of his thigh.

"Here," Chasyn said, stripping off her shirt and tying it around the wound to stem the flow of blood. "Let's get you back to the cabin."

"Let's get back into town," he suggested.

"Mind if I put on a shirt first?" she asked as she helped him hobble back to the cabin.

* * *

A lot happened in the two weeks following the shooting. First and foremost, Chasyn was nursing the mother of all heartbreaks. She had done the smart thing, even if it was a little sneaky. She'd waited until the entire Kavanaugh clan was at the parole hearing, then called a cab to take her to the airport. She'd left Declan a simple note that read, *I'm not what you need.*

Apparently she'd been right, because she hadn't heard a word from him since. She had heard from the Kingdom of Saudi Arabia. They'd contacted her to give her the bounty the royal family had had on Müller's head. Five hundred thousand dollars dead or alive. Dead seemed to be just fine with them. A cashier's check arrived a few days later.

Which was how she ended up staying at The Breakers. A little treat and a great place to run on the beach in the morning and cry yourself to sleep at night. Oh, and the room service was amazing.

Second, and another reason for her heartbreak, was finding out who had hired Müller. When he was searched at the morgue, he'd been carrying a picture of her and Kasey. A picture only Mr. Becker could have supplied. Once she found that out, the rest of the pieces fell into place. Mr. Becker had blamed her for Kasey's death, insisting that Kasey never would have gotten involved in the whole Mary Jolsten murder had it not been for Chasyn. Mr. Becker knew her whereabouts most of the time, so it was easy for him to send Müller toward Purdue after their last call. He'd known Declan's last name and it had been simple for a man like Müller to figure out where they'd been hiding. In exchange for taking the death penalty off the table, Mr. Becker had agreed to let the authorities know all the details behind hiring Müller. This deal had also meant there wouldn't be a trial, which Chasyn was happy to hear.

Finally, she'd decided not to return to Keller-Mason. The place wouldn't be the same without Kasey there and she really had lost her professional drive. Five hundred thousand could do that to a girl.

Chasyn tied her shoes, grabbed her key, and left her hotel room. She went down past the pool, then took the stairs down from the seawall. After stretching, she ran to the sound of the waves lapping at the shore. The sky was blue, the water was turquoise...and she was miserable. But she would get through this. Someday Declan would be nothing more than a memory. Her heart wouldn't squeeze at the mere thought of him and eventually she'd go a whole day without crying. But today wasn't that day. She wiped at the tears stinging her eyes as she made the turn to run the two miles back to the hotel.

The morning sun was bright, so she shielded her eyes to make sure she didn't overshoot the private entrance back onto the hotel grounds. That's when she saw him. Even at a hundred yards, she'd know Declan Kavanaugh anywhere. Her pulse quickened and her heart rate increased the closer she got to where he sat on the seawall. *Be cool*, she told herself. *He's probably just here to drop off my car*. The one she hadn't bothered to reclaim when she got back to Palm Beach County.

"You're a hard woman to find," he said.

His voice was even deeper and silkier than she remembered. "I'm registered under my real name."

As soon as she climbed the stairs, she noticed he had a thick manila envelope with him. Great; he was probably going to claim some of the reward money. Oh well, he'd certainly earned it. "How's your leg?" she asked, careful to keep her tone conversational.

"Practically healed," he answered. "Can I talk to you?"

"Go right ahead."

"I mean someplace more private. Like your room?"

She eyed him suspiciously. "There's no sex in it for you."

He smiled at her and it had the predictable effect. Okay, so she wasn't immune.

"I just need about five minutes of your time, Chasyn. Then if you want me to, I'll leave."

She sighed, knowing full well she should decline. But her mouth formed the word "yes."

He followed her up to her room. It was a small suite with a large bed, and a small table and chaise over by the window overlooking the ocean. Everything was white—white spread, white sheets, white curtains. The maid had tidied up, so when they entered the room smelled of fresh lavender.

Chasyn kicked off her shoes and socks and got a bottle of water out of the mini-fridge. "Want something?"

He simply smiled.

"Something from the mini?" she clarified.

"Just sit and hear me out."

"Okay." She sat at the small round table and he scooted his chair around so their knees touched. To her it was like getting tazed.

"I've had these drawn up and I want you to read them," he said as he pulled a stack of legal documents in blue covers from the envelope.

She glanced at the title of the first one. "Business Partnership Agreement?"

"Just read it."

"I can't go into business with you. If you want half of the money I got from—"

He placed his finger to her lips. "Just read them."

She read the first line, paused and read it aloud. "This agreement between Declan John Kavanaugh and Chasyn Summers Kavanaugh? What is this, some sort of joke?"

"No," he said, taking her hands in his. "I want you to marry me."

"No," she said as she pulled her hands free. "You don't. It isn't who you are. You'd be fine for a while but then you'd learn to resent me for making you change your life."

"You didn't make me change my life," he argued, snatching back her hands. "It just took me a while to figure out that you're different. The way I feel about you is different. I've never been in love before, Chasyn."

"Okay, that's what you start with," she said as she fought back happy tears. "You start with 'I love you.'"

"Really?" he asked jokingly.

"Yes, it goes something like this: 'Declan, I love you.' Then you say—"

"Chasyn, I love you, too. Now what?" he asked, eying the bed.

"Now we decide if we're really compatible."

"I think we already know that." He said as he cupped her cheek.

"I think you want me as a business partner," she reminded him. "Or was that just your guise to get in here?"

"No," he insisted. "I do want you to work with me. Hell, I want you to do everything with me. I want to have babies with you. I want—"

She put her finger to his lips. "I love you."

"I love you, too," he said as he whisked her into his arms and carried her to bed.

After a whirlwind romance, Darby Hayes Grisom married the man of her dreams. Little did she know that one year later that dream would turn into her worst nightmare...

Please see the next page for a preview from EXPOSED.

CHAPTER ONE

Darby's eyes darted around the table, checking and rechecking the two place settings. The placemats were exactly an inch from the beveled edge of the glass table top. Wine glasses and water goblets were precisely placed. Utensils, hand-polished and sparkling, were laid out with precision. She lit the three candles, symmetrically arranged in descending order and then crouched down to make sure the flames flickered at exactly the correct height.

The oven timer chimed. Darby tucked her blond ponytail into the collar of her shirt, stuck a potholder on one hand and eased open the oven door. The smell of fresh yeast rolls escaped on a rush of hot air. Lifting the pan out of the oven, she placed it on a trivet next to the cook top on the center island.

The kitchen, the entire house in fact, was immaculate to the point of being austere. Like most homes in the exclusive enclave of Sewell's Point on Florida's Treasure Coast, the house had a large, open floor plan with picturesque views of the intracoastal. Hutchinson Island, a thin strip of barrier island, separated Sewell's Point from the Atlantic Ocean. It served a more important purpose, buffering the estate homes from the ravages of a direct hit from the hurricanes that roared in from time to time.

Of the five bedrooms, two had been converted into home offices. The master suite was spacious and the decorator had selected a Havana-style décor for the room. It was all muted greens, distressed wood, glass and iron. The only personal item was an eight-by-ten print of the formal engagement portrait that had appeared in the paper nearly fourteen months earlier.

Leaving the rolls to cool, Darby walked through the combination living room-dining room, down the long, narrow hallway. She stopped to absently pluck a slightly wilted petal from one of three dozen roses that had been delivered the day before. She swallowed a wave of nausea as the sweet, heavy perfume of the flowers surrounded her. Normally she enjoyed the scent of fresh flowers, but ever since becoming pregnant she'd found the odor revolting.

Turning the knob, she opened the door adjacent to the master suite and smiled. A soft, pastel mural with fairies and dragonflies had been painted earlier that day and this was the first chance she'd had to admire the artwork. It was perfect. Eventually, she'd have the remaining white walls painted some shade of pink. Or maybe green. She needed to make up her mind. The baby was due next month. Not much time left to procrastinate.

Speaking of time, she glanced down at her watch as she closed the door to the as-yet unfurnished room and went back to the kitchen. A rather uncooperative schnauzer had thrown her schedule off, so she had to keep moving in order to get dinner on the table at nine P.M. sharp. The keep-moving part was proving to be difficult since her belly had expanded. Carrying around the extra weight and girth, coupled with the long hours she worked as a vet, Darby was finding it a challenge to juggle everything that had to get done.

Taking the fresh asparagus from the refrigerator, she gently broke off the woody ends. Spreading the pencil-thin tips in a single layer in a dish, she chopped garlic, added that and some salt and pepper, and then tossed the vegetables with olive oil before placing them in the oven to roast. It wasn't until she lifted the lid on the double boiler that she realized she'd forgotten to turn the heat down on the burner. A good quarter of an inch of hollandaise sauce was scorched and crusted onto the bottom of the pot. "Beyond saving," she muttered.

Her heart rate increased as she furiously worked to wash and dry the pan, and then hang it back on the gourmet rack suspended from the ceiling. Darby used a half dozen paper towels to dry and polish the basin of the sink. At eight fifty-six, she dressed the salad and placed it on the kitchen table. Pulling a bottle of Alsatian *Sélection des Grains Nobles* from the chiller, she filled the Barona wine cooler with ice, then set it on the table next to the salad bowl.

At one minute before the hour, she heard the mechanical

hum of the electric garage door opening. Darby plated the poached salmon and arranged lemon slices in a semi-circle around the platter. Taking the potatoes from the rarely used microwave, she placed them on a small serving dish, then reached for the breadbasket on her fourth trip from the table. She tossed rolls in as she went to retrieve the asparagus.

The minute she heard the door slam, she felt that sick knot of dread lodged in her throat. She turned and did one more visual scan of the table. Perfect. Just the way he wanted it.

Plastering a smile on her face as she pulled the elastic tie from her hair before giving it a fingertip fluff, she turned, folded her hands over the bulge of her stomach in an almost protective gesture, then waited for him to come through the garage entrance.

Sean Grisom was tall, muscular, handsome and smart. Light brown hair framed his darkly tanned skin. His shoulders were broad without being overly muscled. Thanks to good genes, he had a trim frame built for the designer clothing he favored. As usual, he didn't have a hair out of place.

That was one of the things that Darby had noticed about him at their initial meeting. He'd walked into her clinic, carrying a stray dog he'd found injured on the side of the road, and even under those circumstances he hadn't had so much as a speck of blood or dirt on him. When he'd asked for her help his voice had been deep and smooth, but it was his eyes that had melted her on the spot. When Sean Grisom looked at you, he was totally engaged—as if there wasn't another person on the planet. He was generous, too, promising to pay for whatever treatment the dog needed if she would just help him before the poor mutt died from his injuries.

To an animal lover like Darby, hearing the concern in his deep, sensual voice was payment enough. Of course she treated the dog. Some jerk had shot the poor thing with a BB gun. The surgery had been fairly simple and when she was finished, she was surprised to see that Sean had stayed, waiting patiently on news of a dog that wasn't even his. The next thing she knew; they were having dinner. Six weeks later, they were married.

"You worked late again," Sean said.

His voice was still deep but instead of smooth, it was laced with thinly veiled censure. Faux concern etched between his brows. A little over a year into the marriage and Darby knew him well enough to know that everything about this man was calculated and played precisely for whomever his audience happened to be at that moment in time.

Maintaining eye contact, she shrugged. "I had a problem patient but I was only there a little late." Ten minutes talking to a frightened little girl about her old dog's death. A few minutes well spent, as far as Darby was concerned. Except Sean wouldn't see it that way. Nobody should be more important to her than her husband.

"We've talked about this," Sean kissed her cheek as he placed his hand on her belly. "You're pregnant, Darby. It's time you stopped working. That's my child you're stressing."

"Pregnant, not disabled," she teased, hoping to ease the

tension as she moved away from him to get the asparagus before they lost their crunch. "Would you open the wine, please?"

Sean went to the table and uncorked the bottle with practiced finesse. "Have some with me."

"I shouldn't," she said, adding the vegetable dish to the table.

"One glass a week," Sean countered, reciting the passage he'd read in one of her pregnancy primers.

She shook her head. "I had a glass at the restaurant two days ago, remember? Besides, I'm tired and wine would put me right to sleep."

"You're tired because you stand on your feet all day taking care of pampered pets when you should be here, at home."

What could she say? They'd had this argument many times since she'd found out she was pregnant. It always ended the same way—badly. While she was happy about the baby, the pregnancy had been unexpected. She'd been religious in taking her birth control pills but apparently she was part of the point-zero-one percent exception that proved the rule. Giving up her veterinary practice would mean giving up the only piece of herself she had left.

"I'll get a second wind," she promised as she sat in her usual chair and unfolded her napkin. She needed to steer him away from the whole working conversation. A knot was forming in her stomach and she felt the beginning of fear. For her safety and the safety of her baby, she had to calm Sean down before this took a serious left turn. So with a calm belying her true fear, she asked, "How are things at the restaurant tonight?"

Sean's eyes narrowed. "Is that some sort of polite way of pointing out that your practice is thriving while my business is stagnant?"

"Of course not," she said as her heart rate began to quicken. She took his plate to serve him so it would be ready when he sat down to join her. "I was just making conversation." Conversation she hoped would keep him from exploding.

"A new restaurant takes time to build a clientele."

"I understand that." Darby placed a portion of fish on his plate.

"It's going to take time."

She added vegetables and a potato. She tried to sound positive. "It'll be a success."

He glared at her. "Don't patronize me, Darby. I've got serious cash flow problems. Unlike you, I can't serve my guests kibbles and bits."

She drew in a breath and said mildly, "I'd be happy to write another check." Her trust fund was just sitting there. She didn't begrudge him the seed money for the restaurant. Paying him was a far better option than suffering the wrath of Sean.

"I need more than your monthly draw. Almost all of my vendors have upped their prices; some doubled, *tripled* the prices they were charging a few weeks ago." He began to pace. "If this guy I'm meeting in New York in the morning doesn't come through, I don't think I'll be able to keep the doors open for more than a month or so."

"You don't have to go to New York with your hat in your hand, Sean. I can ask my father to increase my allotment."

"Right," he spat, standing perfectly still as his fingers went white where he gripped the back of his chair. "Run to Daddy and tell him I can't support you."

"It's *my* money, Sean," she said as she reached out to pat his arm with her hand. "He's just the trustee and anyway, my father understands a new business requires cash. He knows there are times when you have to spend it to make it. And it is only money. He'll understand. He's a very—"

It took a second for Darby's brain to put it all together. Her cheek was on fire. She was on the ground, the chair teetering on top of her. The back of her head hurt where she'd hit the tile floor. As if in slow motion, she looked up in time to see Sean lifting the edge of the table.

Scrambling to her knees, she skidded along the floor as plates and food rained down on top of her. Shards of glass pelted her skin like a thousand tiny pebbles as the tabletop crashed down, shattering all around her. Darby was vaguely aware of screaming as she curled into a fetal position when Sean yanked the chair off her and flung it through the air. It landed with a thud against the back of the family room sofa.

Then he was standing over her, his feet planted on either side of her body. He began thrashing her with something—the placemat, maybe. All she knew was that each successive snap of fabric bit her through her clothing.

"You stupid, *stupid* bitch!" Sean yelled.

"Sean!" she called, wrapping her arms around her belly as the beating continued. "I'm sorry. Stop!"

She pleaded with him, whimpering over and over. There was no response in his vacant eyes as they narrowed while he continued to thrash at her torso.

Then, as suddenly as it began, it was over. Just like always. Only this time was somehow different. It was the first time he'd attacked her while she was pregnant. She lay there, terrified, wondering if this was just the calm before the storm, or if he still intended to dole out more punishment.

Sean stepped away, tossed the napkin in the pile of food and debris, and then straightened his tie and smoothed his hair.

Darby remained cowering in the corner, following his every move like the trapped animal she was. When he reached for her, she flinched. Annoyance and disbelief were clearly painted on his features.

"Take my hand."

Hesitating for only a second, she reluctantly took the hand he offered. Gently, he helped her to her feet and made sure she didn't lose her footing or cut herself on the glass and food strewn all over the alcove. Sean circled her in his arms and forced her cheek to rest against his chest. She felt his heartbeat. It was even and rhythmic. If she didn't know better, she'd have thought she'd imagined the whole ugly scene.

The feel of his hand stroking her hair as he kissed the top of her head made her skin crawl but she didn't dare pull away. Not when she was this vulnerable. Not when one well-placed punch could harm or kill her unborn baby.

Darby wondered how she'd gotten to this point in her life. She woke up in the morning afraid and fear followed her to bed every night. The only time she felt safe anymore was when she was at work. It was her haven. And yet here she stood, in the arms of her abusive husband, wondering for the umpteenth time how she could get out of this hell of a marriage.

"I forgive you," Sean said.

"W-what?" Darby was startled. What did she have to be sorry for?

Bracketing her shoulders in his hands, he set her back a foot or so and flashed her a brilliant smile. "It's okay," he said, using his fingertip to brush a strand of hair from her forehead. "I know you didn't do it on purpose."

"D-do what?"

"Burn the hollandaise." His finger hooked beneath her chin and he pushed her face up so their eyes met. "I smelled it the minute I walked into the kitchen. You should know better than to try to hide things from me, Darby. That's not how a marriage works. Now, come help me finish packing. I have to stop by the restaurant to pick up Roxanne on my way to the airport."

Darby was fairly sure he was taking Roxanne along for more than just assistance. She was also well beyond caring. As far as Darby was concerned, Roxanne was welcome to him.

"I think taking my assistant along will impress this guy. Send the right message, you know? After all, the key to this kind of deal is making the other guy think you're doing him a favor by letting him get in on the ground floor."

* * *

An hour later, sobbing, Darby dialed the phone, hiccupping as she struggled to speak. "M-Mom?"

"Darby, honey, what's wrong? Is it the baby?" her mother asked. "Will! Pick up the extension. Something's wrong with Darby and the baby."

Then her dad was on the line. "Did you call your doctor?"

"Not...the...baby." She hugged her belly protectively. "It's Sean."

"Something happened to Sean? Is he hurt?"

"No, Mom. He...he *hit* me."

"That son of a bitch," her dad said. "Where is he now?"

She could almost imagine her father's gritted teeth and see his blue eyes narrowed with fury. "Gone. Business trip."

"I'm coming right over," her dad insisted.

"No," Darby said, swiping at her tears with the back of her hand. "Sean won't be back until tomorrow. I'm going to get organized and pack. Then, if it's okay with you two, I'll come over first thing in the morning."

"If it's okay?" her mother parroted. "Don't be silly. You never have to ask to come home, honey. I'll come over to help you."

"Thanks, Mom, but I just need some time to sort through some stuff." *And clean up.*

"Yeah? What if the bastard comes back?" her father demanded. "What then? Has he done this before? Is that why you've been avoiding us the past few months? You need to have him arrested. Now. Tonight."

Darby pressed two fingers to her temple. The peppering of questions was precisely why she wanted some time by herself. "No, he's never hit me before." She lied. They didn't need to know about the slaps or back-handed blow-ups.

"Don't worry. He won't come back. He's already on his way to the airport."

"How can you *know* that?"

"He's got an early meeting with a potential investor in New York." *And Roxanne in his bed.* "He won't bail on that kind of opportunity. The restaurant needs an infusion of cash."

"I've seen the bank statements, Darby," her father said with unfiltered disdain. "You've been infusing a lot of cash into that place. What's he been doing with all of it? Forget it. I don't really give a damn. Screw Sean. Wait until I get my hands on that piece of crap. He won't need any money where he's going."

"Calm down," her mother inserted. "The last thing Darby and that baby need right now is you going off picking a fight with a man more than half your age. Honey, what can we do?"

"You're doing it. I'll come by first thing in the morning. Before work, if that's okay?"

"Would you stop asking?" her mother admonished. "This is your home."

"Thanks."

"Are you sure you're okay, Darby? What about the baby? Maybe we should take you to the ER just to make sure."

"I'm okay. *We're* okay."

"Not if he hit you."

"He just slapped me," she fibbed, not wanting to give them a rehash of the actual events. That could come later, once she was safely ensconced in their home.

"Just?" her father scoffed. "*Just* slapped you?"

She massaged the back of her neck. "Let it go for now, Daddy," she said. "I don't really want to talk about it and the baby is fine."

She heard her father let out a long breath. "Well, I can't think about anything but that creep of a husband you've got. What kind of man hits his wife? His *pregnant* wife?"

"It's over now." Darby breathed in deeply. Feeling discomfort in her chest, she realized she'd cried hard enough to make her ribcage sore.

"It's far from over," her father countered. "I want to know exactly what that bastard did to you."

"I'm totally exhausted right now but I promise to tell you everything in the morning. Promise. I should be there before seven."

"Darby?" her mother asked, her voice so soft and gentle that Darby felt warm tears well in her eyes. "We love you, honey."

"I know. And I'm going to need all that love, mom. I can't, *won't* live this way. And I certainly won't raise my child with Sean and his violent temper. Tonight made that perfectly clear to me. My marriage is over."

* * *

Out of sheer exhaustion, Darby managed a few hours of fitful sleep before the alarm blared her awake at 5:45. Her back ached from sweeping more than two dozen dustpans full of glass-contaminated food and china from the floor, then depositing it in the trash can in the garage. Somewhere in the recesses of her mind, she realized it was a stupid thing to do. But the realization couldn't overcome the automatic reaction to eradicate all evidence of the fight. She didn't do it for Sean. No, on the off chance that her parents or an old friend dropped by, she didn't want to explain why the walls were splattered with salmon.

Covering for Sean had become a habit. A very bad one. As she tossed off the comforter she'd never really liked, she vowed it was the last time she'd make excuses for him. When she entered the adjacent bath and looked at herself in the mirror, she discovered she was smiling for the first time in, well, *forever*.

Rubbing her eyes, then her cheeks, she asked herself, "How did you turn into *this* person?" Holding her hair in a makeshift ponytail, she brushed her teeth and then splashed a handful of water in her mouth. After washing her face, she tossed her nightshirt into the hamper and got the pair of scrubs she'd set out the night before.

After applying just a hint of make-up, she closed her cosmetic case and added that to the suitcase before zipping it shut. It didn't make much sense to pack all her clothes. Most of them didn't fit right now, so she'd worry about that later. When she applied for the restraining order she could get the judge, or magistrate, or whatever you called them, to give her some time alone at the house to get the rest of her stuff. But for now, for today, she was content to take just what she needed for a week. By then, Sean would be back, he'd be served with the restraining order and she'd be on her way to being divorced.

The word was enough to send a shiver down her spine. No, she didn't—couldn't—stay married to Sean. But she'd never failed at anything before. Never.

Darby was smart enough to know that when it came to abuse, past behavior was the best predictor of future behavior. Given that Sean was getting worse by the day, counseling wasn't a realistic solution. No, she had to get out now. Before he killed her and the baby, a threat he'd made on more than one occasion.

After loading two suitcases into the back of her Grand Cherokee, she backed her car out of the driveway. Automatically she reached for the clicker attached to the passenger seat visor and pressed the button. The door descended about two feet before coming to a grinding halt. Then it bounced as the motor continued to whirl.

Sighing heavily, Darby got out of the car to see what was causing the malfunction. It took a minute, but she finally spotted a length of telephone wire looped around one of the slats. "Just what I need," she grumbled as she stood on tiptoe, trying to slap the wire out of the way. Darby gave up after three tries.

Like the house, the three-car garage was as neat as a pin. For once, Sean's insistence on order in all things worked to her advantage. The step stool was tucked between the shelving and the hot water heater. Even knowing that Sean wouldn't have an opportunity to react to any scuffmarks, Darby lifted the awkwardly shaped stool and maneuvered it over to the garage door. Once she had some height, it was simple to dislodge the cord. As designed, a safety feature of the door sent it backward, crawling up and along the ceiling. The phone cord disappeared into the void between the ceiling and the door. Oh well, she thought as she walked back to her idling car. Sean would take care of it. He didn't let things like strangely dangling cords—especially ones that impeded the garage door from working properly—go unattended.

The sun was just bleeding over the horizon as she drove the fifteen short miles to Palm City, the area where her family had owned a home since the 1890s. While the location hadn't changed, the homes certainly had. Her however-many-greats grandparents had built a modest, single-story wood frame dwelling smack in the middle of the original Hayes orange grove.

As the modest grove grew and expanded, so did the size and expanse of the home. She smiled with equal measures of respect and pride as she passed the remains of that first homestead. The only reason part of it was still standing was because of the adjacent cemetery. As common practice until the mid-1970s, all Hayeses had been entombed on that small strip of land. Part of the deal when the groves were sold off to a developer was that the family cemetery would be fenced and appropriately maintained. He'd kept his word.

Darby's stomach felt like a sack of unacquainted cats. She had always been so meticulous about her life. Driven, some would say. After her stint in the Army, she'd gone to college, then to vet school, and by age twenty-eight she had her own business with an impressive client base. How could all those aspects of her life be so right and her marriage be so wrong?

Yes, intellectually she knew that leaving Sean was the safe and only option, but some small crumb in her brain kept harping on the failure aspect of throwing in the towel after less than two years of marriage. It wasn't supposed to be like this, but she couldn't risk the baby's safety, especially now that Sean was getting more violent with every encounter.

Traffic was light as she crossed the bridge over the St. Lucie River. The fresh scent of the ocean air dissipated under the weight of diesel fumes wafting up from the marinas below. Once upon a time in the not so distant past, all of the land on Monterey from Willoughby Road west had belonged to the Hayes family. Little by little, as snowbirds migrated from the north and population swelled up from the south, the groves had been sold off, leveled and replaced by gated communities, indistinguishable stucco homes, strip malls, and golf courses.

Martin County was in transition. More building, more families, less agriculture.

Darby suspected her father held on to one modest grove near Indiantown for sentimental reasons. He'd grown up working the groves. It was more than an exercise in nepotism. William Hayes loved the business. The scent of orange blossoms in bloom; the occasional flurry of activity to fend off an unexpected frost; the rugged machinery weaving through the rows, slicing off the ripe fruit to send it off to market.

Though they ever said it, Darby suspected her parents had thrown themselves into the business because they were married for nearly twenty years before Darby came along. Grace

Hayes had been over forty when she had Darby. William had been fifty-one at the time.

As she approached the small, paved driveway leading to her parents' home, she saw several fire trucks parked at angles, blocking traffic in both directions. Automatically, Darby looked at the sky above the tree line, expecting to see a plume of dark smoke. Nothing. The sky was clear and blue save for a few puffy white clouds rolling in off the ocean.

A cold shiver crept up her spine. It appeared as if the emergency vehicles were in front of her parents' house.

Panicked, she placed the car in park. Darby unhooked her seatbelt and wriggled out of the car. The minute her feet hit the pavement, she did her best to run at the same pace as her rapid heartbeat.

As she neared the fire trucks, she caught sight of a previously obscured ambulance, parked on the west side, its doors open. A man sat on the fender, sucking oxygen through a clear plastic mask affixed to his face.

Holding her stomach to lessen the effects of her vigorous movements, Darby jogged over to the ambulance. She'd moved beyond palpable fear to utter panic.

"You a doc?" the EMT asked, his fingers pressed to the pulse point of the police officer's wrist.

"Vet," she answered. "What happened?" She turned her head, getting on tiptoes in a futile attempt to see her childhood home through the thick shrubbery vining through the six-foot iron fence.

"Carbon monoxide," the EMT explained. "Harry, here, got a few whiffs. The oxygen is just precautionary."

Darby's mind was spinning. Ignoring everything but the dread gripping her chest, she pivoted on the balls of her feet and started toward the house. She got all of maybe ten feet when a tall, lanky patrolman held up his hand.

"Sorry, ma'am. This is—"

"My parents' house," she finished, watching him blanch slightly. "What's happened?"

Crooking his thumb behind him, he said, "I've got to radio the sergeant. Just a minute."

The patrolman turned sideways and whispered muffled words into the microphone clipped to the shoulder of his beige uniform shirt.

"He'll be right here," the patrolman said. "Why don't you come over here. Wait in the shade," he suggested, pointing her toward a small area under a canopy of palm fronds.

Just as she took her first step, four men dressed in street clothes filed past her, pushing two gurneys. The fact that they were in no particular hurry, and that white body bags were neatly folded atop each gurney, confirmed her worst fears. Her vision started to spin and she got that roller-coaster feeling—like her stomach was dropping out. This couldn't be happening. Darby clutched her stomach and felt warm tears slide down her cheeks.

Darby felt her knees buckle, then everything went fuzzy.

As if viewing the scene from underwater, Darby felt the patrolman lift her up and carry her to the ambulance. Gently, she was placed on a stretcher and the EMT who'd been working on the officer turned his attention to her. Though her head was spinning, she brushed his hands away.

"I'm fine."

"You're at risk for shock," the EMT insisted. "Your BP is too low. We've got to get you to the hospital."

"But my parents. Are they…are they…?"

"I'll ask one of the officers to follow us to the ER." He gently lifted her arm and secured a blood pressure cuff, then attached leads to her chest to monitor her heart. The sirens came on at the same time as he reached beneath her to secure a fetal monitor around her abdomen.

"I'm Pete," he said as he fiddled with myriad machines in the ambulance.

"Darby," she said, barely feeling the continuous stream of tears sliding down her cheeks. No one was telling her anything, but she knew. She just knew that her beloved parents were gone.

The EMT offered a weak smile as he donned a stethoscope and listened first to her heart, and then pressed the single-head stethoscope at various places on her bulging abdomen. "What's your OB's name?"

"Meredith Price. Why? Is there a problem?"

He shook his head and patted her hand. "Not that I can see, except for those," he said, pointing to the small red welts on her side. "Look a little like hives. Do you have any allergies? Eat anything new or different?"

Out of sheer habit, she lied, shaking her head. She wasn't ready to admit they were just the latest in a long list of bruises and welts left by her husband's beatings. She wondered if she'd ever have the nerve to tell the whole truth about Sean. It was hard to imagine, since she'd also have to admit that she'd chosen him. For that she felt a twinge of responsibility.

"Said you were a vet, right?" he asked rhetorically. "Any chance something at work might have caused an allergic reaction?"

"Not sure." The truth lingered on the tip of her tongue. The taste was bitter but it was far overshadowed by concern for the fate of her family. "My parents?" she pressed.

The ambulance came to an abrupt halt outside the emergency room of Martin Memorial North. After being rolled into an exam area, Darby waited more than three frustrating hours badgering anyone and everyone about her parents. After what felt like an eternity, a representative from the Martin County Sherriff's office poked his head through the flimsy curtain.

"Mrs. Grisom?"

"Darby Hayes Grisom," she both corrected and replied as she leveraged herself up on the bed with her elbows. "What happened to my parents?"

"First, I'm Sergeant Joe Ciminelli. Secondly, is there anyone here with you?"

"No, my husband is on his way home from a business trip. His flight landed a little more than an hour ago."

The sergeant's brow furrowed. He ran his palm over his bald head, then hooked his hand at the back of his neck. His pale brown eyes were somber and fixed on a point just above her head.

"Is there anyone who could come to be with you?"

Darby's whole body was stiff, braced for whatever news

he seemed so reluctant to deliver. "No. Now, please tell me what happened to my parents."

"I'm afraid there was an accident."

Accident? What kind of accident kills two people? "Excuse me?"

Sergeant Ciminelli moistened his forefinger, then flipped through the small notebook he'd pulled from his breast pocket. "I'm very sorry to have to tell you this, Mrs. Grisom, but your parents passed away in their home sometime during the night."

"How?"

"All indications are that the on-off switch on their car was left in the 'on' position. Carbon monoxide leaked into the home."

"Impossible," Darby said, emphatically shaking her head.

"Ma'am," the sergeant began, his tone sympathetic, "I know this is a terrible shock, but tests conducted inside of the home confirmed a high concentration of carbon monoxide. Unfortunately, it's a very deadly gas. Odorless, colorless. I know this probably isn't much of a consolation, but in most cases, the victims fall asleep, then succumb to the fumes."

Darby raised her hands, waving away his words. "I mean it's impossible that my father would have left his car running. He checked things like that. He was very cautious. Nothing was ever neglected. Were you in the house?"

The officer shrugged his muscular shoulders.

"Did you see a single thing in need of attention? He washed the range hood every single day, for god's sake. This wasn't an accident. He was a detailed person. Practically anal about safety. He would not have left his car running in the garage."

He reached for the small box of tissues and handed her one. Darby looked down at it as if he'd handed her a foreign object. She only vaguely realized she was crying. Tears of sorrow, yes, but salted with disbelief and frustration. "There has to be some sort of mistake. Something you missed."

"Your parents' neighbor was walking her dog and heard the engine running. She used her spare key to enter the house and, well, then she called police. She said your parents were lying comfortably in their bed."

"Something is wrong," Darby insisted.

"I'm very sorry, Mrs. Grisom. There was no sign of a break-in. And now the medical examiner has confirmed the cause of death with blood samples taken from the dec—from your parents."

Darby replayed the last twenty-four hours. Her parents' death was just too coincidental. She'd reached out to them for the first time in her marriage and they'd been dead before morning. Somehow Sean must have known she would contact them. But how could he be in New York and Florida at the same time? Darby didn't know, but she was certain he was behind this. There was no way her father would have been so careless with his new push button-start car. It just didn't make any sense. Darby's sorrow took on an edge of fury when the sword of certainty stabbed through her. "My husband killed them. He knew the garage access code. He must have taken a later flight or something."

"Excuse me?"

"It had to be Sean." She dropped her head, closing her eyes as hot tears fell freely. Her whole body shuddered as sobs wracked her body. Darby embraced her belly, holding on to the baby for dear life. Scrambled, jumbled thoughts raced through her head in a fragmented marathon. Memories: her mother's face; the feel of her father holding her hand as they walked along the beach; the smell of her mother's perfume; the joy in their eyes when she'd told them they were going to be grandparents. Other memories, too, like the first time she'd dropped by the restaurant, unseen and unheard as she watched her husband stroke his fingertips along Roxanne's throat. And the bad, ugly ones: Sean losing his temper time and time again. The cold, emotionless look in his eyes before he exploded in anger. Things being flung against the walls. Finding her beloved German shepherd dead in the parking lot of her clinic—suspecting him, yet deluding herself into believing Sean had had nothing to do with the dog's death. The coincidence had been just too great: the night before she'd found the dog, Sean had *suggested* she get rid of it. According to him, too much of her time was spent walking and caring for the dog. They'd argued to a standoff. The dog had been dead less than a day later.

The similarity now was too great. As much as she didn't want it to be true, it made sense. Brushing at her tears with the backs of her hands, Darby couldn't look at the officer as she quietly said, "My husband killed them."

"It was an unfortunate accident, Mrs. Grisom. Besides, I thought you said your husband was out of town."

"He was. But he did this. I know it." Fueled by grief, conviction, and a sense of security due to her surroundings, she began to open up to the officer. "Sean is a very possessive man. We had a fight last night and he—"

"Apologized."

Darby's head whipped up and her heart stopped as she saw Sean walk into the exam room. Dropping his garment bag in the corner, he came over and gathered her stiff body in his arms.

"Sweetheart, I'm so sorry." He dusted her head and face with kisses. "I should have been here for you. I'm so sorry this happened when I was away."

Planting her hands on his chest, Darby shoved him away. The last thing she wanted was to feel his hands on her. She would never have had the nerve to do such a thing if it wasn't for the officer standing right there. She didn't care what her parents' deaths looked like; she knew Sean was behind it. She looked up at him and saw the raw anger in his eyes and a lot of her bravado faded away. Now she was back to being scared witless. The exchange seemed to intrigue the officer, but Darby didn't care. For all his polish, Sean was a murderer. She saw that truth with absolute clarity. Now her only priority was to save herself and her baby from the lunatic she'd married in haste.

"Get him out of here!"

"Darby—"

"Mrs. Grisom," Sergeant Ciminelli began, "I realize you're upset."

"He killed my family," she said in a deadly calm tone.

Sean backed away from the bed. As he did, he reached into the pocket of his suit coat and produced two rumpled boarding passes. "I've been in New York since yesterday evening." He patted his other pockets, then pulled a folded slip of paper from one and a business card from another. "This is my hotel receipt and the name of the gentleman I met for breakfast."

"See what I mean?" Darby asked. "Who but a guilty man would carry his alibis around in his pockets?"

"Let's step into the hallway," Sean suggested, placing his arm around the shoulder of the officer, guiding him out of the room.

Darby slammed her head against the pillow and again hot tears welled in her eyes. Grabbing the call button, she pressed it over and over until a petite and clearly irritated nurse entered the room. In the split second the curtain was drawn back, Darby saw Sean and the sergeant sharing a handshake.

"Yes?" the nurse asked as she gave cursory glances to the machines tethering Darby to the bed.

"I need a phone."

"We don't allow telephones in the rooms. Is there someone I can call for you?"

"Yes. I need the police."

The nurse blinked, then peered back over her shoulder as she pushed apart the curtain. "Officer?"

"Not him," Darby cried. Too late.

Sean and the officer returned. It didn't take a rocket scientist to see that the sergeant was totally charmed by Sean.

The sergeant took up a position at the end of her bed next to the nurse while Sean moved to the head and draped his arm around her shoulders. "I was just explaining your condition to the policeman." His fingers dug into the flesh at her shoulder.

Ciminelli smiled understandingly. "I've got three kids myself. My wife went a little hormonal with each one. She had all sorts of weird thoughts and cravings. Got so I was afraid to walk in the door after my shift. Never knew what was going to set her off."

"Darby's normally very rational," Sean said, brushing a kiss to her temple. "Don't you have something to say to the officer, sweetheart?"

Darby pressed her lips tight.

Sean squeezed her shoulder harder. "Darby, the officer checked. He spoke directly with Roxanne."

"Roxanne would lie for you," she whispered under her breath.

Sean sighed heavily. "Sweetheart, I thought you might still be…confused, so I made sure the officer called the airline to verify that I was on the flight. The hotel verified that I checked in and even told the officer what I ordered from room service and when it was delivered. The investor I was meeting as well as the restaurant staff verified that I attended the meeting. So, don't you think it's time for you to apologize to the officer for making extra work for him?"

Darby had no idea how he had managed it, but he had. Now she looked like the crazy one. And worse yet, she was at Sean's mercy, which was a terrifying thought. What would happen once they were alone? She shivered just thinking about the potential punishment for calling him a murderer in public. She had that trapped animal feeling again and she couldn't stop crying. No one believed her but she didn't know how he'd pulled it off; she just knew he had. Just as she knew the officer wasn't going to believe a word she said. Darby felt defeated. She gave up. "I'm sorry."

"Don't give it a thought, Mrs. Grisom. I know it was just the grief and the hormones talking. I gave your husband everything you'll need to make the, um, final arrangements for your parents."

"Thank you."

The nurse followed Ciminelli out of the room. Darby braced herself, fully expecting to suffer the wrath of Sean. Instead, he was just looking at her as he arranged the hair framing her face.

"I'm sorry, sweetheart. I always liked your parents," he whispered against her ear.

"Ummmm."

Then calmly and quietly he added, "If you hadn't called them, I never would have been forced to kill them."

About the Author

After selling her first work of romantic suspense in 1993, Rhonda Pollero has penned more than thirty novels, won numerous awards and nominations, and landed on multiple bestseller lists, including *USA Today*, Bookscan, and Ingram's Top 50 list. She lives in South Florida with her family.